A FEW GOOD
FRIENDS

A FEW GOOD
FRIENDS

J. E. Smythe

LEG
Lady Esquire Group, LLC

A FEW GOOD FRIENDS

This is a work of fiction. All of the characters, names, incidents, organizations, and dialogue in this novel are either the products of the author's imagination or are used fictitiously.

LEG books may be ordered through booksellers or by contacting:

Lady Esquire Group, LLC
P.O. Box 790672
Charlotte, NC 28206
www.writeleg.com
1-888-988-4249

ISBN: 978-0-9903418-0-2 (sc)
ISBN: 978-0-9903418-1-9 (ebk)

Library of Congress Number: 2013918802

Printed in the United States of America.

LEG rev. date 04/24/2014

ACKNOWLEDGEMENT

I am so grateful to God for continuously blessing me over and over again, even in times when I didn't feel like I deserve it; He is always there and always right on time.

To my amazing mother, Caroline Jangaba-Nimely, for always being there and never giving up on me. You believed in me and taught me the value of hard work and how to never stop fighting to make my dreams come true. Mamie thank you for all that you are, I love you more than you will ever know.

To my brother, John Frank, you have always been the best big brother a girl could ever ask for. I so appreciate you for always being there. No matter where I am or what I'm doing I always know that if I need you, you will be there.

To the rest of my family, Pookie, Uncle Tom, and everyone who has been such a big part of my life, just know that I love you all and thank God every day for blessing me with this amazing family.

Special thanks to my editor for the work that she did. I am glad we were able to take this journey together. Also, a special thank you to everyone that I've worked with in this process. Thank you for helping make my dream a reality. Your patience and support was amazing, and I will always be grateful.

To my girls, Josey, Niki, and Velice, thank you ladies for pushing me and believing in this story in my head when it was just a play written by a college freshman for the amusement of her three best friends. I love you ladies.

1

Joanna

One thing's for sure, giving a presentation like this was the best part of my job. To these gray-haired old guys, I was the most powerful person. Anyone who can tell you how to make money and grow your business has power. To these fools it's like I'm the only person who holds the key to the Emerald City; that's power for your ass. If you can make someone money, then you can make them do whatever you want. I happen to think that marketing is the best profession in the world. Where else can a little black girl tell a bunch of old men what to do and they actually do it? I'm brilliant and I'm never giving this up for anything in the world. Why should I? This is the best career on the planet. Look at these guys. They're probably thinking, "What an aggressive bitch." Hell yeah I am! I own that. Most women get angry at being called a "bitch" or look at the word "bitch" as this big insult. But shit, I fought hard for my title. Go ahead call me a bitch all you want. All that means is that you're scared shitless of me. Let's be honest, men will play women left and right if given the chance because they feel like they have control. But the moment they come across a bitch, all that changes. They know not to play with her and no matter who the man is or what he has accomplished, the bitch is always in control.

So hell yeah, I'm a bitch and a sexy ass bitch at that. I see how they're sitting in here staring me down trying to picture me naked. I bet they wish I could give them some, but sorry fellas, I don't do white. Well, maybe once . . . . Ok sometimes I do, but I definitely don't do old unless he's really hot or rich.

I bet they're wondering where this big-hipped, big-tittied, mocha-skinned, hourglass-shaped sistah came from; right here in B-More, baby, born and raised. I didn't even go far for college, just right up the street to the first university I found. That was the best decision I ever made. How else would I have met my three best friends Nicole, Jessica and Victoria? Hell, I found myself in there, too.

Growing up, I never found my strength. I grew up in this run-down apartment with a single mother who worked two jobs to make life better for us. I guess I just didn't believe there was anything more than that.

But damn, look what happens when you seek more than your eyes can see. I hold an MBA. I have the most accounts at my firm. I make my own money. I live in an expensive loft overlooking the Inner Harbor, and I bought my mom a cute little house all her own. I mean, no one really cared what I had to say when I was younger, but now, these old white men who use to drive by my apartment complex in their all-too-expensive cars are now applauding me as I finish my presentation. Finding out who I am and not being afraid to scream out loud has gotten me here, and I do not plan on shutting up anytime soon.

"Thank y ou all f or y our a ttention. I will leave a c opy o f the presentation along with some figures with you. Please feel free to contact me with any concerns," I said as I passed out individual reports to each of them.

"Thank you, Ms. Stuart, for that amazing presentation." Mr. Stephens, my boss, came over to me and shook my hand. That was the sign for me to leave so that he could close the deal.

"It was my pleasure, Mr. Stephens."

As I left that room, strutting those legs that I pay my gym way too much for, I could hear how impressed they are; I could also feel their eyes on my ass. Men will always be men no matter their color or age. That's why I don't have any. They just waste your time and suck your energy and all they care about is getting between your legs. People always wonder if the reason I don't have a man is because I can't get or keep one. Hell no! I'm the sexiest fucking bitch walking plus, I'm smart and I can cook; I get plenty of men. Hell I've been on five or six dates this week. I just don't want a man. I like my life. I'm alone, free, and at peace; no damn drama. Besides, there are absolutely no men around that even comes close to being Mr. Perfect.

Well, all except one—David. I knew he was something special ever since the first day I saw him in college. He's Jessica's cousin and the most magnificent man I have ever known. I remember when I first saw David; it was at a frat party and I went to a black college so the fellas were on point. I was this too-grown-up-for-my-own-good freshman, and I was ready to take them all on, one lick at a time. But all of a sudden, I turned my head and saw the most gorgeous back I had ever seen in my life. All I could do was stare and wait eagerly for him to turn around. In my mind I was hoping his front looked as good as his back. Then something strange happened to me when he turned around. I saw his face, we made eye contact and the first thing I thought was Oh my God, that's my husband. That shit scared me. I was looking at this six-foot, two-inch, caramel-skinned, low haircut muscular man and all I could think was this is my husband? What the hell had happened to me? I mean it wasn't as if I was a hoe or anything, but I kept a man on standby and still do. I love sex, especially with sexy men, but all of a sudden I was looking at this man like a possible husband. My heart just took hold and I couldn't control it.

After that, I spent a good month running from him and I had no idea why. There was just something in me that was so afraid of him-of the possibility of him and me. Every time I would see him on campus, I would go the other direction-but not far enough. I still wanted to watch him walk and smile and do everything else, but I just didn't want him to see me. I guess I'm still that freshman girl who is scared of the possibility of having this amazing man love me.

But David has always been the man of my dreams. Every man in my life got the D-test, and if he didn't measure up he was out of here. I've dated a few men, but no one ever came close to passing the D-test. How could they? They weren't him.

"Ms. Stuart, why do you do this every time?" My secretary Laurie, was this incredible woman who kept me together at all times. I don't know what I would have done without her. She was a tall, slender, black woman with a hint of gray highlighting her jet black hair and her eyes always showed that she had lived a good and interesting life. Laurie always treated me less like her boss and more like her daughter who needed constant attention; I really needed that.

"Do what Laurie?" I asked.

"Smash your face against your desk like that. Sometimes I wonder about you." Laurie said letting out a slight chuckle as she walked over to me.

"I just need a minute where no one is watching me or looking me dead in the eye." I lifted up my head just enough to look up at her face. I could see that she was holding some small pink papers in her hands and realized that all that meant was more work.

"Well you take your minute, and I'm going to leave you alone. Here are all your messages." Laurie laid the pink papers on the desk in front of me and walked out of the room. As she was leaving, I managed to get out a soft thank you before laying my head back down.

Sometimes I loved my life and sometimes I hated it. I wanted to complain and then I thought What the hell do I have to complain about? There aren't that many black women in my position. Hell, there are not that many women period in my position. I would sometimes catch myself wondering if something was missing. Everyone was always talking about marriage and love and children. Well, I have none of that. Do I need it to be complete? Does any woman? Especially in this day and age where women can do everything for themselves. Why isn't success in career and finances enough for people? I'm so sick and tired of being judged by some primitive rule and thought to be unwomanly because I spent twelve hours a day at work and not with a man, or because I spent money on really cute shoes and not on children of my own. I think happiness comes in many forms, and I know this happiness. I don't know another one. Who's to say I won't get married, have kids, and be the most miserable person on earth? I've seen that happen. I'm not saying I'm completely pleased with my life as it is, but it's what I got. It's what I've created for myself and I'm ok with that. I mean people are not coming out and saying "your life sucks," but I've seen the looks. Maybe I want to see the looks. I don't know anymore. As much as I love my life, there is a loneliness that comes with it. My mother always talked about how you want someone to be there and go with you on your journey-having your support system. I guess I've gone on my journey by myself for so long that I don't know how to allow someone else to come with me. But if I did bring someone with me it would definitely be David.

It must have been almost five in the evening when I realized that I had been working nonstop for hours.

"Honey, you are too young to be putting yourself though this. It's Friday. You should be out there having fun." Laurie came into my office making her proclamation after she noticed that everyone was getting ready to leave for the day except me.

Working nonstop was what I needed to do. In order to be the best in my field, I had to endure the pain that came with success, even if it meant working myself into a coma. You have to work hard in order to make your dreams come true. But people aren't willing to do that. They just think that it's all easy and the world is at their feet. We women get told so many lies these days like it's possible to have a career and a family too. Bullshit. How many successful women-I mean *really* successful women-have a husband and kids? It takes sacrifice. You need to decide early on what you want. Is it a career or is it a family, cause you sure as hell can't have both. Do you see men worrying about any of that? They will work twenty-four-seven if they have to and that's why there's that glass ceiling; women just aren't willing to do the same. They're too worried about finding a husband and having kids.

"Well are you at least gonna leave early tonight?" Laurie sounded more like she was demanding rather than asking. But before I could respond, the phone rang and Laurie immediately reached for it. "Joanna Stuart's office. Yes, she is, Mrs. Combs. Please hold." Laurie handed me the phone and left.

Sometimes you have to take a few deep breaths to prepare yourself for Victoria, and something told me that this was one of those times. She can be the most amazing friend; when no one else shows up, Victoria will. She figures out what you need and finds a way to help you get it. But Lord, that girl can work a nerve.

"What's up Vickie," I tried to sound joyful when I answered, but everything in me was telling me that Victoria wanted something, as always.

"Nothing. I was just wondering what you have planned for tonight."

"Uh, nothing. Why?

"I was wondering if you wanted to go on a date with a cute, successful man who has a wonderful career, loves the Lord, and has great values." Victoria sounded as if she was a used car dealer fighting to make a sale, and if she had to convince me that badly, something must be wrong with this man.

"No."

"But why? He is an amazing man, who is sensitive, and I told him all about you and he saw your picture and . . ."

"Oh shut up Vickie, I'll do it."

Victoria could wear a person down to the point of absolute surrender. Even if you disagreed with her, you'd end up doing what she wants just to get her to stop talking.

"Thanks girl! You won't be sorry."

All I could do was roll my eyes.

"I hope not. When and where?" I asked. I hated blind dates, but since I was the only single one, Victoria thought it was her mission in life to fix me up with the first man she came across.

"He will pick you up at eight."

"Vickie it's already five. I cannot be ready by then."

"Of course you can. Besides, it is too late now for me to call him and cancel. So just go home now and get ready and everything will be cool."

I sat in my chair for a few minutes after hanging up the phone wondering what I had just gotten myself into. Victoria has never known what I liked in a man. For all I know, I could be about to go on a date with Chewbacca. But it was too late now. I turned off my computer and picked up my briefcase. As I left the office, I turned to Laurie. "Looks like I'll be going home on time tonight."

"It's about time." Laurie flashed me a grin as I entered the elevator.

2

Victoria

After hanging up the phone with Joanna, I prepared myself to go on stage and give my speech. I couldn't believe how many people were here just to hear me speak. Some people might say that I don't have a real job or that I went from living off my father to living off my husband, but I do have talent. I'm Victoria Combs, the best political fundraiser in all of Baltimore-no, in all of Maryland. Sure, my husband, Mitchell, has money. After all, he's a senior partner at one of the nation's most prestigious law firms. But I made him who he is. Everyone in Baltimore knows and respects my family. I gave Mitchell the clout he needed to become who he is now. I am the ultimate woman behind the man. Mitchell ought to be grateful that I do what I do. My status in Baltimore has become solidified and no one can ever tell me I don't do anything. I've just gotten a room full of Baltimore's richest and most powerful people to not only sit through my entire speech but now they are about to part with their money; all because I asked them to. No one is better at getting people to give away their money than I am.

I surveyed the room searching for familiar faces among the sea of strangers, but the only one I saw was my mother's. Nothing I do seemed quite as important to anyone but her. No one really took me seriously or perhaps they're just too jealous to celebrate my work. I'd hate to think that jealously is the reason. I mean I get it; Mitchell is a busy attorney, Joanna is a high-power executive, Jessica is an overworked doctor, and Nicole, well, she has kids. It takes a lot to be a mother and I don't think I can do that right now. Although Mitchell has certainly been pushing that agenda, I just tell him, we already have it all. Why give people even more to envy?

All of my life, people have, how do they say it, hated on me. I was the quintessential rich, tall, skinny, light-skinned girl with long hair. I've always been more mature then everyone else. I guess that's why I never really made friends easily. That was until I met my girls.

I remember all the times we've shared together. They made my college years so enjoyable. When I was with them, I wasn't Victoria; I was Vickie, and Vickie laughs and acts silly and cracks jokes and busts out dancing for no reason whatsoever. I liked being Vickie; I liked being with them.

But life changes and we've changed. Being an adult isn't always about laughter and having fun. As my mother would say, life is about building a legacy. That has to be my priority, even if I am doing it alone. Sometimes Mitchell shows absolutely no interest in being on the same path. He is just so content with going through life working day in and day out with no purpose whatsoever. I needed a purpose, and building the Combs legacy will be that purpose.

I ended my speech with "Have a blessed day and may God be kind to you all." It is my signature closing. I figure a speech isn't memorable without a signature closing and since the church is such a significant part of my life, I thought my signature closure should somehow reference the Lord. That way people will know that I'm a woman of faith.

I shook hands with almost everyone in the room before leaving. I had been given an office for the day so I could prepare for my speech. I so appreciated it right now because I needed a moment to decompress. I quickly made my way to the office where I was met with the glare of disapproval.

"Mother how did you get here so fast?" I didn't know why, but I was actually confused as to why my mother looked as though I'd just made a fatal error. Everything went well or so I thought. What could I have possibly done wrong? Sometimes I felt nothing I did was right for my mother. For years I've been living by her rules just so she would be proud of me. My life is exactly how we planned it. Everything that we discussed about my future, I have. So maybe I'm the problem. Maybe I'm just not living up to her expectations.

"I left before the end of your speech," my mother said. At that moment, it occurred to me that my mother was about to tell me about how awful my speech was. So I sat at the desk and braced myself for the backlash. Everything about my mother's demeanor screamed disapproval.

She is a handsomely beautiful woman who always took great care of herself. She's always been poised and well put together. Her hair is about as long as mine, just below her shoulders, and her skin is even lighter. My mom would often be mistaken for a white woman and I sometimes think that some part of her actually liked it. She has this way of looking at me with one brow raised and a glint in her eyes that makes me feel like hot beams are shooting out of them and right through me.

"Victoria, where was your husband?" My mother sat in the chair across from me and folded her arms.

"Excuse me?" I was not quite prepared for my mother to ask that sort of question.

"Those people in that room are some of the most powerful people in Baltimore, sweetie. He should have been there."

"Mother, I'm sure that he had a good reason why he wasn't here."

"A good reason? One that is more important than building your status in this community?"

"Mother please. Leave it alone."

"I can't, sweetie, because it's not just me noticing. I mean, people are starting to talk."

"People like whom, Mother?"

"Like the people at the church and at my country club and . . . ."

"Mother, please."

"No, this could hurt your status. No one wants to be associated with people who come from a broken marriage."

"Mother, my marriage isn't broken. It's just fine."

The words had just left my mouth when the door opened and there was Mitchell standing there in his dark suit and chocolate skin with a bouquet of beautiful long-stem roses in his hand. I was so glad he showed up, if for no other reason than to shut-up my mother. I wouldn't say Mitchell was drop-dead gorgeous, but he wasn't a fright to look at. He's shorter than average with a few extra pounds, but he's a good man and I always admired the way he shows up when needed.

"Great speech, Vickie," Mitchell said.

"Oh you heard? It's funny, we didn't see you sitting there in the front row like you should have been." My mother spoke so quickly that she didn't even give me a chance to thank Mitchell for the flowers or for even showing up.

"Mother," I called out, trying to stop her from talking.

"Well hello to you too, Lynn. I apologize for being late, but I'm sure if Vickie checks her voicemail, she'll see that I left her a message. I was stuck in court all morning."

"Thank you for coming, Mitchell." I had to acknowledge that he was here, because I could see the sincerity in Mitchell's face.

I'm sure he would have been here earlier if he could. If nothing else, Mitchell is an honest man. That's why I married him. It wasn't love at first or second sight, but I knew that I could trust him; he got me and he allows me to be me.

"Yes. Mitchell. Thanks for showing up and working your wife into your busy schedule." My mother said with an attitude.

"My pleasure, Lynn," Mitchell replied. "Well, I have to get back to work. Again Vickie, great speech."

"Thanks, Mitchell, but it's a little late. I mean, why would you go back to the office at this hour?"

"Because I have some work to finish. I should be home shortly."

I looked at my mother as she rolled her eyes and folded her arms in complete disbelief of what Mitchell had said. Then, I watched as my husband left the room looking and feeling just as much as a stranger as he did when he entered the room. I took a sniff of the roses he had brought me and realized my mother was right. My marriage was broken. There was this distance between Mitchell and me that made us feel awkward whenever we were around each other. How does that happen in a marriage?

"Do you see what I mean Victoria?" my mother asked. "You would think he would show a little more gratitude for us elevating him the way we did. Hell, when you met him he was some lowly public defender. The least he could do is show up when we say show up and act accordingly."

"Mother, it's alright. He's been busy."

"Busy? Victoria, what's going on between you and Mitchell?"

I found it difficult to explain to my mother what the problem was between Mitchell and me, especially since I didn't know myself. He went from being the short, dark, chunky guy who chased me for months to being my husband who has now become just my roommate. How could I explain to my mother who had been married to the same man for over thirty years that my own marriage may be in serious trouble? I wasn't even sure there was a marriage at all any more.

"I don't know what's wrong mother. It's just not working."

"Well I've been hearing that he's not coming home nights. Is that true?"

"How did you ..." I wasn't surprised that my mother was so well informed of my personal life. She always has been.

"Don't worry about that. Is he?" My mother came close to me as if she was waiting for me to tell her a big secret.

"Yes, sometimes he doesn't get home until late, but he does come home."

"You know, sweetie, something like this could ruin you." My mother came even closer to me and placed her hand on my shoulder.

"Something like what?"

"The scandal of an affair of course."

"Mother, Mitch is not..."

"Sweetie, you should always check your facts first and protect yourself."

I couldn't believe what my mother was saying. There was no way Mitchell was having an affair. I knew him; he was just not that type of man. But Mitchell's behavior did match the actions of a cheating man. I sat back in the chair as my mind replayed every action Mitchell had taken and every word he had spoken. I didn't want to believe it, but perhaps my mother was right. Perhaps Mitchell had grown tired of our well-oiled machine of a life. At some point people do look for something new and exciting; I can't fault him for that. I just wished I knew for sure. What should I do? Hire a private investigator to follow him around or just come right out and ask him?

"Why don't you call your friends and go out tonight? Take your mind off things for a while." My mother's smile put my mind at ease for a moment, but nothing could make this alright.

"Well, I've set Jo up on a blind date tonight so she's not available."

"Oh really? With whom?"

"With this guy named Bryan Roberts I met him some time ago through Mitchell. His firm does some architectural work in the city."

"That's excellent. If they hit it off, then you have him and his firm in your back pocket. Good thinking. Well maybe you and Jessica can go out."

"Yes, I can find out what she and Nicole are doing tonight."

"No, sweetie, not that Nicole person." This look of panic crossed my mother's face as she let go of me and sat back down.

"Why not her? She's one of my best friends."

"I know. But being around her is not a good idea."

"Why not?"

"Well because, being around someone like that could hurt you way more than a cheating husband can."

"Someone like what?"

"You know. Gutter People. They bring society down."

I was infuriated by my mother's ignorance, but said nothing to defend my mother's classification of Nicole. The truth was I knew that being seen with Nicole was a disservice to me. I was known for my lavish lifestyle and constantly being around someone who lived in the slums of lower-class Baltimore could prove detrimental to my image. As much as I loved Nicole, I had to think about me and my family. I was building my life; that's something that Nicole needed to learn how to do. I couldn't feel guilty because she chose to give herself less.

Excluding Nicole was always the hardest thing that I could ever do because we were best friends, and Nicole, more than anyone, had been there at some of the lowest points in my life. I'd do anything for her but my mother was right; I had to keep my distance for now.

3

Nicole

"Tekeshia and Devonte y'all come on in the house and stop messing with that dog. We need to get ready!" It seems like I am always making sure people are doing what they're supposed to do. I have to make sure my two kids are raised right. I have been so worried about them being happy that I hardly find time for myself. Shit, I gave up on my dreams the moment my doctor told me I was pregnant with my first child, Keshia. And all my career goals went out the window when the preacher declared Steven and me, husband and wife. No time for regrets now 'cause, hell, the shit's done. Don't get me wrong I love my kids and love being their mother, but my life is so damn predictable. It's the same endless tasks day in and day out; I'm tired of it. But there ain't shit I can do until the kids can take care of themselves. I learned that I just gotta put up with the bullshit. My biggest problem is being married to a man who thinks that I got pregnant just to keep him. Who the fuck wants his tired ass anyway?

Every chance Steven gets, he reminds me how miserable he is. Well shit, I'm miserable too, but you don't see me throwing it up in his face. Maybe I should, then maybe he'll get out of my face and go somewhere.

The truth is I never thought that my marriage would turn out to be a disaster. When we did this whole marriage thing, we both decided that we would raise our kids right. He said I should stay home and take care of the baby; now, he's acting like I am this lazy bitch he's stuck with.

I mean, sure, I knew that neither of us was in love; marriage was the first thing our parents thought of when they heard I was pregnant. I didn't have the balls to tell my parents that my pregnancy came from one night of stupid unprotected sex with a guy I'd known for only a few

13

days. All they thought was that Steven and I had been dating while I was away at college. Shit, that's all they needed to know. All the other stuff was none of their business. Hell, my mama would have killed me if she found out I was one of the most popular students to *never* step foot in a classroom. I had a ball in college, but if someone would have told me that the price I had to pay was a life with a man I hardly liked or respected, I would have been the biggest damn nerd anyone had ever seen. My fucking ass would have stayed in the damn library. Then maybe I would have avoided Steven's trifling ass all together.

As my kids ran in the house I tried with all my might to smile so that I could cover up my anger at having to use my long braids to cover up my black-eye and wear a long-sleeved shirt in eighty-degree weather to cover up the bruises that ran up and down my arms. I couldn't believe that I was in this situation. I was the last person anyone would assume would put up with this; hell, I'm the last person I would assume would put up with this. People always think that it's those skinny white chicks having to deal with the crazy man putting hands on them, but I'm a tall sistah standing at almost six-feet with some weight on me, and here I am dealing with this bull.

A few months after Keshia was born, I became mixed up in this never-ending battle with my husband. Shit, with Steven, I can't even classify that asshole as my husband. We would fight constantly sometimes for no reason at all, only to prove who really wore the pants. And that motherfucking bastard needed to know that I wear the pants. Ain't no man fixing to run me.

I watched my children push and shove one another, as children do, and my mind wondered back to the first time Steven and I fought. We first started by screaming and cursing at each other. But soon that bastard got pissed and backhanded me across the face like he was my pimp and I was a fucking whore who didn't turn enough tricks by the end of the night. The hit was so hard that it felt like someone had taken a brick and threw it against my face. My eye was throbbing.

Steven had yelled, cursed, and even called me some God-awful names, but he had never hit me before. Being hit by my husband was not part of the bargain. I refused to take it from him; so I got up and began hitting him back with everything I had, and before long, we were having one of the most violent fights that I had ever experince.

When that bastard realized that I was about to kick his ass, he got mad as hell and slammed me against the wall. He was about to put his fist through my face when the baby started to cry. I pushed Steven away and went into the room. I was not going to let that bastard make me cry. But I had to get out. The only thing was, I couldn't go to my parent's house. I knew they would think it was all my fault. I picked up the phone and began calling everyone I could think of. Finally Joanna answered her phone.

"Hey girl. How long you gonna be in your room?" I asked.

"I'm in for the rest of the night. Why?"

"Me and Keshia are coming to visit you."

By the time I arrived at Joanna's dorm room, my eye was already red and swollen from the slap from Steven. I grabbed some shades out of the glove compartment of my car and put them on. I hoped that no one on campus would notice.

The minute I entered the door, Joanna asked, "Why are you wearing shades in the middle of the night?" I tried to ignore the question by walking past Joanna and took my sleeping baby to Jessica's bed. When I turned around, I saw Joanna's nosy ass sitting on her bed watching me. The look on Joanna's face told me that she knew what the hell had happened. I knew that I had to come clean. So I sat down on the bed next to my daughter and took off my shades. "Oh shit!" Joanna gasped as she jumped up to take a better look at my eye. She then ran to her small refrigerator and grabbed an ice pack and placed it on my swollen eye.

"You're not going back to that son-of-a-bitch," Joanna said to me.

"Well that son-of-a-bitch is my husband I ain't got a choice."

"But he hit you!"

"Just a little bit, Girl. I got a few good licks in myself, believe that." I tried to make light of what happened but Joanna was not going for it.

"But Nic—" I already knew what her next words were going to be and I didn't want to hear it.

"But nothing, Jo. I just came over here to calm down; everything is gonna be ok. It ain't no big deal."

The truth is, I didn't know what the bastard would have done if I had stayed. I didn't know what I would have done either.

"Well at least you could stay here for the night. Jess is gone for the weekend, so you and Keshia can use her bed."

She seemed disappointed that I didn't decide to leave Steven right then and there, but where the hell was I going to go?

"Jo promise me that you ain't gonna tell nobody."

"Why?"

"Cause I don't want nobody to know that's why."

"Alright."

"No, promise me. You know your ass can't hold water. So just promise me."

"Ok I promise. I won't tell anybody."

I should have left Steven's ass that night. I should have taken my baby and never looked back. But I didn't. I knew then that shit wasn't right. My gut told me not to ever go back, that it wasn't worth it. But the next morning, after I thought Steven had calmed down, I took my baby and went home.

For a while after that, everything was ok. Me and Steven were cordial - enough so that I ended up pregnant for the second time. But after Devonte was born, everything just got more stressful, and me and Steven seem just to hate the sight of each other.

A lot of the time I used to hang out with my girls as much as I could. Since Joanna knew what was really going on I stayed with her more; cause there were no questions like, Why ain't you with your husband? or Why you and your kids never home? Joanna even gave me a copy of her room key, just in the off chance I needed a place to stay. But when those heffas graduated, got jobs and went to grad school, things changed. I found myself running out of places to go. That's really when my life became more about taking care of my kids and holding boxing matches in the middle of my living room.

"Y'all kids stop making all that damn noise!" Steven yelled as the kids ran past him. Why the fuck was Steven home? I just wished he would go somewhere and never bring his black ass home. He's so fucking sorry. He'd better not be yelling all crazy at my kids. That's why he's got that big-ass knot on the side of his head. He's just sitting on the sofa like a big ole dirty lump as if nothing had ever happened.

That motherfucker really wanted to try me last night. Yeah, I got a black eye, but I swear he almost lost consciousness when I popped him on the side of his head with my shoe. That's what he gets for always trying to put me down. He ain't shit himself, but he tries to make me feel like crap. Fuck him.

The motherfucker actually tried to tell me that I ain't smart enough to go back to school. It wasn't like I wanted to, but, hell I could if I wanted. Fuck him, black bastard. At least I started college; his dumb ass ain't even seen the inside of a classroom. Man, why am I even worried about what he says anyway? He ain't shit.

"Where the fuck y'all going?" Steven decided to take a break from watching TV to get up in my business.

"To mind our business. Why?"

"You always taking my kids places I don't know about."

"And when was the last time you cared anyway?"

He was just trying to get under my skin. I could feel myself getting pissed, but I decided I was just going to ignore his ass.

I sent my kids to their room to get ready, and I started getting my shit together. It was early evening and I knew people were probably just getting home from work. I didn't want to pop in on just anybody right now, but I need to get out of this house and away from this bastard. I figured Joanna was probably working late. Damn, that girl would work till midnight if she could, and the bitch probably has.

"We're ready, Ma." My daughter came out the room holding her brother's hand.

"Alright, come on let's go." As I led them out of the house, Keisha turned to Steven.

"Bye, Daddy," She said. My babies were still at a place where they just loved their daddy. Too bad he's sorry as hell.

"Your daughter's talking to you."

"Yeah, bye." He couldn't even lift his eye to look at her or muster the strength to give her a smile. Sorry bastard.

"Come on y'all, let's go."

He's just gonna sit there and watch TV like the jackass he is. He could have at least answered his daughter. Damn, he don't care about nothing.

"Hey, I hope you leaving something for me to eat!"

I stared at him. What the fuck? Did he really just scream that shit at me?

"Why don't you eat your dick and choke on it, bastard!" I made sure to slam the door behind me.

I'm glad Joanna didn't live far. It took me no time to get to downtown Baltimore. Joanna's loft was dark and quiet; I knew that heffa hadn't gotten home yet. My kids had fallen asleep in the car, so I just went and put them in Joanna's guestroom.

When I came back downstairs, I lay on the sofa and stared out the window at the city lights. The shit just seemed to dance to some magical beat that no one hears but everyone feels. It was peaceful and calming and before I knew it, my ass had fallen fast asleep.

4

Jessica

"Dr. Mathews, please report to room 3A, code blue. Dr. Jessica Mathews, room 3A, code blue." The sound of my name being called sent a surge of adrenaline running through my body. It was as if I was moving in slow motion, just like those silly doctors shows you see on television; you know, the ones where the patient is cured in an hour or less. It always seemed ridiculous to me because problems just don't get solved that easily. There are no grand morals to the story of life; it's just life, and sometimes life doesn't play fair no matter how much you wish it would.

That's just one of those on-the-job things you learn - you know the ones they forget to tell you about in medical school. I mean what's fair about a little girl fighting for every single breath she takes? It's moments like this that I forget about this white coat and see her as if she were my own child. I can't let her die, not like this, not without experiencing all that life has to offer. She is so pure and innocent. She knows nothing of the bad or the ailments of the world. All she knows is that she was sick and now she's not. That's all that matters to her. Her mother brushed the hair from off her forehead and looked up at me whispering the words "thank you." It's funny how those two words can give you such a sense of accomplishment and make you feel as if you have a purpose in this world. I always wondered why we don't say them more often and to more people. A mother's thank you is all it took to make me feel special and appreciated.

I walked out the room feeling the same rush of eagerness and empowerment I always got ever since I began my residency in the E.R. I felt important and respected. People had actually needed me and wanted to hear what I had to say. These were practically strangers who, for a moment in time felt like I was the most important person in the world; and for that same moment in that same time, they made me feel like I mattered.

But why doesn't the man I love most in the world see me the same way? I give Michael all of me, and all I asked in return was his heart and loyalty. I just don't know if I have either. It is driving me crazy not being able to trust my own man. I would find myself leaving my patients' bedsides just to call and check up on him. The moment he answered with that deep bass voice of his, my heart would just melt, and my knees buckle when he said "I love you baby." But damn it, when he doesn't answer, I can't function. My mind is left wondering where he is and what he's doing and who he's with. My soul needs this man. My body aches for this man. It's like I'm an addict and he's my drug. Anything that Michael asks of me I'm willing to do. He's my everything, and he has been my everything since the moment I met him all those years ago in college.

There was just something about Michael that made every woman who came in contact with him yearn for his touch. Maybe it was the silky darkness of his skin or the deepness of his voice or the tattoos that ran up and down his arms. Or maybe it was those dark brown eyes that seemed to caress every inch of my body whenever they look at me. Whatever it was, it belonged to me—all of it.

When Michael and I first met, there were women all around him. I just knew I didn't have a chance. But then he walked over to where Joanna and I were standing and spoke to me. I couldn't believe that he left all those women behind and chose me. He gave me a sense of self worth that day. The moment Michael chose me, I knew I was beautiful. And when he said he was willing to wait until I was ready to have sex for the first time, I knew I was worthy.

I loved Michael with everything within me. I guess that's why people think I'm stupid. But I'm not. I know Michael cheats constantly. There are always women around him. He's always in the clubs and out late at night. He says that it's all part of his job and that those women mean nothing. But they do. I know Michael loves me, and I know there will come a day when I will be enough for him. But until that day comes, I'm just going to love Michael more than any other woman could.

Once my shift was over, I started to wonder what Michael was doing. Maybe we could have a date night or just spend some time alone together. We hadn't done that in such a long time. Michael's phone seemed to ring an extra long time before his voicemail came on and I was forced to leave a message rather than talk to him.

"Hey, Baby. It's me. I just wanted to see if you were free tonight. Well, I'm on my way home so maybe I'll see you there. Bye. I love you."

It's strange how we share a home, but we hardly ever see each other. I guess that's what happens when you and your man have busy schedules. That I can deal with. I'm just finding it difficult to deal with the constant wondering whom he's with and what he's doing. I live my life waiting by the phone just to hear his voice. It's so pathetic.

Right now I just need to go home wipe the day away, clear my head and stop worrying about Michael. I had just gotten into my car when my phone rang. For a moment, I got excited thinking it might be Michael. But my hopes were soon diminished when I realized it was Victoria.

"Hey, Vickie. Watcha want?"

"What are you doing tonight?"

"Vickie, I just got off work and need to be home. Why?"

"I just wanted to go to the movies and needed some company."

"I don't know, Vickie I'm pretty tired."

"Come on Jess. You can rest in the theater. I need the company."

"Alright Vickie as long as it's not a long movie."

"Great. I'll pick you up in an hour."

"Make it an hour and a half. I have to stop by Jo's."

Joanna had just arrived home by the time I got to her loft. She must have seen me when she got out of her car, because she was waiting for me at the entrance of the building.

"Girl hurry up!" Joanna shouted.

"I'm coming."

"What are you doing here? I thought you had to work?"

"My shift just ended. I wanted to get that pullover sweatshirt I loaned you."

"Now?"

"Yeah, I'm going to the movies with Vickie and need it to cover up my head so I can sleep while she watches the movie."

"Oh, so she takes you to the movies and sets me up on a blind date." "You're going on a blind date? When?"

"In a few hours."

"Oh, wow."

"What?"

"Oh, nothing."

I couldn't help but laugh at the fact that Joanna trusted Victoria enough to let her set her up on a blind date. This could be interesting.

5

Joanna and Jessica woke me up when they came in the door laughing like some damn hyenas. I didn't expect to see Jessica. I hoped she wouldn't see what my eye looked like. I thought the swelling had gone down a lot, but there was still a mark there. I knew Jessica, and she could over-dramatize shit. The bitch was annoying.

"What you bitches laughing at?" I sat up trying not to face them.

"Jo actually let Vickie set her up on a blind date," Jessica said through her chuckle.

"That damn Vickie wouldn't let me get out of it," Joanna responded.

"Girl, you know better than to let Vickie set you up. You remember what happened the last time." I had to remind Joanna about the last guy Victoria tried to set her up with. It was an absolute disaster. I couldn't believe she was letting Vickie do it again.

"Oh yeah, Nic. It was the wannabe preacher who swore up and down that Jo was ordained to be his fist lady?" Jessica plopped down on the chair across from me. She looked right at me, but I guess she was laughing so hard that she hadn't notice my bruises.

"Very funny you two. Anyway, it was too late to get out of it. Where are my babies?" Jessica may not have noticed my bruises, but Joanna did and went to get an ice pack. It wasn't until I put the pack on my eye that Jessica saw and immediately stopped laughing. But me and Joanna kept on talking like nothing had happened.

"In your bed," I answered.

"They stopped pissing in the bed, cuz those are some expensive sheets," Joanna said with a smile.

"Shit, have you stopped, bitch." I could see that Jessica was trying to figure out what the hell was going on.

"What happened to you? And why are you both acting like I'm the only one who can see this." Once Jessica asked that question, the whole damn mood in the room change.

"She's alright," Joanna answered.

"No she's not, Jo!" Jessica came over to me to do her doctor shit. I swear ever since that girl became a doctor she thinks she's the only one that can fix people.

"Who did this to you?" I didn't want to answer her and could see that Joanna was gonna follow my lead. It ain't that I didn't want Jessica to know. It's just that she's so damn dramatic. I ain't got time for the explanations and arguments. I know what I'm doing. I don't need to hear the fussing. I quickly switched the subject to Joanna.

"Jo, ain't you got to get ready?"

"Girl, yes, and I don't have a clue what I'm wearing." Joanna sat back in the chair and folded her arms like she was beginning to change her mind about leaving.

"Wait Jess, I thought you were supposed to be at work." Since I was sure Joanna was not gonna continue on the subject of my fucked up eye, I had to make sure that Jessica got the memo to leave shit alone.

"My shift is over," Jessica replied.

I could tell by the way Jessica's voice was low and sounding detached that she didn't get the memo, and she was nowhere near done with the subject. So I braced myself for Jessica's attempt at sound advice. If I didn't let this bitch do this now, then she wouldn't let the shit go.

"Go on Jess let me have it." I turned to face Jessica preparing for what she had to say. I just knew she was going to take it some place that it just didn't need to go.

"Alright, I can't believe this was going on and the two of you didn't say anything," Jessica said.

"It wasn't for me to say," Joanna answered, finally getting up and walking off as if she didn't want any part of this conversation.

"Uh huh. So if he would have killed her then that's what you would say over her casket, Jo?" Jessica got up and followed behind Joanna. It seemed as if her beef was with Jo and not me.

"Wait a damn minute now, Jess. You're going a little too far. Ain't nobody 'bout to kill nobody," I said to her. By that time all three of us were standing and our voices were slowly getting louder with every word.

"No I haven't gone too far, Nic. Do you know how many women come into the E.R. because of domestic violence? And not all of them leave." I knew Jess was going to take it too far.

"Jess, I can handle myself. Nothing like that would ever happen to me. We just like to fight that's all." I didn't know why Jessica was acting so high and mighty all of a sudden like I didn't know that shit happens.

"No, that's not all, Nic. You need to find a way to break free from him and hiding out with Jo isn't it."

"Jess, she's good. Just let her be," Joanna calmly said as she made her way to the stairs.

"Jo, you really think she's good? Because I don't. This is serious and somebody has to deal with it." Jessica sounded even more upset.

"But, Jess it's not for me or you to deal with. If Nic says she's good, then she's good," Joanna replied.

"And my ass is good. So you bitches need to stop talking about me like I ain't here." I had to let them know so we could put an end to this whole stupid conversation.

"Nic—" Jessica started to say.

"Leave the shit alone. Damn, Jess!" I yelled.

"Fine if the both of you say it's good then it's good."

This was exactly what I was trying to avoid. That's why I didn't want nobody to know. It ain't that serious and people were acting like the whole fucking world was about to end.

Jessica got what she came for from Joanna and left without saying anything. I know the bitch was mad, but it ain't her life. It's mine, and I got this under control. Her ass will get over it.

6

OnceVictoria and I were at the movie theater, we argued over what movie to watch. I started to get frustrated with Victoria's lack of compromise. To avoid the argument, I just allowed Victoria to do whatever she wanted to do. That seemed easier than listening to her complain about not liking the movie all the way through the movie. Besides, I had too much on my mind with this whole Nicole thing to even entertain Victoria's demands. I didn't want to tell Victoria about Nicole. She would make this more complicated, and Nicole does not need that. I just had to figure out a way to make her understand how dangerous her situation is. Until, then I hoped Joanna was right and Nicole did have everything under control. I just couldn't help but be afraid for her. There were so many women in that situation who thought that they had it under control but they didn't. It's almost as if they've convinced themselves that it's ok to be in that situation, and I think that's what has happened to Nicole. She feels that's how her life should be. But she could be so much more and do so much more. I just wished she knew that.

The movie theater was so packed that I found it interesting just watching people pass by. While looking around, I saw a friend who was once Nicole's roommate in college and spent a lot of time around us.

"Hey." I nudged Victoria. "Isn't that Monique?" Victoria looked over in the direction that I was pointing.

"Oh yeah. It is." As we began to walk towards Monique, we were stopped by the sight of her hugging and kissing a man who looked a lot like Michael. Victoria held my hand.

"Come on, Jess, let's go," she pleaded. I couldn't leave. My eyes were stuck on Monique and the man she was kissing so passionately. I had to make sure what I was seeing, so I just ignored Victoria's plea and walked up to Monique and Michael.

"What's going on here!" I shouted pulling the two of them apart.

"Jess, baby. I just ran into Mo and was telling her hi." Michael tried to explain but I was so angry that I barely heard a word he said.

"I can't believe you, Mo." My eyes were glued to this home-wrecking whore. How could she do this to me?

"Jess, it's not that serious." Monique replied as if she was waving me away or as if my feelings didn't matter.

"Not that serious, Mo? You're with her man." Vickie must have seen how stunned silent I was and how much I was ready to jump on this girl, because she moved me back and stood between Monique and me.

All I could do was stare in disgust at Michael. He had done it again; he had broken my heart. In the past when he cheated, at least it was with women I didn't know and sometimes never saw. But this time not only was he being open with his adultery, but he was with someone I considered a friend. I just knew that this was definitely the end of our relationship. I could no longer be with someone who showed such disregard for me.

"Come on Jess, let's just go." Victoria pulled at my hand trying to lead me away from Michael and Monique. This time I went with her, but not before slapping Michael across the face.

The drive home seemed to go by fast. All the way to my house I could feel Victoria trying to think of something to say but I guess there was nothing to be said. When the car stopped at my row house, Victoria got out too and began to follow me. I didn't know if she thought I needed an escort or maybe she felt as if I would completely fall apart right on my front porch.

"Jess, you want me to stay with you for a while?" Victoria asked while wrapping her arms around me. "Mitchell is working late and I'll be in that big old house all by myself anyway."

"No. Go home, Vickie. It's late and Mitch is probably wondering where you are. I'll be fine," I answered.

"No, trust me. He's not even thinking about me right now; it's all about work. Maybe you can come stay with me for the night. I mean, since we missed the movie, we could pop popcorn and watch a DVD," Victoria offered as another option.

"No Vickie really, I'm fine. I'll call you later." I needed my heart to feel the pain and allow myself to cry, and I knew I wouldn't be able to do that with Victoria around. Even though I knew Victoria meant well, there was nothing she could do. There was nothing anyone could do. My heart was torn out my chest and left on the floor of that movie theater. How could a friend fix that? How could I, a doctor, fix that?

After Victoria left, I put the chain behind the door to make sure that I kept Michael out. But I still didn't feel comfortable being in the home I shared with him. I needed to just gather my things and go to the only place where I really feel in control; like I mattered. I decided to make my way to the hospital. I didn't even remember my ride over there. The only thing I could feel were the tears falling down my face.

I made my way to the doctor's lounge and lay on a bed. I tried not to make eye contact with anyone because I didn't want them asking me why I was here when I wasn't scheduled to work. I just needed to bet there at that moment. Going to a place where you feel welcomed can sometimes pick you up when you are at your lowest point; I hoped this was one of those times.

The hospital bed was a familiar comfort and I soon fell asleep. I was awakened, in what seemed like moments later, by a voice saying, "Jess, I just want to let you know you are my world. I may not be a perfect man but I'm your man and you're my woman. So please forgive me. We belong together."

"Michael!" I looked up and my eyes quickly began to search around the room for him. How the hell could he have made it past security to get to the doctor's lounge? Then I realized that Michael wasn't really there. It was his voice over the radio. I had fallen asleep listening to the stupid radio station where he worked as a DJ and his show had come on.

"Somebody must really love you," a male voice said. I glanced around and saw Dr. Todd Reynolds sitting on the sofa getting ready to start his shift.

"What?" I asked still feeling a bit confused.

"That message. By your reaction I'm assuming you're the Jessica he's referring to."

"I guess."

Dr. Reynolds sat at the edge of the bed.

"You want to talk about it?" he asked.

I really didn't feel like getting anybody's sympathy. I just hated how pathetic my life was, and I didn't need someone, especially someone I barely knew, confirming it.

"It's nothing, thank you." I knew that Dr. Reynolds meant well and I didn't mean to shut him out; he's a great guy, tall, good-looking, and very patient. But I needed time to process everything before hearing the advice of others. I needed to be sure of what I was feeling. I needed my heart to speak to me.

7

It had been well over two hours since Jessica left to go to the movies with Victoria and I still wasn't ready for this blind date. I'd been sitting around my loft with Nicole procrastinating and now that man would be here any minute.

"Jo, I can't believe you let Vickie's crazy ass set you up." I was glad Nicole was over at my apartment as I got ready. She has this way of calming me down and making me laugh all at the same time.

"What? Vickie has good taste, sometimes."

Nicole was the around the way friend that every girl needs. She would cuss someone out, slap them, or hit them with a bat if they ever try and mess with you. Of the four of us, Nicole and I were a lot alike. We both talked a lot of crap and were always down for a fight. No matter what happens, I know she has my back and I have hers. At the end of the day that's what friendship is all about. It doesn't matter what you and someone have in common, all that matters is who's going to show up when you need them the most. Since the first day we all met, those three women have shown up every single time I needed them.

Ever since we were in college, when one of us had a date, the others waere always there to make sure we knew what the guy looked like, what car he drove, his height, weight, and any distinguishing features just in case the police needed the information. The only person I ever trusted to get that information was Nicole. She didn't play.

"Vickie ain't never picked no decent looking guy. Even Mitch is kinda of a mess," Nicole said, and she had a point. Victoria always found the ugliest looking guy to be cute as long as he drove a Benz and wore Armani. Not that her husband Mitchell was ugly. I mean, he's the nicest guy you will ever meet. He's always there for Victoria no matter what she needs, covers for her when she goes into her selfish mood, and through the years, he has always done what he could to make sure our friendship stayed intact. Once he said, "Vickie needs you ladies to stay grounded. I don't know what kind of wife I'd be coming home to if you ladies were not around." He's a really great guy but he was far from my type. I mean I don't tend to go for the short pudgy type.

I took a long deep breath and looked at myself in the mirror. The dress I chose was a black wrap around that hugged my body in all the right places. It fit me like a glove. I picked a gorgeous pair of Louboutin shoes that made me look less like five-seven and more like six-feet. I wore a matching pair of earrings and necklace that made my light brown complexion glisten. I placed my hand on my stomach to make sure that it was not sticking out.

"You ain't got no stomach, heffa." Nicole yelled out.

"Yes I do. It's right here," I said pointing at it.

"Bitch, please. Try pushing out two kids like me and then we can talk about a stomach."

Before I could continue finding imperfections, there was a knock at the door. Nicole leaped off the bed and ran down the stairs to open it. Standing on the other side was a tall, light-skinned perfectly built brother.

"Damn, baby, come in." Nicole pulled the man into my apartment.

"Hi," he said to Nicole. I came quietly down the stairs and hid around the corner until I made sure he really looked good and that it wasn't just my imagination.

"Are you Joanna?" the Man asked Nicole.

"I could be." Nicole replied.

"No she's not," I say as I ran from around the corner. "I'm Joanna- Joanna Stuart and you are?"

"Bryan Roberts, and these are for you." Bryan handed me a bouquet of long-stemmed red roses.

"Thank you, they're beautiful," I said, taking the flowers from Bryan and giving him what I felt was my sexiest smile.

I diverted my attention to Nicole who was busy staring lustily at Bryan.

"Hey, Joanna Number Two." I said to her.

"What?" Nicole asked, not taking her eyes off Bryan.

"Could you put these in some water please?" I tried to hand the flowers to Nicole, but she was so focused on Bryan that she didn't even notice.

After all these years of being around her, I knew exactly what she was thinking and it was strictly X-rated.

Nicole didn't budge. Instead the lusty look in her eyes turned to confusion and she folded her arms.

"I don't get it. You know, Vickie?" she asked.

"Vickie? Oh, Victoria, I know her husband Mitchell; his law firm represents my firm. Victoria called me up and asked if I would be interested in a blind date." Bryan then turned to me and said with a smile, "I'm glad she did." I smiled back and flung the roses into Nicole's arms.

"Lock up when you leave," I told her.

His story and Victoria's story didn't match up but he was so fine that I decided to worry about it later. I took Bryan by the arm.

"Are you ready?"

"After you," He replied.

We got to one of the most upscale restaurants in Baltimore around eight-thirty, and by that time it was packed with couples trying to be romantic. The restaurant did not disappoint on the romance. It was dimly lit, and all the tables had candles that sat inside of crystal holders. Everyone seemed to be in their own space, and while there was talking, it was so soft as if each table were miles away.

I was so impressed by how charismatic Bryan was. He never took his eyes off me, paid me compliments, and had been holding my hand the entire time. The whole evening was going perfectly. We were talking and laughing and we'd even discovered that we had a lot in common. He was passing the D-test with flying colors; oh yeah, he was definitely getting some tonight.

I was excited that Victoria finally got it right and came through for once. I couldn't wait to see what he was like in bed. I began having fantasies of his strong hands caressing my body and his plump pink lips searching me slowly until they found that right spot. But before I got completely wet, I noticed a commotion at the front door. I realized that it was a woman who was trying to get in but obviously didn't have a reservation. "Would you look at that. Some people think they can just bully their way through anything." I pointed out the commotion to Bryan who turned to look at the door then quickly looked away and buried his face in his hand.

"Oh shit ... it's my wife," he said.

"Your what? You're married?" I waited for him to begin laughing and saying that it was just a joke, but the motherfucker didn't.

"Yeah, well separated, but she doesn't seem to understand that," he answered.

I couldn't move. I wanted to slap the shit out of him, but I felt a little confused. Is he married? Separated? Is she stalking him? What the hell was this fool up to?

Pretty soon, the woman managed to plow her way through the hostess and walked right up to the table.

"Bryan, what the hell is this?" the woman asked, shouting to the top of her lungs.

"Baby, listen, it's not what you think," Bryan replied.

"Oh, it's not what I think? Well it looks like you're on a date with this stink hoe." The woman said.

"Ok, wait a minute." I started to say, but quickly caught myself from getting completely ignorant. It was one thing for her to be mad at her man, but calling me out my name was something different.

"Baby, this is just a business dinner," Bryan said as he stood up to grab hold of the woman's hand.

"Business!" The woman and I both yelled at the same time since this being a business dinner was news to the both of us.

"Ok, you know what, this is way too much drama and I'm out," I said. "Girl, I didn't know he was married; you can keep him" I stood up and could see everyone in the restaurant staring at us; some of them were even laughing.

This was so embarrassing, and I had to get out of there. I grabbed my purse and walked out. Outside I hailed a cab and left. Once the cab began to move, I immediately took my cell phone out of my purse and called Victoria.

"Hello," Victoria answered, sounding as if she were half asleep. "How could you do that to me?"

"Do what?"

"Send me on a date with a married man."

"He's married? Oops, sorry."

"'Oops sorry'? That is not an oops, sorry, Vickie. That's an I'm gonna kick your ass when I see you, that's what that is."

"Well, he's a friend of Mitch's, I really don't know him."

"Vickie, next time don't even mention my name to any man. As a matter of fact when you see a man, just forget that you even know me." I hung up the phone without giving her time to respond. Victoria was never going to think she did anything wrong. That's just how she is. All I needed right now was a sympathetic ear so I had the cabdriver take me to David's house.

As usual, David let me in. The sight of him made my body quiver. The minute he opened the door and looked at me, it was as if he were looking right to my soul.

"Where are you coming from?" he asked me.

It was obvious that he was either getting ready for bed or just spending the evening lounging on the couch because he was dressed in sweat pants and a t-shirt. He made loungewear look damn good.

"I was on a date."

"Oh really? With who?"

"Some married guy Vickie set me up with."

"Did you know he was married when you went out with him?" David looked at me like he was shocked that I would do such a thing.

"Of course not. It was a blind date."

I told David everything that happened and watched as David began to roar with laughter.

"Oh it's funny? Me being embarrassed in front of a restaurant full of people is funny?" The sight of him finding humor in my anguish amused me a bit. I felt myself starting to crack a smile.

"I'm sorry Jo, but that shit is funny as hell," he said as he walked over to his sofa and sat down.

"No, it's not," I said sitting next to him.

"Oh, come here girl." David reached over and put his arms around me. I laid my head on his shoulder and allowed him to hold me. David's arms felt so secure that I didn't want him to let me go. This is where I should have been tonight. Not with some random guy but with this guy—my guy.

8

A couple of days had gone by without seeing or hearing from Michael, and I had finally come to the conclusion that our relationship was over. As Nicole would put it, "good riddance to the dog." Tonight it was going to be all about me. I was off and could just relax in my living room doing absolutely nothing. I put on my sweats and lay on my sofa watching television. Still I couldn't help but wonder where Michael was and what he was doing. The pictures on the wall of the two of us reminded me of better times, and I wished we could go back there. The pain of losing him was killing me, and it was getting harder for me to hide my feelings. I couldn't stop reminiscing about the days when he and I were blissfully happy - the way he loved me, the way he held me. As tears began to fill my eyes, I heard keys in my front door. When the door opened, it was Michael with a bouquet of flowers in his hand. I wasn't sure how to feel at the moment. On one hand I was so happy he was home, but on the other hand I couldn't believe he had the nerve to come into my home after what he had done. It was much too soon, and I still needed to figure things out. The sight of him standing before me looking as if nothing had changed made me burst into tears.

"Baby, please don't do that. Just listen to me," he said as he came through the door closing it behind him.

"Listen to what - some more of your lies?" I asked as I stood up and tried to walk away from him.

"No, Jess, that's why I'm here. I want to be upfront and honest with you, so ask me anything and I'll tell you the truth. I swear." His eyes looked at me and made my heart long for him, his touch, his smile, his love.

"Ok, did you sleep with Mo?" My whole body dreaded hearing the answer. I had to cross my arms just to hold myself together. I feared my legs would give out so I leaned against the wall that separated the kitchen from the living room.

"No... ok... yes...but just once that's all," he answered.

"That's all?'" I couldn't believe that those words just came out of his mouth. How could he possibly think that one time didn't mean anything?

"Yeah, baby, and the thing is, I thought about you the entire time." Michael sounded as if he had done something I should be proud of. Like thinking about me while fucking some bitch was a good thing.

"You thought about me? But you didn't think to not sleep with her?" I asked.

"Baby, I love you more than anything and these past few days have been pure hell without you." Michael was walking towards me like he expected me to jump into his arms.

"Michael, just leave." By now tears were so full in my eyes that I could barely see.

"No, baby, I don't want to ever be apart from you again." Michael put his arm around my waist. His touch was my kryptonite and he knew it.

"Well, you've already made that choice so—" I tried to push him away but he wouldn't let me. Then Michael said something that made my whole body shake.

"Marry me?" Michael got down on his knee and pulled out an engagement ring.

"What?" I asked in complete disbelief.

I had been waiting for the day that Michael would propose to me and make our relationship official. But this wasn't the way I expected it to be. For years, I dreamed of a lavish dinner in a room full of roses and violin music and I would look into Michael's eye and see nothing but love, not guilt. This was not the way I wanted it or imagined it.

A part of me was angered that Michael took that dream from me. How dare he? But that side of me that tells me that Michael could be the man that I wanted him to be was talking to me again. He proposed. That meant he's now ready to change. When I looked into his eyes, there was love there and that made everything seems right somehow. He was not perfect or close to what I needed, but he was the man that I wanted and I knew that one day he would be the man that I deserved.

"Yes. Yes, I'll marry you."

9

As the sun rose, I turned to face Michael who was peacefully sleeping beside me. Making love to Michael always seemed to leave me in a cloud of confusion. He felt so right as if he was made just to be with me. But I couldn't help but wonder how many other women felt the way I did after they'd made love to him. I ran my fingers across Michael's face and tears filled my eyes again. He was the only man I'd ever loved, and I had waited for the day when he realized that I was all he needed. I wanted to hold him and know without question that I was the only one.

I looked down at my engagement ring and could no longer fight back the tears. I got out of bed and locked myself in the bathroom. Pretending to trust Michael after what happened with Monique was probably the toughest thing I had ever had to do. My head and my heart were at war and my heart seemed to be winning. How could I let go of a man who holds such a vital part of me in the palm of his hand? I loved him too much to lose him. How could I ever let him go?

I turned on the shower and stood underneath it. Michael's touch lingered against my skin as the water ran down my body. I closed my eyes and went back to the place when I first loved Michael and he first loved me.

"Baby, why you got the door locked?" Michael's voice yelled from the other side of the bathroom door.

I came to myself and yelled back "I don't know I'll be out in a sec."

"That's alright, I'll use the guest bathroom."

I was glad that Michael didn't come in the bathroom with me. It never occurred to me that sex with Michael would leave me with such conflicting emotions. I remembered when my whole body would quiver with just the touch of his hand. Whenever he entered me, it was like I heard angels sing. That's how I knew he was my soul mate-the one that was made just for me. Now it almost seemed forced, like we were both obligated to each other.

I was nearly dressed when Michael came back into the room wrapped with a towel and still dripping wet from his shower. Looking at him half naked took me back to a time when I believed that he was much too good looking to be with me. Now I wondered why I was with him. What was it about him that made me cling to him with all that is in me? The words that he said and the way that he said them could possibly be the reason. Michael walked over to me and caressed me in his arms, and then he kissed me gently on the lips. Maybe that was the reason-the way Michael touched and kissed me made me dream of happily ever after with him.

"Baby, my car is acting up. How 'bout I drop you off at work and use yours," he said after letting me go.

"How will I get home?" felt the after effects of his embrace. It was like little shockwaves ran from my head right down to my toes.

"Baby come on, do you think I would leave my best girl stranded at work?"

"Alright, I guess that's fine. I need to be in soon so you better hurry up and get ready."

Michael dropped me off on time and promised to be just as prompt when he picked me up after my shift. I stood on the sidewalk in front of the hospital and watched as he drove off. Something inside me was saying that I never should have trusted him enough to give him my car, but I dismissed that feeling and figured that if I loved him enough to agree to marry him, then I would have to love him enough to trust him.

The entire workday went by very quickly. I was consumed with so many patients that I barely thought about Michael at all. It wasn't until almost the end of the day when I realized that I hadn't heard from him yet; he didn't even leave me a voicemail. I tried my best to block all thoughts of what Michael could be doing. Neither my patients nor I could afford the distracting thoughts of a painfully dysfunctional relationship. I had to believe that Michael would be waiting outside for me at the end of the day just like he'd promised.

Finally my shift was over and I went into the doctor's lounge to gather my things. I thought that if I took my time, it would give Michael enough time to arrive. Once outside I saw a car that looked like mine parked a few feet from the hospital entrance. I felt such relief as I began to walk towards the car. But the closer I got the more I noticed that the car was not mine and the person sitting in the driver's seat was not Michael. I stopped walking and looked around. There were no sign of my car or my man. The hands on my watch showed that ten minutes had passed since my shift ended and still no Michael. I didn't want to panic. Maybe there was traffic or maybe he was running late at work, or maybe he had to make a quick stop somewhere. So I just waited patiently. Another ten minutes went by and still no Michael. Then another and another. I covered my face with my hands and wanted so badly to burst into tears. Just then I heard someone say "Everything alright?" I turned to see Dr. Todd Reynolds standing behind me with a look of concern across his face.

"It seems that I have no ride," I responded.

"Sure you do, I can take you home."

"I don't want to bother you. I'll just call a cab or something."

"It's no bother. Come on. I won't even charge." Todd's smile made me feel a little better and gave me the courage to push back the tears.

The drive was soothing for me; there was something about Todd that made me feel comfortable around him. As he drove me home, Todd said just the right things to put a smile on my face. By the time I got home I had laughed so hard that I wasn't even thinking about Michael or how much he had let me down.

"Thank you for the ride."

"It was my pleasure. Anytime you need anything, you just have to ask." That was the first time during this drive that I saw Todd with a serious expression on his face. The whole ride home he seemed as though he realized how down I was and was trying his best to pick me back up again. I gave Todd a smile and then got out of the car. As I walked to my door, I turned to see Todd still waiting to make sure I got in all right. It was the sweetest and most gentlemanly thing that any man had done for me in a very long time.

It must have been more than two hours after I had arrived home when I heard Michael come in. I didn't say a word to Michael because my anger wouldn't allow me to show restraint. Instead, I turned my back to him and pretended to be so intrigued with what was on the television that I hadn't even noticed he was home.

"Oh baby, I'm sorry." He said as he came over to sit by me.

Still I didn't speak. Every word out of Michael's mouth was a lie and I didn't have the strength to listen or accept it right now.

"Come on baby say something. I just didn't know when your shift was over," Michael said in the most innocent voice he could muster.

"What!" I had to give him my attention at that moment because that lie was just so obvious.

"What I mean is I thought you were working a double shift. I'm sorry," he said.

"Just get away from me," I replied pushing his hands off me.

But Michael didn't give up. He pulled me close to him and began to hug and kiss me saying "I'm so sorry baby." There's that touch again. Before I could stop myself, I had allowed him to break down my defenses and defuse my anger. I allowed him to lay me down on the sofa and kiss every inch of me as he slowly took off my clothes. Once again I was making love to Michael and right back to feeling like I did when I woke up that morning.

10

"Hey girl," I answered my phone after just one ring once I saw that it was Jessica who was calling. It was already late on a Saturday afternoon and I had done all the sleeping I could possible do and now I was bored. So I was really excited that Jessica had called. At least I could talk on the phone for a while and add some sort of sound to the echoing silence in my loft.

"What are you doing, Jo?" Jessica asked me, as if she were excited about something.

"Nothing, just eating and sleeping. That's about it."

"You sound bored as hell."

"Yeah but—" I started to say.

"But what?"

"I just can't stop thinking about something."

"About what?"

"There's a promotion that I may be up for and I really want it, Jess."

"Jo, what are you worried about? You're the only person I know who always get what they want no matter what."

Jessica's words were reassuring, but I still had massive amounts of doubts. It was hard enough getting to the position I was currently in. I was absolutely certain that if the partners at my firm could find just the right white man for the job, I would be completely disregarded and all my hard work would have been for nothing. It wasn't as if I was giving up hope. I knew that there was no one, man or woman, who could do the job I did. But the good ol' boy network reigned supreme and someone like me who already fight two battles-first as a black person and then as a woman-had to rely on hard work and a little bit of luck. Since luck never seemed to be in my favor, hard work was all I had. But now for the first time in my career I distrusted even that. The moment Mr. Stephens told me about this opening for a marketing director I wanted it and I hoped that all my hard work would pay off.

"Hey listen, you remember my aunt who lives down in Columbia, right?" Jessica asked me.

"Yeah what about her?"

"Well she's having a little get-together tonight and I don't want to go alone. So you need to come with me."

"Why do I need to come with you?"

"Because I don't want to go by myself."

"Why?"

"Will you stop asking questions and just say you'll come."

"I don't know Jess, I—" Just as the excuses of why I couldn't go began to fumble around in my brain, Nicole walked through my door smiling yet still looking as if steam was about to fly through her ears. I took one look at her and knew that she and Steven had probably had another fight, but thought it best not to ask and allow Nicole the opportunity to volunteer the information. That was just how we've always done it. I didn't press for information, and Nicole gave me the information she thought I should have and nothing more. As long as she wasn't all bruised up, I could let it slide.

Once I told Nicole what Jessica had planned for the night, it was as if a big beam of light hit her face.

"Well shit, let's go," Nicole said, seemingly happy about having something to do. I really didn't feel like leaving my loft. I preferred to stay alone with my own thoughts tonight. My goal was to do nothing else but concentrate on work until I knew one way or another if I'd gotten the promotion. But my friends' persistence made me give in and I soon agreed to go with them.

"Alright, I'm going to pick you guys up in a few." Jessica hurriedly hung up the phone.

"Damn, I ain't even got nothing to wear." Nicole looked at the jeans and plain t-shirt she wore to come see me.

"What's wrong with what you got on?"

"Look at this shit," Nicole pointed to the clothes she had on as if they were absolutely disgusting, "I just left my house with this shit I've been wearing all day. I went to my momma's house to drop the kids off and did some work for her with this shit on. Now you want me to go out looking like this?"

"Go upstairs and find something then." I instructed. Nicole sometimes aggravated me with the way she would put down everything about herself. Nowhere in the conversation did Jessica say that this was some formal event. To me, jeans and t-shirt were just fine.

While Nicole was rummaging through my closet, I was trying to call Victoria. I thought that it would be more fun if we could have a girl's night out, just the four of us. But Victoria didn't answer any of her phones, so I left a message telling her where we would be on the off chance she wanted to join us.

"Who you calling?" Nicole asked me as she came down the stairs fully dressed in one of my black leggings and a blouse that was covered in animal prints and loose enough to hide the imperfections of her body.

"I was just trying to call Vickie," I answered.

"What for?" Nicole asked, looking disgusted.

"Because she's our friend and if we are going out, then she should, too."

"You know damn well that if Vickie comes along she's gonna complain about every damn thing. I say leave her ass where she is." Nicole took a seat on the sofa and turned on the TV.

I figured that Nicole's resistance to Victoria coming along was more about the two of them not being able to get along for more than five minutes and not so much about Victoria's dissatisfaction with all things that were not part of Victoria's world. Nicole and Victoria had serious problems with each other, and I didn't have the strength it took to deal with the two of them at the moment. I had more important things to think about. I ignored Nicole's comment about Victoria and went to get dressed. Before long, Jessica had arrived and the three of us were headed down I-95.

When we arrived, the three of us exited Jessica's car and the first thing I saw was David's car parked just a few feet from where we were.

"David's here." I felt a sense of pure joy.

"I swear you can sniff out that man from a mile away." Nicole said.

"No bitch, I just saw his car." I cut my eyes at Nicole and walked away.

Behind me, I could hear Nicole and Jessica snicker but it didn't bother me. I was too busy trying to quickly get into the house and find David. Unfortunately, the three of us were detained at the front door by Jessica's aunt who kept asking us questions and wanting to know what we were up to now. My eyes searched the room as Jessica's aunt talked.

I was hoping to spot David among the crowd of people, but there was no sight of him. Finally Jessica's aunt stopped talking long enough for us to come into the house.

Inside, my eyes continued its search as I slowly walked past acquaintances who greeted me with hugs and warm hellos. At last, I spotted David talking amidst a group of people. Our eyes met and he flashed me one of his sexy smiles.

"There goes your man," Nicole whispered in my ear.

"Shut up, Girl."

I began to feel the same nervous anticipation I always got whenever David came around me. I placed my hand on my stomach and took several slow deep breaths. "You better go on over there and talk to that boy," Nicole told me. I began walking towards David, but was stopped by a very aggressive admirer.

"Damn, baby, you fine," The man who was dressed in a bright yellow shirt and brown pants said. When he smiled, his gold tooth nearly blinded me. "Them jeans are fitting you in all the right places," The man's eyes wandered over my body that was dressed in tightly fitted black jeans and a blue wrap around shirt. "Girl I can sop you up with a biscuit you look so good." I rolled my eyes and looked back at Nicole and Jessica who were laughing almost to the point of tears. Somehow I was always the one who ended up having to deal with the weird mac daddies and my friends constantly found it funny.

"I'm not interested, but thanks for the compliment. Ok." I tried to walk past him but with no such luck.

"Wait a minute now, baby. You don't even know what I got, so how you know you not interested?" the man said.

"Cause I know what I need and you sure ain't it." I tried to be as stern as possible, but some men just don't get it no matter how you say it.

"Damn, baby, you starting to hurt my feelings," the man replied.

I shrugged my shoulders and made another attempt to pass by him, but once again he prevented me from doing so. Just then, David walked up behind the man and patted him on his shoulders saying, "Hey Curtis, I got this, man." I gave Dave an appreciative smile and mouthed "thank you."

"Damn. Dave man. How many woman you gonna have?" the man said and finally walked away. I was puzzled by the man's question but

I was so glad that David came to my rescue that I never thought to inquire about what the man meant.

"You have saved me and I thank you," I said to David.

"Well you're welcome. I'm always happy to save you, Jo," he replied.

Hugging David was such a comforting feeling. I was always in control and tended to overpower those I came in contact with. But whenever David held me, his body sucked me in and I would get lost in his arms; I felt small and protected. That was the only time I was able to let go and allow someone else to lead.

"David." A woman's voice called softly from behind him. David let me go and wrapped his arms around the woman. I stood back to give the woman a once over and gave David my "who the hell is this bitch" look. I waited for David to tell this other woman that he was talking and she needed to leave, but instead he said, "Tiff this is Jo, one of my really good friends." Good friends? When did we only become "good friends?" I felt the ghetto coming out of me. It took everything I had not to snatch the bitch bald.

"Nice to meet you," the woman said and held out her hand.

"Likewise," I replied in the most insincere voice I could muster. I barely wanted to touch her, but when my hands met hers I wanted to squeeze it tight and swing her around the room like the rag doll she looked like.

Nicole and Jessica who had been watching the entire event unfold came up beside me.

"Hey, cuz," Jessica said as she gave David a hug.

"Oh, I see you finally took some time off, huh, Jess," he said to her.

"'Bout time, ain't it," Nicole said to David, then gave him a hug as well.

After every hug, David placed his arms back around the woman, and I watched in contempt at the way the woman held onto David and gushed as he introduced her. I refused to say anything for fear that my true feelings would flow through my words. Instead, I just listened as the woman told Nicole and Jessica all about herself and how she and David met. I grew increasingly irritated at the sound of the woman's voice and wanted to be far away from her and David or at the very least tie her ass in a corner somewhere so she could get the hell away from my man. But as long as the woman didn't include me in the conversation, then I figured I would be spared from having to actually speak to this person.

"So, Joanna, what is that you do?" Oh no, this bitch didn't just address me. I thought for a long time and was about to blurt out, I kick bitches' asses who try to steal another woman's man. But before I could say anything, my cell phone rang and I simply excused myself.

I made my way to the porch and answered my phone. It was Victoria calling me back to say that she couldn't make it. But I really wasn't up to talking to anyone at the moment. I was feeling much too hurt and angry to hold a conversation. So I simply said, "It's ok, Vickie. I understand. Talk to you soon." But Victoria kept on talking about her day.

"Vickie, I really got to go," I finally said. Although I had gotten Victoria to hang up, I still held the phone up to my face and wrapped my free arm tightly around my waist. Every time I saw another woman standing beside David, in a spot where I should be standing, something inside me died a little. At that moment, I hated my ambition. If I wasn't so driven, then I wouldn't pull away from David and it would be me holding him and gushing.

"Hey Jo, you still on the phone?" I heard David's voice from behind me.

"Ah no...no...I'm done."

"Well, what was so important that it couldn't wait?"

"Umm . . ." I struggled to find the words. I didn't want to say that it was only Victoria. I knew that David might accept that as a reason for me running out but not as a reason for me being so upset. "...its just work."

"Today's Saturday, Jo."

"I know, but I'm up for this promotion and so I got to be ready twenty-four-seven." It's funny how every time I tried to lie to David, I never could look him straight in the eye. I always found a reason to bend my head or to look in another direction.

"Oh, a promotion. You really want it?" David's eyes searched my face until they caught mine as if he knew I couldn't lie to him while looking directly at him.

"Of course." I bent my head again this time. I didn't know why because I do really want the promotion. "I've sacrificed a lot not to want it."

"Then I hope you get it."

I looked up at David and gave him a smile. I didn't know if he realized that the sacrifice I made was not being able to be with him. If I lost out on the promotion, then denying my heart its one true desire would have been for nothing. I knew I was missing out on probably the most amazing man. But my life was centered on my career. I didn't know how to make time for anything else, and David deserved a woman who was able to put him first.

David took me by the hand and led me back inside. I spent the rest of the evening avoiding Curtis the gold tooth bandit and watching David as he enjoyed the company of someone other than me. I felt as though I was crying, but there were no tears coming from my eyes and my lips shivered every time I smiled. Maybe this was the woman who would make him happy. Maybe tonight was the night that I'd finally lose David forever.

11

"My lord! Why on earth would you put that there?" I had to take the chair out of the hand of one of the workers I'd hired to set up for a fundraising dinner party I was hosting at my house.

"There are too many chairs at this table! Can't you see that?" My nerves were beginning to get the best of me and every little thing was setting me off. This fundraiser was just so important that I couldn't afford anything to go wrong. There were going to be some of the wealthiest and most influential people in the state of Maryland at my house. This was huge; everything had to be perfect. I could not allow anything to ruin this for me.

I took a look around the room to make sure every table had the right amount of chairs. Then, I put my personal touch on each and every decoration. I was proud that I could turn my home into something of shear elegance. Why else would I have made Mitchell buy me such an extravagant home if not for days like this? The ballroom in my house had been turned into an enchanted oasis. Earlier, I made the housekeeper clean the wall of windows that ran from floor to ceiling so that as night falls, the twinkling lights from the stars will dance across the dimly lit room. Each of the tables were centered with white hydrangeas nestled inside a crystal vase and circled by small white candles.

My next step was to ensure that the chef was preparing the most exquisite meal money could buy. The food's scents already filled the house. The sweet aroma of herbs and spices made it seem as if I were on some far away Caribbean island.

As I made my way to the kitchen, I saw Mitchell on his way out the door. I was stunned that Mitchell would leave at a time like this. He knew how important this all was to me. What was more important than ensuring that we make a good impression on people who could change our lives?

"Where are you going?" I asked him.

"To the office."

"But I could really use your help here."

I was not completely convinced that the office was where he was headed. It was a Saturday afternoon; late afternoon. Who goes to the office at this time?

"Vickie, you know that I'm working on a major case. Besides, it looks like you have that all under control," he said, sounding as if I should never have questioned him.

"I know, but I just assumed that you would put off going to work for one night. But then again why should my needs be on your list of priorities?"

I tried to sound as calm and as patient as I possibly could, graciously walking away from Mitchell and continuing my journey to the kitchen. From behind me I could hear the front door slam as Mitchell left. I stopped walking for just a moment to catch my breath. It felt as though all the blood had drained from my entire body and I grew weak. It was a struggle for me to gain my composure again but I was determined not to give Mitchell the satisfaction of distracting me from what mattered most.

I put all thoughts of Mitchell out of my head once I entered the kitchen; it was back to business and I decided to deal with all the other stuff later. Right now every entrée the chef prepared had to be tasted and every appetizer approved. It is without a doubt going to be a perfect dinner party. Everything is as I wanted it to be and no one could find fault with anything.

"Victoria, sweetie. Where are you?" Hearing the sound of my mother's voice made my heart sink. I knew that if just one thing was out of place my mother would make me start from scratch.

"I'm in the kitchen, Mother!" I took a minute to look everything over one more time.

"Oh, sweetie, there you are. Everything looks wonderful."

I found myself being pleased that my mother approved of the decorations and hoped that the same would prove true for the food. My mother was very particular about what she ate and what she served. But I felt confident that she would be satisfied since she was the one who recommended the chef in the first place.

"So, Sweetie, what's on the menu for tonight?"

That was a bit of an odd question since she was the one who suggested the menu. Nevertheless, I showed her all of the food the chef had prepared. It seemed as if my mother admired the meal, but looks could be deceiving when it came to her.

"What do you think, Mother?" I knew there wasn't a thing that she could possibly find wrong.

"Well, not bad. I can live with it." That was the best that I could expect to get out of her. Exuberance was not one of her character traits, so that "not bad" meant that my mother was pleased.

"Oh, sweetie, look at the time. You have got to go upstairs and get ready before your guests start to arrive," she said to me.

I quickly made my way up the stairs and began to dress. My mother had bought me a beautiful navy blue pantsuit that was enhanced by a fur-like collar on the jacket. I took a look at myself in the mirror-sharp. I put out my best Louboutin stilettos and headed back down stairs. The minute my mother saw me, she blurted out, "Marvelous." I was glad that she approved. Then she began to stare at me up and down.

"There's something wrong," she said.

"What? Everything looks good to me."

"No, your hair."

"What's wrong with it?"

"It needs to be down, that suit just cries for you to let your beautiful long hair flow down your back." My mother walked over to me to take the pins out of my hair. She brushed my hair until it was silky smooth with just a hint of soft curls. Then she stood back to admire her work.

"That is absolutely gorgeous. Not many black women can say they have hair like yours, sweetie. You wear it well."

While I was admiring my hair in the hallway mirror, the front door opened and Mitchell walked in. He stood still for a while and just stared at me. I didn't know what to make of his expression. It was as if he had just seen an old friend for the first time in years. I could feel myself blush a bit and started to feel the connection between the two of us that had somehow gotten lost.

"Mitchell, where on earth have you been?" My mother was stern with her questioning of Mitchell.

"Relax, Lyn, I'm here now," Mitchell said as he walked up to me with a faint smile.

"Well, it would have been highly inappropriate for you not to have been here, Mitchell," my mother said.

"Mother, it's alright he's here now." I was barely able to take my eyes off Mitchell. The way he looked at me, or rather the way he used to look at me, always made me feel like a queen.

"No, Victoria, it is inappropriate, isn't it?" My mother gave me a stern look, and I know that I hadn't any choice but to agree.

"You shouldn't have left, Mitch," I said. As the words flowed through my mouth, I stared at my mother. I hoped that Mitchell would see that it was my mother, not me, who felt this way. I somehow thought that maybe later we would have a good laugh about it and Mitchell would look at me that way again. Mitchell instead shook his head and didn't say a word. He made his way past both of us and went up the stairs.

"Mother, you shouldn't have done that." I tried to admonish her, but she just always had her own way of looking at things.

"Done what? Tell the truth?"

"Mother you know what I mean." I said. I am so frustrated at my mother's constant behavior towards Mitchell. All I could do at this point was to walk away from her.

"Sweetie, have you forgotten that he is the adulterer in this house," she said as she followed after me.

"Mother..." I don't want her to go there again. I get it. She thinks Mitchell cheats and perhaps he does, but I just do not have to be reminded of it over and over again. I was just about to enjoy a rare moment with my husband and she ruined it.

"No, you listen to me. If his presence in our lives wasn't key, then I would tell you to get rid of him; but even the dirtiest of dogs serve their purpose. But don't you dare fall for his charm. I did not raise you to be easily fooled." My mother put her hand under my chin and lifted up my head.

"Remember who you are, my love. He is lucky to have you as his wife. That man should be kissing the ground you walk on."

I looked at my mother's face and could do nothing but agree once again. For a moment, I forgot that Mitchell was unfaithful, and I'm thankful that my mother was there to remind me.

I shook off any thoughts of the connection I felt with Mitchell when he walked through the door as nothing more than a momentary lapse in judgment on my part and I could not let that happen again. It was

Mitchell who was in the wrong, and I need to worry more about the people coming here tonight and less about my husband.

—⁓•⊶⊷⊶•⊷⊶•⁓—

Soon people started to arrive, and I turned into the ultimate hostess, only surpassed by my mother of course. The two of us worked the room like a well-oiled machine. We greeted and hugged and kissed everyone who walked through the door. I was on cloud nine because the best of the best were in attendance; senior level senators and congressmen, the lieutenant governor of Maryland, and even my father who hated things like this made an appearance. It was fabulous. Everybody knew that this was my house, and they all came because I invited them.

As I spoke to a very rich and powerful businessman from DC, I heard my mother say, "What on earth is she doing here?" I turned in the direction that my mother was looking and saw Nicole standing there as if she was completely lost. Then I saw Joanna walk in and stand beside her. I couldn't help but smile at the sight of my friends. I knew that they are here to support me, and I was so excited. Before I could walk towards them, my mother stopped me.

"Sweetie, why don't you stay and continue your conversation, I'll make sure they're comfortable." I watched as my mother went over to my friends and gave Joanna a hug but only smiles at Nicole. Then I saw my mother take Joanna by the hand and pull her away from Nicole. I felt awful watching Nicole stand there all alone. I didn't know why my mother always treated Nicole like that and if I could have stopped her, I would have. My focus was so much on Nicole that I excused myself from the conversation I was in and went up to her.

"Hey Nic." I wanted her to see how happy I was that she was here.

"This is nice, Vickie. You did good." It felt pretty good getting Nicole's approval.

"Thanks, it was hard but..." I started to engage Nicole in a conversation, but my mother came over and grabbed me by the arm.

"Victoria, Senator Johnson has been asking for you," she said, once again ignoring Nicole's presence.

"I'll be right there, Mother. Let me finish talking to Nic first." I tried to get my mother to go away and leave Nicole and I alone, but my mother was insistent.

"Victoria, you can't keep a US senator waiting. I'm sure your... Nicole would understand."

"It's alright. Vickie, go ahead, I'll be here." Nicole graciously allowed me to leave even though doing so would mean that she would be all alone.

I followed my mother's lead and before long I found myself completely forgetting that Nicole was even in the room. When I finally did remember, I looked around to see if she was alright. I saw her standing in a circle of people beside Mitchell talking and laughing. Soon Joanna joined them and the three of them seemed to be enjoying each other's company immensely. For the first time all evening I felt left out. My husband and my two best friends were having the time of their lives at my party without me. Even during the dinner, Mitchell was supposed to sit near me and Joanna was supposed to sit at a table next to her boss, an arrangment I made to help Joanna get the promotion she wanted. Instead both Joanna and Mitchell sat at the table with Nicole; a table filled with the lesser-known people.

I was completely livid. How could my friends and my husband disregard me at my own party? I couldn't wait to tell them how I felt, but Joanna and Nicole left without even saying goodbye, and Mitchell kept his distance for what was left of the evening.

After everyone had gone home, I found myself sitting alone in our living room. An evening that was supposed to be all about me, ended up making me feel as though I were the odd man out. All I wanted was to have a moment that showed me in my element, at my best. Is there anything wrong with that? Why couldn't they just give me that? I made my way upstairs to my bedroom where I found Mitchell putting on his clothes for bed.

"I'm not quite sure what the three of you were doing but it wasn't appreciated," I told Mitchell.

"What are you talking about?" Mitchell tried to sound as if I was losing my mind, but he knew very well what I'm talking about.

"You, Joanna, and Nicole made me look terrible tonight."

"Look terrible? Did you look as terrible as Nicole felt when you totally disregarded her?"

"What are you talking about? I spoke to Nicole, but I had more important guests to tend to."

All the while Mitchell and I were talking, I could feel the anger build up in him and had no idea where it was coming from. After all, he was the one who had wronged me. I just don't get Mitchell anymore. When it was about him, when he was building his career, I did everything he asked of me just to make him look good to the other partners. I went to all the events and I shook hands with all the right people. I mean, I was the perfect wife. Now that I was doing me, doing something that's important to *me*, he acted like this.

"Vickie, sometimes I don't even know who you are any more." Mitchell sounded as if he had reached the end of his rope as if I'd done something wrong to him.

"I'm not the one who's changed."

"You're right. Maybe we have both turned out to be different people who see things differently."

"Yes, I think that's quite possible." I waited for Mitchell to say that despite that, we would be able to work things out. But instead he headed for the door.

"I'll be sleeping in another bedroom from now on." Mitchell voice was soft and almost seemed to crack with each word.

"What are you talking about?" Where was this coming from? Why did he feel the need to sleep in the other room? I didn't know what I should do or say.

"I think we both need our space from one another." Mitchell said.

I couldn't believe that Mitchell was doing this. He had always promised me that he would love me forever. That he would never leave me or let me go. Now he's turning his back on me, on us. What's going on? I was pissed.

"Well, just make sure that you don't have your slut with you!" I slammed my bedroom door and locked it. If he was going to turn his back on me, then I would turn my back on him. I refused to be one of those women that constantly begged a man to come back to her. I was not desperate or pathetic.

But I had never in my life been in such silence. For the first time, I realized how much trouble my marriage was in and I didn't know how to fix it. I dropped to my knees and began to pray:

> *Lord, I can't lose my husband. He's my entire life. Please help me to find a way to make this right. But if it's truly over, please give me the strength to take him for everything he's got. Amen.*

12

"What the shit you mean you cutting back some of my benefits?" Why couldn't nothing get done with these damn welfare people unless you yell at their asses?

"Mrs. Bennett, your husband makes more than the allowable amount. You can't continue to receive all of your services." My caseworker made no fucking sense. If she only knew that the damn dog didn't give nobody nothing. I depended on those benefits to take care of my kids. These bitches were fucking around with food to feed my kids and insurance for them to see the doctor. Now they're saying they ain't going to be able to do that. What the fuck?

"That's bullshit, I got two kids who I need to feed, and now you telling me I can't!" I yelled at the caseworker - a fat, short black lady with a manly haircut.

"I'm sorry, Mrs. Bennett, but those are the rules. As long as your husband is in the home and is making enough to sustain a family of four, then there's nothing we can do," she said.

"He only makes a couple of dollars over the limit," I said. But trying to reason with these people was like hitting your head against a brick wall.

"A couple of dollars over is over. I'm sorry," she replied.

"What about the insurance? Do they still get that?" I asked her.

"Well Mrs. Bennett, our records indicate that your husband works full-time, and his employer should be able to cover insurance for your kids," she said as she looked through some folder on her desk.

"If that was the fucking case I wouldn't have needed your asses in the first place!"

"Mrs. Bennett, I get that things are tough, but rules are rules." She was looking at me like I had better get out of her office and leave her the hell alone.

"Well fuck your rules you fucking bitch!" The anger that had been brewing in the pit of my stomach came out all at once and I had to let her have it. Grabbing my kids by the arm and storming out of my caseworker's office probably didn't do much to help me out, but it sure was a lot better than ending up in jail for punching her in the throat.

I couldn't even put my key in the ignition before the tears started to come. The entire reason behind me losing almost all of my benefits was Steve's pathetic ass, and the reason I needed benefits in the first place was cause he don't do what he supposed to do. We were basically living off the benefits I got from the state. Sure, Steven helped out, but what he gave was always what he wanted to, not what we actually needed. I depended on the food stamps to feed my kids and the extra money to help pay the rent and bills. What the hell's going to happen now?

"Mammy, are you ok?" My daughter's voice snapped me back to myself.

"Yeah, baby, I'm fine." I knew that no matter what, I had to figure out a way to take care of my kids and that gave me the strength to actually start the car.

On the drive home, I could hear the sound of Steven's voice. It was like daggers in my ears telling me that I'd once again screwed everything up. I wished that Steven would never have to find out, but I knew that I needed to tell him, so that we could try and make some kind of a plan. But the idea of dealing with that son-of-a-bitch made my head hurt.

Once I got home, I lay on the couch waiting for Steven to get home and go over in my head what I was gonna say to him. I still felt like this could get ugly. With my temper and his, ain't no telling how this conversation was going to turn out. I heard Steven's car pull-up and my heart started to beat faster. I wasn't scared of the motherfucker, but damn I just didn't feel like dealing with his put-downs or going through the battlefield.

"Y'all go into your rooms and watch TV," I told my kids. I figured it was best to get them out the way in case something popped off.

"Ok, Ma," my kids responded.

"Y'all close the door!" The last thing I wanted was to have my kids caught in the crossfire.

Steven came through the door; the look on his face told me that he had had another bad day. So I decided not to deliver my announcement just then. But once Steven finished eating, I prepared myself.

"Steve," I called.

"What?" By the way Steven answered, it sounded like the sound of my voice was the last thing he wanted to hear.

"Nothing, don't worry about it." I decided to just sleep on it and tell him when he was in a better mood.

But the next day was the same thing. Steven came home agitated and was ready to bite somebody's head off. The day after that was more of the same and so was the day after that. Pretty soon, a week had gone by and food was in short supply not to mention the fact that the rent would be due any day. I had no choice but to tell him and pray we would be able to handle it like adults.

This time though I wasn't going to wait till he got home; I would call him at work and maybe that would be better. I sat at the dining room table, holding the phone to my ear and nervously tapping the table with the other hand.

"Steve, I've got to tell you something." I didn't even say hello the minute he answered the phone.

"It couldn't wait till I got home?" Steven sounded like he was pissed that I called him at work. But I really didn't care cause this way was much easier for me.

"Nah 'cause it's important. We...um...we lost a lot of the benefits from the state."

"How the fuck that happen?"

"They said you make too much money."

"Man, that's bullshit!" Steven held the phone for a while without talking.

I was almost afraid of what he would say next so I also just held the phone and didn't say nothing. Soon I heard Steven yell "SHIT!" then the line went dead. It was almost too good to be true. He hadn't blamed me for anything and although he shouted, it really didn't seem like it was directed at me but at the situation.

Still I didn't want to push my luck. I had to get money from somewhere to pay rent and get some food. But I didn't know how I was going to get the money. I thought about asking my parents for some money, but it was embarrassing. They would ask a bunch of questions that I didn't feel like answering.

Then I thought about my friends, but the last thing I needed was for them to see me down and out again. So I figured I could sell something around my house, but there was nothing in this house worth shit.

My mind was searching for something to do for me to get money when my phone rang. For a minute I thought that Steven had time to think and decided I was at fault and was calling with bullshit. But, much to my relief, it was Joanna.

"Girl, you scared the shit out of me." I couldn't do nothing but laugh at myself for acting like one of those women who shake whenever their husbands come around.

"Why was that?" she asked.

"Nothing girl it's just stupid."

"Nic, you OK?"

"I guess."

"Alright, come on what's going on?"

"I just lost some benefits from the state, that's all." It actually felt good to tell someone I know what was going on and not feel shame.

"Damn, Nic. So what are going to do?"

"I don't know. I'll figure out some way to pay rent, I guess."

"Nic, how much will help you get by at least two months?"

"Jo don't. I can do this myself," I said. I didn't need anyone feeling sorry for me.

"Nic, how much?"

"At least a thousand. You got that laying around?"

I could hear Joanna's mind turning. I sure could use the help but I felt bad having my friends give me money all the time.

"Nic, I'll see you later." Joanna hung up the phone before I could tell her not to do anything. I refused to be a charity case to my friends. There had to be something in this damn place I could sell.

I searched my entire house, and by the time night came, I figured out that I had absolutely nothing. Who the hell doesn't have at least one thing in their house that is valuable? Me, that's who. I sat on my sofa thinking about what I was gonna do when the doorbell rang. Jessica and Joanna were standing on the other side with big, Kool-aid smiles on their faces. I was actually excited to see their stupid asses.

"What you bitches doing here?" I asked.

"We can't come see you anymore?" Joanna asked as she walked in with Jessica following close behind.

Once inside, both of them stood facing me and Joanna handed me a white envelope. I couldn't believe my eyes; the envelope was full of money.

"What's this?"

"Uh, money." Joanna always tried to be so damn sarcastic.

"I know that, jackass, but what for?"

"To help you out." Jessica came over to me and put her arms around me. I thought I would feel bad taking money from them again, but I guess when someone gives you something from a place of love you can't help but to be grateful.

"Well, this looks like more than a thousand."

"Yeah, it's a thousand from me," Jessica answered.

"And a thousand from me and a thousand from Vickie," added Joanna

"Vickie! Why she ain't here?"

"Well, um..." Jessica always had hard time giving people information that she thought would be hard for them to hear. How her ass became a doctor I'll never know.

"Girl, that heffa said she can't be seen in your neighborhood." Joanna on the other hand ain't got no problems with it.

"But she still cared enough, that's something." Jessica's Mary Poppins ass could see the good in everything. That shit can get annoying. If something's wrong, it's wrong; if something hurt, it hurts. Sometimes you just have to say shit happens now let's deal with it.

Joanna and Jessica stayed with me for a while and even ordered pizza for my kids to eat. We were having a great time; this was the first time that I could remember that my friends actually came and stayed for such a long time. But our fun was cut short when Steven came home, mad that Joanna had parked her car in his spot.

"What, you think because you drive a fancy car, you can park it where ever you want?" Steven yelled and then walked past us.

"Girl, we 'bout to go before something jump off in here cause I'm ready to slap the shit out of your man," Joanna said. She and Jessica left and I was feeling really good. I wanted to tell Steven why they were here, but he was in one of his moods, and I was not about to let him ruin this for me too. Three weeks after losing mostly all of my benefits, I received a letter in the mail from my caseworker:

> *Mrs. Bennett,*
>   *This letter is to inform you that you will begin to receive full benefits as of the date of this letter. Please call me if you have any further questions.*

13

I barely wanted to turn over in my bed. It felt so good. I can't remember the last time I got to sleep in late. Today I was off, not on call, not coming in late just completely and totally off, and I was going to make the best of it. My plan was just to lie in bed and think.

Michael was gone and there is nobody around to disturb me. This was my time to wonder where my life had gone so wrong. I almost cried thinking about how stupid I had been. I guess love is stupid. In order to get to the good there has to be some bad, and well, this must be our bad.

After lying in bed for a while feeling sorry for myself, I got up to run some errands. It was pretty early in the afternoon and everyone seemed to be at work, everyone except me. I loved those days when I could go places like the grocery store and not have to worry about running into some girl who claimed to have had my man.

There was just a sense of peace and stillness throughout the city. I started my car and right away I noticed that Michael had left it on empty. I found my way to the closest gas station and begin to fill my tank. While pumping gas, I looked inside my car and decided that it could stand to be vacuumed a bit. I pulled in close to the vacuum machine at the gas station and started to clean my car. When I got to the backseat, I noticed something shiny that was lodged between the seats. I stuck my fingers between the seats and pulled it out. To my surprise, it was a gold necklace that appears to belong to a woman, but it wasn't mine. As a matter of fact, I've never seen it before in my life. Squeezing the necklace in my hand, I tried to think whose it might be. I thought that it might have been Joanna's or Nicole's because they were the last ones in my car. So I called Joanna to ask.

"Hey Jo," I said the moment Joanna answered her phone.

"What's up?"

"Did you lose a necklace in my car the other night?" I was hoping she would say that it was hers.

"Nope. I wasn't wearing a necklace, why?"

"I just found a necklace and was wondering if it was yours. I'll just ask Nicole."

"Well, it's not mine, and Nic don't really wear jewelry like that."

"What are you trying to say, Jo?" I asked knowing what she was trying to insinuate; that this necklace had something to do with Michael and some girl. I could feel Joanna's judgmental look coming through the phone. But there was nothing that pointed to Michael havine done anything wrong. Joanna was just someone who jumped to the craziest conclusions. Her mind could take her places where she had no business going, and that always got her into trouble. I was not going there with her.

"Nothing, Jess, I hope you find who it belongs to."

"I will, I'm sure it...I will." Until I knew for sure this had something to do with Michael, I chose to remain positive.

After I hung up the phone with Joanna, I called Nicole and again hoped that she would say that the necklace belonged to her.

"Girl ain't nobody got no damn gold necklace." Nicole replied. Sitting in my car, I thought for a long time as to whom the necklace could belong. I decided to call and ask Victoria. I knew it was a long shot because Victoria hadn't been in my car in months, but I had no idea how long the necklace had been there; it could have belonged to Victoria.

"No baby," Victoria said. "I don't wear anything but diamonds." I sat in my car and the tears began to roll down my face. Maybe Joanna's conclusion was right. I couldn't think of anyone else who this necklace could belong to.

It was Michael who had my car last and who never showed up to pick me up from work. I was tired of crying over the same old thing. It was draining to constantly go through what I was going through with him. It was enough. I didn't feel that I should have to go through so much pain. I was a good person with so much love to give and didn't deserve to endure all the betrayal. So I went to Michael's job to confront him. It was something I'd never done before, but waiting until I saw him was not an option. I needed him to see me in all my anger, but more important, I needed to see him at this moment when I was determined enough to end our relationship.

When I arrived at Michael's job, I saw him standing outside surrounded by a mob of women. This infuriated me even more. That was just the end; I was no longer going to be Michael's naive little girlfriend any longer. I honked my horn furiously to get his attention. He realized it was me and pulled himself away from the crowd of women and quickly ran to me.

"Baby what are you doing here?" he asked me. I could hardly speak and didn't want to. I knew that anything I said would be twisted by Michael and would make me forgive him all over again. So I picked up the necklace and threw it in Michael's face. Before pulling off I yelled to him "I want you and your things out of my house!" I drove away and didn't bother to look back. I was proud of myself and satisfied with the decision to cut him loose.

I took my time going back home so I drove around for a while and cleared my head of all the thoughts. But by the time I got home, Michael was already there waiting for me.

"Baby let's talk about this. I don't understand what happened," he said to me.

"Get away from me," I said walking by him with the anger still boiling up inside me.

"What did I do?"

"Michael I'm just tired of it all, so it's over."

"What because of a necklace? Because I can explain that."

"Oh you can? Whatever." The thought of Michael concocting another lie was starting to make my head hurt. All the lies were just too much.

"Yeah I can; it's yours." He said with a side smile as his eyes searched my face for a reaction.

I looked at the way Michael told a bold face lie with such an expression. I was disgusted. How could he possibly think that I was that gullible?

"Michael, I know every piece of jewelry I have and that isn't one of them!" I could hear myself shouting and it really felt good.

"No, baby, it's yours because I bought it for you. It was supposed to be a surprise but I lost it," he said as he held the necklace up for me to get a better look at it.

"What?" I was so confused. If this was my gift why wasn't it wrapped or in some kind of a box? How do you just lose it in the back seat of your car? How the hell did it get there? I had so many questions, but Michael looked like I should be satisfied with everything he just said.

"I was hoping to find it before you did but...I'm so sorry baby," Michael said and made another attempt to grab for me. This time, I let him put his arms around my waist and soon I was allowing him to kiss me. Once again he managed to defuse my anger and like every other time before, I gave in to Michael and let myself make love to him again. There was something about this man that I just wanted to believe every lie he told.

14

"Hello." I answered my phone as soon as it rang thinking it could be someone important or about something important.

"Hey Nic, how are you?" The voice on the other end asked.

"Who's dis?" I asked, even though I recognized Victoria's voice the moment she started talking. I just couldn't believe she was actually calling me. We ain't talked on the phone to each other in a minute.

"It's me. Victoria."

"Vickie, what the hell you want?"

"I was just checking on you."

"Well I'm good."

"Good . . . good. And how are the kids?" She continued to ask.

"Everybody's fine, Vickie, but that ain't what you calling for." Ain't nobody got time to make small talk with this girl. Whatever she called for, she just needed to get on with it.

Vickie don't just be calling me for no damn good reason. We don't roll like that no more. This bitch was up to something and I was in no mood to play twenty questions with her ass. She needed to get to the damn point.

"Well I know that you had some issue with your welfare benefits, and I just wanted to make sure all that was alright now," she replied.

This bitch just couldn't let it go of the fact that my ass ain't got what she got.

"If you cared, Vickie, you should have came when Jo and Jess came."

"I was busy and couldn't make it, but I think I did more than my share."

"What the fuck does that mean, 'more than my share'?"

"Well, I made a couple of phone calls and . . . well, I hope it helped."

"What do you mean by a coupld of phone calls?"

What was this girl getting at?

"Well, I just happen to know some of the people in certain positions and I convinced them to give you your benefits back."

BAM! there it was. That bitch was calling to gloat. All she wanted to do was throw it in my face that she was the one who got my benefits back. I hoped she didn't think I was gonna go out like that.

"So what the fuck? You want me to kiss your ass 'cause you got my benefits back?"

"I don't need you to do anything of the kind, Nic. But I think you would at least say thank you. I mean, just be a little bit grateful," she said with this superior tone that always got on my last nerves.

"I ain't saying thank you 'cause I ain't asked your ass to do shit. I can handle my own business, Vickie. Don't nobody need your ass to come to the fucking rescue."

"You know what Nic, fine. The next time you find yourself in trouble I will not be there to help you out," she replied sounding as if she was the only one who be giving me stuff. Like she's my mamma or something, and I couldn't survive without her.

"Yeah, fine bitch I don't need your help."

I wish there was a way to slam down a cell phone so people could really feel it. I just can't stand her ass. Why do people always do that shit? They just can't give somebody something without wanting something in return. Vickie's the worst one. She didn't do nothing for you without throwing it back in your face like you should be at her mercy 'cause she's done something that ain't nobody ask her to do in the first place.

That's why I couldn't stand being at other people's mercy. Everybody just gets on my nerves with that shit. I'm glad I decided to look into this whole school thing and get serious about getting myself together. Once I get my degree and I'd be good. I could start working and making good money to take care of me and my kids. Then nobody would have nothing to throw in my face.

I was on my way to the college downtown when that damn Vickie called-bitch almost made me have an accident. The college was huge. I didn't even know where the hell the admissions office was. I found the first person I saw sitting at a desk and went up to her.

"Hi, I wanted to speak with an admissions counselor," I said to the girl sitting behind the desk. She was so young she looked like a student.

"Sure, have a seat and someone will be right with you," the girl said to me.

Everybody that came in and out that office looked like they just got off breast milk. I ain't never felt so old. What am I gonna do around all these kids? They gonna look at me like I'm a fool.

"Hi, I'm Mrs. Spencer the admissions counselor. What can I do for you?" This tall, skinny, blond-haired, blue-eyed lady said as she reached out her hand for me to shake.

"Hi, I'm Nicole-Nicole Bennett. I just wanted to get some information... see what you had to offer," I said to her as I stood to shake her hand.

"Sure. How about you come into my office." Mrs. Spencer led me past the desk where the girl was sitting and into an office with a desk full of files and a huge window that looked straight onto the busy street.

I didn't know why I was so nervous. I could barely open my mouth. This damn bitch had all these degrees on her walls. I bet half of them were just for show. Ain't nobody got that many damn degrees.

"So, Mrs. Bennett, how about you tell me a little about yourself."

I think I told her more than a little. She caught me in that I-just-feel-like-talking mood. I damn near told her how both my kids were conceived.

"Well, Mrs. Bennett, this school certainly does cater to an older student population. We offer nights and weekend courses and some online courses as well. As a mother, that may work best for you. We would have to take a look at your transcript from your prior college to see exactly where you would have to start from."

This lady just kept on talking about all the courses and majors and everything else. I didn't even know how I was paying for all this. This shit didn't make no sense to me. I didn't even know why I was there. Then Mrs. Spencer handed me a bunch of papers talking about it's their application. That shit looked long as hell. At that point, I knew I didn't belong there.

I must've stood in the hallway outside the admissions office for at least twenty minutes before I decided to leave. This whole thing was so damn foreign to me.

"Nic?" I heard a voice from behind me call and I turned to see who it was.

"Mitchell? Shit. What the hell you doing here?" I was shocked to see Mitchell standing there in one of his very expensive suits with his briefcase in hand.

"Well that's a long story," he said.

"I like long stories."

"Okay then, how about I buy you lunch," he said with a smile.

I didn't know what Mitchell was up to but I was sure glad he was buying me lunch 'cause my ass was hungry. I was just going to go to my mother's and raid her refrigerator when I went to pick up my kids, but, hell, this was even better.

Mitchell took me to a restaurant right on the harbor and we sat at a table next to the window that looked right onto the water. It must be nice to have money.

"So, Nic, you thinking about going back to school?"

"Thinking about it."

"You should, Nic. Don't tell Vickie this but I always thought that you were the one with the most potential out of the four." Sometimes Mitchell could be full of shit. But you had to love him 'cause he's always trying to make people feel good about themselves.

"Mitch, stop trying to gas me."

"I'm not. You have so many different talents. It's just a matter of picking one."

"Well thanks, Mitch but I think my time done passed."

"I know the feeling. But I can't help but think that it's never too late to live your dreams."

"Well I ain't got no real dreams."

"Of course you do. We all have dreams, Nic. We just have to be brave enough to go after them." Mitchell's eyes looked so damn sad like he was lost inside himself somewhere. I ain't never seen Mitchell like this before. I bet that damn Vickie got something to do wit it.

"What's going on with you, Mitch?"

"You mean besides having a wife that drives me crazy?" He said with a chuckle.

"Hell, your wife drives everybody crazy so that can't be your problem."

"I know...um...I've been teaching nights over at the law school and I really like it," he said with this glint in his eye that I hadn't seen in a long time.

When I first met Mitchell, he was working at legal aid for less than nothing. He had that same glint in his eye. Then I messed up and introduced him to Victoria. They got married, and he became this big-time lawyer, making a lot of money, and, well, somewhere along the way, he lost his glint.

"That's good. But why is that a problem?" I asked him.

"The problem is a law professor's pay is nothing compared to a lawyer's pay...and well..."

"Your bougie-ass wife is going fall out when she finds out." I knew exactly where Mitchell was coming from. Victoria loved herself some money, and if she thought that she may lose some of that money, well hell, the girl might spaz the fuck out.

"Yes, exactly. Especially if she finds out that I want to stop practicing law and start teaching full time," he said as he turned his head to look out the window.

"Oh shit. Please let me tell her or at least let me be there when you tell her." I am kind of excited that this news may just make Victoria lose her mind completely. Hell I may just hear her cuss for once.

"No Nic. Come on seriously. I know you and Vickie got your issues, but you guys know each other...I mean I just need to know."

"Know what?"

"Does Vickie really love me-I mean, love me enough to let me do something for me for once?"

"Vickie loves you, Mitch, but the bitch is crazy as hell. Shit, loving you and accepting a pay cut are two different things."

"I know. I think she senses something is wrong, but I don't think she even cares. I think it may be time for me to move on from this marriage," he said with a sad tone.

"Mitch you ain't cheating on Vickie are you?"

"Of course not. I love her way too much to ever hurt her like that. I just sometimes have my doubts that she loves me the same."

Mitchell looked really disappointed. I swear he's the last of a dying breed-a man who actually wants to see his woman happy and would give up his own happiness to make it happen.

Vickie didn't know what she had. I felt so bad for Mitchell. I could tell this whole teaching thing was something he really wanted to do but that damn Victoria would never let him. It's hard when your heart wants to do something but someone or something is stopping you.

"Look, Mitch, just go on ahead and tell Vickie, and then live your life. If her crazy ass don't want to stay for the ride, then tough. You can find someone who will."

"That's easy to say, Nic, but as crazy as it sounds, I don't want anyone else but Vickie. I know that if she doesn't want me to do this, then I probably won't."

I just sat there the rest of the time listening to him talk about how he doesn't know what to do and how fed up he is, but just loves Vickie too much to do anything drastic.

That's why I treated Vickie the way I did. She just never got it. If I was Mitchell, I would leave and take all my money with me. But he's too good of a guy to do that, last of a dying breed.

15

I should've been fast asleep at such an ungodly hour, but instead I was pacing around my room waiting to hear my husband come home - how undignified. My mother would explode if she were to see me right now. Women should never belittle themselves by waiting on a man. Yet here I am waiting on my husband to come home from "work." That is utterly laughable, *work*. Who works until after midnight? What law firm is still open at this time anyway?

I finally heard the front door close, although he tried to shut it softly. I could even hear the creaking of the stairs as he tried to tiptoe up them. "Hello Mitchell, late night again?" I stood outside our bedroom door. I wanted him to look me in the eye and tell me that he was only at work and not doing something that could ruin our marriage.

"Hi Vickie. Yes it was," he said in an exhausted voice."

"So then why don't you tell me all about it?"

"All about what, Vickie?" he asked, looking as if he just didn't have time for me or this conversation.

"Your day, tell me all about your day."

"Like you care."

"Why wouldn't I care? You're my husband."

"Do you really care, Vickie? I mean screw my day. But do you care about me?"

"What kind of question is that to ask, Mitchell? It's absurd."

"Absurd? Right. Well how about this, do you love me Vickie?" Mitchell asked, seeming to press for.

Mitchell's face was tight. He looked as if the survival of the whole world depended upon my answer and no one would be able to proceed through life until I opened my mouth and said something. What was wrong with him? Why has he chosen to put me on the spot in such a way?

"I'm going to bed Mitchell." I turned to enter my bedroom door.

"No, you stand here Vickie and for once have the guts to answer me!" Mitchell stood in front of me preventing me from entering my bedroom. He had never yelled at me before. He had never been aggressive towards me before. I don't know this Mitchell. I don't like this Mitchell.

"Mitchell, I don't know why you are acting this way. Perhaps you're tired and need some rest. So I'm going to bed and I suggest you do the same." I tried to be as calm as possible.

"Yeah Vickie, I think I will be going to bed now. Besides I've gotten my answer anyway."

Mitchell walked into his room slamming the door behind him. He left me standing there alone in our hallway wondering what just happened and why I hadn't answered. Obviously I love Mitchell. Why wouldn't I? He had given me everything I had ever asked him for. If he loved me, he would know that I am not the type of girl who goes around shouting to the world that I'm in love. That sort of behavior is for the unmannerly. The fact that I'm still with him should be enough to let him know how I feel. Why do I need to say it all the time?

—⁓•⌒◦⌒◦⌒◦⌒•⁓—

The next morning I awoke to find that Mitchell had already left. It's probably for the best. There was no need to repeat the fiasco of last night. We are educated enough to know that we should never act based on emotion. Sure we were angry but anger passes. I was sure by now Mitchell had gotten over whatever it was that was bothering him, and we could go on living our lives as if nothing happened. Hopefully.

I was almost dressed when my housekeeper knocked on my bedroom door, "Mrs. Combs, a Pastor Freeman is here to see you." I had completely forgotten about my meeting with my church pastor to discuss raising money for the church. Today was just not a good day. But like my mother always said, no matter what's going on in your life, you must put on a smile and keep moving forward. So that's exactly what I decided to do.

"Pastor Freeman welcome to my home please have a seat," I greeted.

"Thank you, Sister Combs," the pastor replied as he took a seat on the sofa in my main living room.

I was trying my best to be a good hostess, but for the life of me I couldn't hear a word he was saying. I know he was here about the church's fundraiser, but the details of his conversation were a blur. It was eating me up inside how Mitchell and I had left things. I was sure he was over it by now, but maybe I should have answered him. Why did he feel the need to ask me how I felt about him? Mitchell had never asked me how I felt about him before.

"Sister Combs, are you alright? You seem a bit distracted."

"Um, Pastor how does one know when they are doing the proper thing?"

"Well God provided each of us with a conscious for that exact reason. If your conscious is telling you that something is wrong, then, well, you're probably doing the wrong thing."

"But what if you're still so confused?"

"Then you get on your knees and take it to God."

"Thank you, Pastor."

"You're welcome. But is there something specific that you need to talk about? Sometimes it helps to get things off your chest," he said.

"No, everything's fine. Could we table this discussion for a later date? I'm not quite feeling like myself." I said to him.

"Sure. If you need anything just give me a call." He said as he got up to leave.

After Pastor Freeman left, I went back to my room and lay down on my bed. I took the covers and put them over my head. This was where I wanted to be for the rest of the day.

16

Another long workday. I couldn't believe that it was almost three in the afternoon, and I hadn't even taken a break to have lunch. There was still a pile of work left on my desk. It was going to be long night.

"Hey Laurie!" I called through the phone intercom.

"Yes, Joanna?"

"Would you please run out and get me a sandwich or something?"

"You know eventually you will have to detach yourself from that desk."

"I know and believe me I can't wait."

"Alright I'll be right back in a few."

"Thanks and please let the phone go to voicemail while you're gone."

"No problem."

I did need to take a break, but I couldn't - not if I wanted to get the promotion that I deserved. There was no way that I could slow down and let this chance pass me by. I've worked hard and it was time for me to start seeing some results.

Sometimes I wondered what if I woke up one day and realized that I have lived a life filled with regrets. I've never been the girl who had her wedding all planned out or already knew what I would name my kids. I just never wanted anything else but what I have right now. I've always told people that I can't afford to get distracted with all that other shit. But what if all that other shit is what makes life livable?

I've never really dealt with heartbreak, because I never really took the time to give my heart to anyone. What if I'm missing something?

Since I could remember, I've lived by the mantra that sometimes the best way to prevent pain is never to become vulnerable to its sources. So that's what I did; I avoided the sources of pain.

But that damn thing called love always seems to take hold of me whenever David was around. I always wondered what my life would have been like had I pursued a relationship with him. My heart ached daily to be loved by David, but my mind worried that I would lose my independence. I don't care what all those crazy sitcoms say or even what Oprah says, there is no way that I could be loved by David or even love David fully and have this perfect marriage with beautiful children and still be where I am in my career. That's impossible. What successful woman is married with kids? Sure, Oprah has Stedman, but Oprah don't have kids. Condoleezza Rice has never been married and she doesn't have kids, and look at where she is. I just wanted my dreams to come true. I mean what woman doesn't want a man to sweep her off her feet? Sure, sometimes I get lonely, but I just want my dreams.

I wondered what my girls are up to. I figured I'd call Jessica just to stop all the crazy thoughts that were running through my mind. As Jessica's phone rang, Laurie came into my office.

"Hey, here's your sandwich and a soda. I'll be at my desk if you need me for anything." She said.

"Thanks, I really appreciate this."

Jessica's phone must have rang for what seems like forever before she finally picked up.

"Hey, Big Head." Jessica sounded cheerful yet sad. I didn't know what to make of it. I wondered if she was just having a rough day at work or if something more serious was going on and she didn't want me to know about it.

"Hey, Shorty." I tried to meet her voice tone without letting on that I was worried about her, but something didn't seem right.

"What's up?"

"Nothing I just hadn't heard from you guys for a while."

"Well, I'm fine, can't speak for anybody else though."

The way Jessica sounded didn't convince me that she was fine. Jessica spoke like herself but her tone was almost somber, as if she was trying her best to hide something.

"Are you sure you're fine?"

"Yup, why?"

"Nothing. Um, where are you?"

"At the hospital in the doctor's lounge, I've been here all night and decided to take a little break."

"Oh OK, well—"

"Jo, let me call you back later. They're paging me," Jessica said cutting me off.

Jessica hung up the phone so fast that I couldn't say goodbye. Something just didn't feel right. Jessica has never hung up the phone that fast even when she was being paged; she'd at least say bye or make some kind of a joke. Maybe I should call her back? My hand reached to dial Jessica's number again, but then Laurie came on the intercom.

"Ms. Stuart, Mr. Winthrop is out here for you."

Mr. J.B. Winthrop was one of the founding partners of the marketing firm and whenever he came around, the conversation could either be good or bad. I've worked too hard for the conversation to be bad. Still my nerves began to kick in. "Thank you Laurie. Please send him in."

Mr. Winthrop came into my office and looked directly at the pile of work on my desk.

"That's what I like about you, Stuart," he marveled.

"What's that, sir?" For some odd reason he felt the need to always call me by my last name. At first I thought it was cute, but now I really believed he couldn't remember my first name.

"You always stay focused on work; that's what's going to take you far with this company."

"Well, thank you, sir. Is there something you needed?" I tried to remain in control and seem calm, but every inch of my body shook with anticipation.

Mr. Winthrop was on the elderly side and often had a problem getting to the point of his visits. People needed to have immense patience when dealing with him. Fortunately, I had all the patience in the world, especially when it came to my future in this company.

During this particular visit, he felt extremely chatty and went on and on talking about the company. He gave me a history lesson on how the company first came about and what it took to get them to where they were today. He laid out a comprehensive plan for the direction he felt the company should be going in, all the while pacing up and down my office floor. At some point during his lesson, I think I zoned out and it wasn't until he said,

"And that's why, Stuart, I feel you are the right person for the job." I didn't hear a word Mr. Winthrop said and wasn't sure what he was talking about. I could have played along and pretended like I knew, but this was way too important.

"What job?" I asked.

Mr. Winthrop finally sat down and replied, "The job of marketing director." His voice lowered and he stared right into my eyes.

"Oh, ok." If that old sucker wasn't watching me right now, I'd be doing cartwheels and jumping on the top of my desk.

"You were interested, weren't you? At least Stephens felt that you were." He said.

"Yes, sir I am. I just wasn't aware that you would be filling that position so soon." It took everything within me not to burst out of my chair, grab him by the neck and scream, what the hell took you so long!

"Well we've decided that we needed someone to fill that position as soon as possible."

"This is quite sudden. I would have to think about it." Business 101 taught me that you should never seem too eager over a potential deal; that would give your opponent the upper hand. But, shit, for that job there was no thinking necessary. He could have told me to give him my first born for the job and I probably would've.

"Well, Stuart you have until Monday, we need someone in the office by then." Was Mr. Winthrop trying to call my bluff?

"In the office? I would have to move my office?"

"Stuart, you would have to move all together. The job will serve our needs better in our L.A. office."

"L.A. as in Los Angeles, California?"

"That's correct." He replied as if it were no big deal.

I had prepared for this moment and thought of every scenario but never once did I consider that maybe I would have to leave Baltimore and to move so far. How could I pack up and leave behind everything and everyone I cared about? I guess I really would have to think about this.

"If I don't take the job, then what?" I never considered turning the job down until now. I didn't know what leaving Baltimore would mean for me.

"Then nothing. You would keep your old job here," Mr. Winthrop said, "but I hope you understand the importance of this promotion."

"I do, but L.A. is very far."

"Listen, think about it over the weekend. As a matter of fact I'll give you until Tuesday."

I was so confused that I didn't think Tuesday would be enough time. Mr. Winthrop must have seen the confusion on my face.

"Why don't you go away this weekend and use the company beach house in Ocean City? It might help you to decide," Mr. Winthrop added. He then took out keys and laid them on my desk. It was clear that he really wanted me to take this job because the beach house is nothing more than a bribe, but one that I was perfectly willing to take.

After Mr. Winthrop left, I sat back in my chair still confused. This was the opportunity I'd been waiting for, but why did I have to go across the country? I didn't know what to do, and I knew that if I told my girls they would panic and make me feel guilty for getting the promotion. Maybe the best thing would be not to tell them until I made my decision. But how would I make my decision without having someone to talk to? This was one of those times when I wished I had a man in my life. Then we could discuss big decisions like this together, in bed, while he gave me a massage.

I figured the closest thing I had to that was David. He was always so clear about everything. His confidence made me confident.

"Dr. Mathews' office." David's receptionist was an older lady who always had the most soothing voice.

"Hey Renée, is he in?" I asked her.

"Hi Joanna, I'll put you through."

After a couple of minutes, David came on the phone. The sound of his voice made me smile. No matter what I was going through, just hearing David's voice made it seem all better. I knew that he would be able to help me make up my mind, like he had so many times before.

"Hey stranger, where have you been hiding?" David inquired as he came on the phone. Every time I called, no matter the time, David sounded like he was happy that I did.

"Nowhere, you just haven't been looking."

"Oh, alright then fair enough." He chuckled.

"What are you doing later on tonight?"

"Nothing, why?"

"I was wondering if you wanted to get a drink with me, I really need your help with something."

"Uh oh. What do you need my help with, Jo? You and the girls fighting again?"

"No nothing like that. It's just that, um, well I'll tell you tonight."

"Ok, now I'm worried. Why don't you tell me now, Jo," he said sternly.

"Um, well, I got the promotion," I said with a big smile on my face as if he could see me.

"That's great, Jo! Why would you need my help with that? It's what you wanted, isn't it?"

"Yeah, of course, but the job is located in the L.A. office. I have to move." The words came out of my mouth so quickly that I barely gave myself a chance to catch my breath. I listened for David to say something, but he didn't.

"Are you still there?"

"Yeah, yeah, I'm still here."

"So then, what time do you want to get together tonight so you can help me figure all this out? I mean just telling my girls alone would be a problem and then figuring out...." I began to ramble, thinking that if I talked long enough I could cut this tension I was feeling between us.

"Jo? I just remembered I did make plans tonight."

"What plans? Are they so important that you can't cancel them this one time? I really need you."

"Jo, I made these plans a few days ago, and it would be rude to cancel at the last minute." His words didn't sound believable. It sounded like David was searching for an excuse not to go out with me.

I couldn't believe that David was blowing me off at a time I needed him the most. Didn't he understand what I was going through? I was so furious with David that I hung up the phone without telling him bye.

I couldn't understand why he wasn't more interested in my problem. The only thing I could think of was that it was because of some chick; it was the only thing that made sense. If he was just hanging with his boys or doing something work related, then he would have said. David normally just doesn't blow me off like that. I bet it was that trick from the party the other night. She sure had her claws in him and was not letting go. If David was so serious about that bitch, more so than helping me in my time of need, then forget him. This is why I chose not to give up my dreams for no damn man.

I could barely finish out the rest of my day. My mind kept wondering why David felt this woman was more important and if it wasn't a woman, then why would he completely blow me off.

I looked at my clock and saw that it was almost six-thirty at night. I figured the best thing for me to do was to go to David's house. If it was another chick, then at least I could put her on notice that I was around and I wasn't going anywhere. If it wasn't a chick, then I needed to find out why the hell he blew me off. Either way he was going to get an earful from me.

On my way to David's house, I planned out exactly what I was going to tell him and how I was going to tell him off. I knew David; if I got mad enough he would cancel his plans and be with me. So all I had to do was make him feel bad.

I arrived at David's row house and parked right behind his car. I looked to see if there was another car that didn't belong, but none of the cars parked on the street stood out as suspicious.

I marched up the stairs to David's front door and rang the bell. When David answered, he was dressed in sweatpants and a t-shirt. His attire looked strange for someone who should be getting ready to go out. I knew that if David was going out, he would be grooming himself very well. I figured that maybe the girl was there and they were planning on spending time alone in his house.

"Jo, what are you doing here?" David asked with a surprised look on his face that I couldn't explain. After all these years as friends, he should have known that telling me no would only piss me off.

"I need a reason to visit you now David?" I stood in the doorway waiting for him to ask me in.

"Not really Jo, but I thought I told you I had plans."

"You did." I got tired of waiting for his ass to let me in, so I just pushed passed him.

I began looking around David's apartment to see if anything was out of place. Then I began to sniff around to see if I smelled any woman's perfume. As I searched, David closed his door and took a seat on the sofa.

"Let me know when you're done."

"Done with what?"

David put his feet up and stared at me. He seemed as if he was fed up with me. But I was not going to let that deter me from telling him just what I'd plan on telling him.

"You know what, I just came here to tell you one thing. I did not appreciate the way you blew me off and don't think for one moment that I didn't know that's what you were doing. Whoever the trick is that caused you to blow me off well I hope she's worth it because it will be a long time before I forgive you for this and that's all I have to say." I stood back and waited for David to apologize profusely for what he had done, but for some reason my speech didn't work. David had a skeptical expression on his face, as if he didn't believe that I was bothered by the fact that he chose to be with someone else. Maybe he just didn't care.

David got up and walked towards me. I was sure that he was going to put his arms around me and tell me he was sorry and that everything was going to be just fine. But David didn't. As a matter of fact, he stood within an arm's length of me and never reached out his hand to hold me, not even once. He just stood there with his arms folded and stared at me coldly.

"Jo, you don't need me to tell you what to do. You've already decided to go to L.A., so go." He said coldly.

"Just like that?"

"Jo, if you're going just go. I can't keep doing this." David's voice became haunting. "Just leave."

"David, do you want me to leave your house or the state or your life?" I didn't know whether to cry or slap him across the face.

"The choice is up to you, Jo. I can't tell you what to do anymore, not this time. You have to make the choice because you're the one that has to live with the consequences."

"Um, I think you have plans so I'll leave and we can talk about this later."

I began walking towards the front door, but I really didn't want to leave. I didn't know where he was coming from or why he was turning on me. I couldn't believe this was happening. But to put the final nail in my coffin, David opened the front door for me to walk through and leave him behind.

"Do me a favor, don't come back until you're ready to stay."

"Are you serious?" I asked him, too afraid to move my feet.

"Very serious."

I began walking out, but then stopped to look at David one last time and make sure he wasn't joking. I would have given anything for him to say that he was just playing or that it was April Fools' joke or some stupid shit like that. When I saw that his eyes were disconnected from me, I knew he was serious. David wanted me gone.

I was crying so hard while driving that I could barely see my way home. I parked my car by the harbor and began walking. I passed by the Hard Rock Cafe and saw a couple inside laughing like it was the most natural thing in the world. Soon I found a vacant bench overlooking the water and sat down. I felt as if someone had just died. I could literally feel my heart coming apart. So this was it, this was what a broken heart feels like. No wonder I had been running from it for so long. I had hoped that I would get through my entire life and never have to feel that way. It was the worst thing I ever felt. I wanted to drop to my knees and scream to the top of my lungs and get rid of all this emotion inside me. My tears seemed to fall out of my eyes uncontrollably, and I had no strength left to wipe them away. It was as if someone was carving my heart with a knife and I could feel every painful cut. It hurt so bad, and I didn't know how to make it stop. All I wanted was David. When my cell phone rang, I thought it was him calling.

"Hello"

17

This must've been the first time I had rested in almost twelve hours. Lying on this old sofa felt so good that I didn't even care how lumpy and smelly it was. No one could mistake the doctor's lounge for being the Hilton, but as exhausted as I was, it sure did the trick. I couldn't remember the last time I had been this tired. The funny thing was I didn't think it had anything to do with work. Dealing with Michael could sometimes take a lot out of me. Right now all I wanted to do was close my eyes and sleep for a while, then maybe everything would become clearer once I was well rested.

The problem was I couldn't close my eyes. I just lay there with thoughts running through my head and they all seemed to focus on Michael. I wondered if he was sincere and if he had changed his ways. I had to assume that he was no longer cheating on me and that he was completely devoted to our relationship; after all, he had asked me to marry him. How much more devoted can a person be? I was convinced that my relationship with Michael was meant to last, and we had weathered the rough times that every couple goes through.

"You look completely rundown." Todd said as he walked into the doctor's lounge so upbeat and awake that it completely annoyed me.

"Well that's a nice thing to say," I responded as I picked myself up from the lumpy sofa.

"All I mean is that you should go home and get some real rest so that you can go back to looking like your usual beautiful self," Todd said.

"God, you're a smooth talker, aren't you? But I can't. I still have a few more hours left," I replied.

"Well I don't think you'll be much help. Besides, we're completely covered," he said.

"Really?" I asked.

"Yeah, go ahead. If anything happens I'll call you personally and if anybody asks, I promise to cover for you."

"Ok, I guess I could go home for a couple of hours."

When I walked out the hospital doors it was completely dark outside, but the night air felt great. The cool breeze helped to wake me up a little bit, at least until I got home.

I opened my front door and was shocked to see how quiet and pitch dark my house was, especially since I saw Michael's car parked in front of the house. Maybe he had fallen asleep; after all, it was nine o'clock at night, and he really didn't expect me home this early. I tiptoed into the living room to lay on the sofa. My sofa felt so comfy and the sleep started to come quickly, but what the hell were those weird noises coming from my bedroom? Maybe Michael fell asleep with the TV on. I decided I had to go in there after all, because I sure as hell couldn't sleep with all that noise. The noise sounded so clear like maybe it wasn't the TV at all.

What the hell was wrong with me? I was standing in front of my own room door scared to open it. Get yourself together Jessica just turn the knob; it's just the TV.

But it wasn't. There he was, Michael, going at it with another woman in my bed. I couldn't breathe, I couldn't speak. The sounds of screams were clogging up my throat but nothing seemed to want to come out. I was just standing there like a statue frozen in place. The funny thing was, they were so into it that they hadn't even notice that I'd come home or that I was standing over them. He didn't even give a damn about me. I couldn't breathe. There was no air coming into my body, and the room was starting to spin. I had to get out of there. I had to get some air.

Why would he disrespect me like that, in a house that I bought so that we could have a place to call home and start the family that we had always talked about having? Somehow I found myself standing in the kitchen and searching for something, anything to fuck him up. There's nothing here or anywhere that could hurt him the way he hurt me. What was I supposed to do? He needed to get out. As much as my body was shaken and my face was soaking wet from the tears, I needed to get him out now. So I sat there and waited. I didn't know what I was waiting for, but I just couldn't bring myself to do anything else.

When Michael was done, he came running down the stairs half naked as if he had just discovered a new world. He didn't even see me sitting there in the dark.

"You need to get out now." The voice that came out of my mouth was almost unrecognizable. I guess that's why it scared Michael.

"Baby....what...what...." Michael's words stumbled over each other.

"You need to get out now."

"Listen, baby, let's talk about this."

It seemed like this force had taken over me and I could hear myself screaming. "You need to get out now!"

That must have gotten to his little friend because the bitch came out of the room and had the nerve to have one of my good sheets wrapped around her.

"Ok, I'm going. Just let me go put some clothes on, alright?" Michael ran up the stairs and pulled his little friend with him. I waited for five minutes before the both of them came down still dressing.

"Hey baby listen..."

"Get out now," I said again. Michael looked at me as if he were confused, as if I had been the one to do something wrong.

As they walked out, I slammed the door as hard as I could. Why couldn't he just love me? Why wasn't I enough for him? How could I have been so stupid? Only an idiot could love a man so hard without him ever loving her back.

All the crying must have knocked me out because it wasn't until Joanna called me that I woke up and realized that I had slept all night and into the afternoon. I tried to sound as upbeat as possible. I knew that if Joanna got wind of what was going on, she would flip out then tell Nicole, and she would definitely flip out. The last thing I needed was the two of them plotting on how they will deal with Michael. In the middle of talking to Joanna, there was a knock and then the door opened. Standing before me was Michael with a bouquet of flowers in his hands. I rushed Joanna off the phone by telling her that I was being paged. The truth was I was at home and this son-of-a-bitch wouldn't leave me alone.

"Hey baby, I hope I'm not disturbing you," Michael said, looking so pathetic that I almost felt sorry for him.

"No you're not disturbing me, Michael. What are you doing here?"

"Well I just wanted to see you and give you these." Michael handed me a bouquet of flowers and went to give me a hug.

"Why?"

"Why what?"

"Why did you feel the need to come here today and bring me flowers?"

"Because I'm stupid and weak. I don't know why I treat the woman I love the way I do."

"The woman you love, and who might that be?"

"You, of course. It has always and will always be you," Michael answered. That whole sentence was so comical I had to let out a little chuckle.

"My world was complete the day I met you. You mean everything to me," Michael said, obviously not getting it. But he had never expressed himself like that before. He was saying everything I wanted him to say. His timing just completely sucked.

"Well I don't know what to say," I replied.

"You don't have to say anything; I just wanted you to know," he said and then proceeded to give me the gentlest kiss on the lips that he had ever given me before leaving. Michael had made me feel love again. I couldn't figure out how he did it, but he was the only one who could make me feel content. He had this mind-boggling ability to shatter my life in a million little pieces and then put it all together again as if nothing had even happened.

But this time I was just cold. I couldn't even go upstairs to lie in my own bed. The only thing I could do was curl up on the living room floor until the day turned into night. Every time I tried to get up, I would fall back down into the same position. The phone rang and the answering machine picked up. Joanna's voice came on the other end. I tried to get up and reach the phone to tell Joanna that I needed help, but I just couldn't move. My body wouldn't let me. All I could do was to cry out, "Help me. Please, help me." It was as if I were paralyzed. Nothing worked on my body; even my heart seemed to have stopped beating.

18

I should've been coming up with ideas for the church's fundraiser, but all I could do was think about where Mitchell was again last night. Every time I tried to fall asleep, my eyes would hit the clock, and I would notice how late it was getting. I wasn't waiting up to ask him where he had been. We had barely made it from our last encounter and I didn't need to revisit that mess. I just wanted to know that he was home. I kept hearing the sound of my mother's voice telling me that he was being unfaithful, but how could I blame Mitchell? It wasn't as if our marriage had been much to hang on to. We spent our days away from one another and our nights sleeping in separate bedrooms.

I still didn't know how this could've happened. We had such a magnificent lifestyle. People would kill to live this way. Our marriage should have been perfection. I wasn't going to let our lives shatter. I could feel that Mitchell wasn't connecting to me emotionally. But what really hurt was the thought that he might have found someone who he could connected with.

What was I supposed to do about that? How could any woman change that? It was impossible. There were times when I felt as if I should just accept it and move on. But then why should I? I had put so much time and energy into this marriage. The most important thing was for us to that we keep our marriage. I thought, maybe I should just tell Mitchell that I knew about his affair and it would be ok as long as he stayed married to me. That might sound stupid to people, but my mother and father lived like that for years and they've made it work. I'm sure Mitchell and I could as well; after all, everyone needs some intimacy in their lives. If Mitchell felt as if he couldn't get it from me then he should be able to get it from someone else. Maybe that's just how things work in a relationship. Mitchell was the first guy I had ever been with. So I just don't know what should happen.

All I knew is that I wanted my marriage and I was willing to sacrifice what I had to in order to keep it.

I really wanted to call Mitchell at work and tell him about the decision I'd made, but there was a knot in the pit of my stomach. I knew that if we were to do this arrangement, it would be the best for all concern. I knew he'd see that. But what if he didn't? I sat there staring at the phone for what seemed like forever until the phone rang. For a second I thought it was Mitchell until I looked at the caller ID and saw that it was my mother. She was the last person I wanted to speak with.

"Hello," I answered.

"How are you, sweetie?" my mother replied.

"I'm alright, Mother."

"Then why do you sound so disturbed?"

"Mitchell didn't come home last night."

"I see and how long do you intend to allow this to continue Victoria?"

"I don't know, Mother."

"And why didn't you call me last night?"

"I just didn't want to bother you with my problems."

The truth was I didn't feel like hearing my mother say that I needed to take control of the situation. I knew that I had to take control, and I thought I'd figured out how. I just didn't want my mother pointing out how inept I was.

"Well Victoria I told you that..."

"Mother, I have to go. I'm expecting company any minute, and I have to make sure the house is prepared." If I were to let my mother finish her statement, it would do nothing but make me feel worse then I already did. I couldn't handle her and her advice right then.

After my conversation with my mother, I decided to go sit on my lanai and have a glass of wine. The beauty of my garden soothed my thoughts and brought me tranquility. I felt at peace.

"Victoria!" I heard a voice call from behind me.

"Mother, what are you doing here?" These were the times when I regretted making Mitchell buy a home so close to my parents.

"You know I don't appreciate being hung up on."

"How did you get in my house?"

"Well, that's a nice question to ask your mother. Your housekeeper let me in."

"Oh... Mother I'm sorry I just had..." I began to say.

"Victoria, I know you think that I don't understand, but I do," my mother said as she sat down next to me.

"Mother I decided to let Mitchell have his other woman. I figure it works for you and Daddy, it may work for us as well," I said to her. My mother let out a slight chuckle, as if she was remembering a joke that nobody else knew but her.

"Yes it works for your father and me because our marriage was a business arrangement. Everything we do is about what is appropriate. When it was appropriate, we got married. When it was appropriate, we had a child. And when it is appropriate, we'll get a divorce. Are you alright living like that?"

"Mother, all I know is that I want my marriage, and if that's how we have to live, then yes I'm alright with it."

"Well then, I suggest you talk to Mitchell sooner rather than later, because the one good thing that your father and I do is that we tell each other everything no matter how painful."

"I will, Mother."

My mother and I hadn't really talked like that before. She wasn't telling me what I should do; she just listened and talked to me not as her daughter, but as another woman who really understood.

———❦———

Later in the night, I tried to wait up for Mitchell, but once again he hadn't come home. It must have been really late when I was awoken by a noise coming from my closet. I got out of bed to see what was going on and I was startled to see Mitchell rummaging through what used to be our closet. When Mitchell turned and saw me standing behind him, he looked as if he was caught doing something horribly wrong.

"Sorry to have woken you. I tried to be quiet," Mitchell said.

"What are you looking for?"

"Um, I thought I might have left some shirts in here."

"Everything that you had in there I told the housekeeper to take out, so maybe it's in the laundry or something."

Mitchell shook his head as he walked past me but I was not going to let that distract me. I had to talk to Mitchell now. Even as I saw him about to walk out the bedroom door, I couldn't let him go without telling him that I wanted this marriage. I was willing to let him do what he wanted just as long as he stayed with me.

"Mitchell," I called to him.

"Yes," Mitchell answered looking back at me, and he waited for me to say something. I couldn't decide how I wanted to start. All of the words became jumbled in my head, and I needed time to get them straight. I could see that Mitchell was getting irritated.

"I think we should discuss how we could amicably handle this situation between us." The words didn't seem to come out the way I intended, so I hoped he understood what I was trying to say.

"Amicably, Vickie. you mean a divorce?" he asked, obviously not understanding, and I didn't know how to explain it. Mitchell and I had never had deep conversations.

"That's not...we should just...." I honestly didn't know how hard this would be. We're married for Christ sake. We should be able to express our feelings to each other. I should be able to tell him that I don't want a divorce.

"There's no need for discussion, Vickie I get it."

"You do?" I asked feeling confused.

"Yes I do, and I think you're right."

"I am?" I asked again still confused.

"Yes and I'll have the divorce papers drawn up and sent to you in a few days. Is that amicable enough for you?"

"What...I...." The words could barely come out of my mouth and Mitchell didn't even give me a chance to say anything before slamming the door behind him. I just stood there in disbelief staring at the closed door. My marriage was over. Divorce wasn't what I wanted. The life I had built was what I wanted; Mitchell was what I wanted. But all that was gone now. I had failed.

I managed to walk over to the bed and lay on top of the covers staring at the ceiling and praying for God to rescue me. I felt lost and broken. I never thought it would be over. Mitchell loved me too much. How could anything be over with someone who loves you that much? The sound of the ringing phone scared me. As if it were God's signal that the final bell had rung and there was no more Mitchell and I. When I heard the soften tone of Joanna's voice I knew something else had gone wrong.

"SHE'S WHERE?"

19

The kids were at my mom's house, and the bastard was at work. Damn life felt good. Ain't nobody around me needing nothing or expecting nothing. Ain't no arguing or fighting. It almost felt like my ass could breathe. It had been a long time since I felt this good. My stupid ass siat there all by myself at my kitchen table smiling and shit like somebody done said something funny. I almost forgot about all the shit going wrong in my life. Sometimes people just wake up in a good damn mood; well, I guess this was my day.

The only thing about being all alone was that you can't help but think about all kinds of stupid shit. For some reason I was sitting there thinking about Victoria's dumb ass. I couldn't believe that she was one of my best friends, and we were talking on the phone like we barely knew each other. Shit, at some point one of us was gonna have to admit that this friendship ain't working. Obviously she don't too much care for me, and to tell the truth, that heffa got on my damn nerves. But I still kinda missed her and her nagging. Didn't no one stay on me about doing better then she did. Hell I was acting like she was dead or something. I guess it was our friendship that was dead. I couldn't blame Vickie, though. I was the one who made a mess out of my life. If I could go back in time, shit, I'd change everything, do things different.

I needed to get back to being me, whoever that was. All I know was this person ain't her. There was something out there better for me, and I was sure as hell gonna find it. Forget what that dumb ass Steven said. I ain't just gonna sit here looking at these walls forever. I knew I could make it. Shit, I almost made it before. All I needed to do was to get focused. I sat there looking at those college applications like the answers to all my problems were somewhere on one of those pages.

But what the hell was college gonna be like now? I was in my thirties, I had kids, and my girls ain't gonna be there. We had a ball and I liked hanging around them. It was the best time I had ever had in my life. There would be no more passing notes to each other with the answers on them or midnight study sessions with pizza and a little "something" to drink or even the post mid-term parting. Them bitches really helped me. It gonna be hard to do this without them. But I gotta make this right for my kids and for me.

Oh man, I didn't realize how late it was. That son-of-a-bitch was home. I just knew we gonna start arguing as soon as he walked through the door.

"Where the kids?" Steven asked the moment he walked through the door. What the fuck! He couldn't even say hi or how was your day or some shit like that?

"They at my mother's."

"Why the fuck you send them there for?" I could do nothing but look at his dumb ass.

"Ain't that their grandmother?"

"So that mean they gotta be over there all the time?"

"Man, whatever."

Steven walked his trifling ass into the kitchen and started looking around. When he saw that I hadn't cooked, he got all pissed.

"What the fuck! You've been home all damn day and didn't even fix me nothing to eat. You lazy ass bitch." I was not even going to look at him. I was just going to keep working on my application and ignore his stupid ass. The minute I looked at him, he was gonna feel like he just did something good. But shit, if I didn't say nothing then he was gonna think I was gonna take that shit.

"You're standing in the kitchen. Fix something yourself, trifling dog!"

I knew he ain't gonna let that shit go but please lord just let him go into the room and fall asleep or better yet leave and not come back. I didn't know why his stupid ass was even coming over here to me. He was always looking to start something. He stood over me like somebody should be scare of his punk ass.

"What the fuck is you writing that's so goddamn more important than you fixing me something to eat?"

"None of your business." I said, trying to push the application under my arms but his nosy ass yanked it from me.

"What, you dumb-ass bitch. You trying to go to college?" He asked when he saw what the papers were.

"Give me my paper back!" I was trying so hard to remain calm and ignore him 'cause I knew he just trying to get me started.

"Hell no. I'm throwing this shit away. You letting your bitch-ass girlfriends juice your head up when you can't even do the thing you supposed to do, man please."

"Give me my paper." I had to stand up now 'cause this motherfucker wanted me to lose it.

"I said hell no!"

The minute he pushed me back down, I could feel the tears starting to form. I am fucking pissed. I jumped up fast and lunged at him to get my application out his hands. But that bastard pushed me even harder and instead of falling into the chair, I went straight back and hit the wall. He should've known that shit wasn't gonna stop me. I lunged at him again and grabbed the hand my application was in. This time Steven pushed me with so much force that I landed on the ground. By this time my whole back hurt, from my neck to my ass. It felt like somebody just rubbed it raw and then rolled me over hot coals.

"You crazy bitch!" Steven yelled. This mutherfucker had the nerve to stand over me ripping my application and then throwing the pieces of paper in my face.

"You son-of-a-bitch. I'll show you crazy!"

Everything seemed to go black and my whole head was turning. Before I had time to think, I was on my feet and in the kitchen with my hand on the broom. The room went from black to bright red. I could feel this hand on my back pushing me over to him. The broom was in the air and I heard this voice yell, "You ripped up my paper now I'm gonna rip you up!" The next thing I heard was Steven yell, "What the fuck is your problem?"

Then again that voice, "You're my fucking problem and I'm about to solve it!" Then there was a loud scream and Steven took off running. That hand was on me pushing me again and I seemed to be chasing him. All I hear was furniture breaking and screaming. The redness in the room was so blinding I couldn't see anything. I don't know what is going on. Why was Steven yelling like that? Who the hell was breaking my furniture?

The banging on the door made the redness go away, and I could finally see. The broom was broken and had blood on it. Then I saw Steven lying on the floor bleeding and rolling around.

The screams were coming from him. What the fuck just happened? I stood stuck in one spot watching as Steven crawled over to the door. He kept repeating, "She's trying to kill me! She's trying to kill me!"

I didn't even realize that I still had the broom in my hand until one of the cops asks me to put it down. I throw that shit on the ground and hear that voice again, "that dog had it coming."

"Ma'am, do you have any other weapons on you?" The cop asked. I could feel the cop searching me. He pushed his hands on my back, and it burned so bad that I almost jumped out of my skin.

"Ma'am, are you alright? May I see?" The cop lifted up my shirt a little to see what was wrong with me. "Ma'am what happened here tonight?"

"He already told you. I tried to kill him."

"How did you get those bruises on your back?"

"It don't even matter."

"Why did you hit your husband?"

"That dog had it coming."

The police officer left me alone with the paramedics. The minute he opened the door, all I saw was the dark night air and all my nosy-ass neighbors trying to get a look inside. I knew I needed to call someone, but I couldn't remember anybody's phone number. I was trying so hard to remember, but that damn paramedic kept talking in my ear about if I wanted to go to hospital or if I could move in this direction and how bad was the pain. He just needed to shut the fuck up so I could think. Then to make matters worse, the cop came back into the house talking about how Steven had accused me of assault and that they had to place me under arrest. Then that stupid-ass cop started to read me my rights. The only merciful thing was that he handcuffed my hands in the front and I didn't have to feel that fucking pain in my back-well, at least not as much. I went from having a good damn day of planning my future to being led away in handcuffs, stepping on the pieces of my application as I walked out the door.

20

"Nicole Bennett!" the female cop called and opened the cell doors to let me out. I had spent the whole night on a bench with some chicks, who I guessed were prostitutes. I couldn't wait to get out of there. That bitch cop looked at me like I was the worse damn criminal in the world. Shit, I don't even understand why they had even arrested me; I was merely defending myself. It seemed as if everyone was against me. I couldn't even remember what happened. But here I was being led into a small, windowless room with two chairs and a tiny table.

"What am I doing here?" I asked the grumpy looking cop.

"Just have a seat." She said. This damn bitch acted like Steven was her man or something. I wished I could slap the shit out of her.

"Nic, are you alright?" I was so glad that when that door opened it was Mitchell standing on the other end.

"I think so, how did you know I was here?" I asked him

"Vickie woke me and told me you may need my help."

"Mitch, I ain't got no money to pay for no lawyer."

"Nic, you know you don't have worry about that."

"Good, then when am I going to get out of here?"

"Well, your bail was about five grand."

"What the fuck. Mitch I said I ain't got no money."

"It's being taken care of."

"By who?"

"That doesn't matter right now. Just tell me what happened."

If this wasn't Mitchell, I wouldn't say shit. But since I knew that he was trying to help me, I explained what I could remember.

"Did a doctor look at you?" Mitchell asked me after I was done explaining.

"Yeah, they sent me to the infirmary when I got here."

Mitchell was so sweet. He looked like he was so scared for me. Shit, I was scared for myself. I'm just glad my kids were at my mother's house. This whole shit would have been even worse if they had been home to see it.

"Alright Nic, you're going to get a trial date, but I'll see if something can be worked out with the DA. Right now we need to go sign some papers and get you out of here."

Mitchell walked with me over to the main desk. That damn bitch of cop was stuck on me all the way there. I don't know if she thought I was going to make a run for it or what. I had to make sure that all the things they took from me were there. I actually really didn't care. They could keep all that shit if they wanted it, I just couldn't wait to leave. All I wanted was to put this whole damn night behind me.

"Hey, gangsta bitch." I heard Joanna's voice and turned to see all three of my girls standing behind me. Judging by the fact that Victoria looked like she was still in her nightgown, they must have been here all night. I ain't never been so glad to see them before in my life.

Having them put their arms around me was the only thing I needed at that moment. I didn't even care that my back hurt like hell. When they finally let me go, I could feel Jessica wiping the tears from my face.

"Are you alright?" she asked.

"Yeah, girl."

"Well did they treat you alright?" Victoria asked actually sounding like her ass cared, "I mean didn't nobody mess with you did they?" Lord, Victoria got this shitty habit of going from caring to asking too many damn questions. That's some of the annoying things about her that got under my skin.

"You didn't sit down on any thing did you? Cause there's a lot of germs and diseases in there."

"Vickie! Let it go," Joanna said. I was so glad Joanna said something, because Lord knows, I couldn't afford to catch another charge.

"Alright ladies. I think we're all set here," Mitchell said hugging all of us, except his wife, as he left. I knew they had issues, but for Mitchell not to even acknowledge Vickie made me think that their issues had gotten worse. I bet he told her about his plans and the bitch flipped. I knew Vickie, and she couldn't think of nobody else's happiness but her own. She's lucky I got my situation going on right now, 'cause I would cuss her ass out for treating Mitchell the way she did.

"Why don't we go get Nic something to eat?" Jessica suggested.

"Jess it's like six in the morning. What's open?" Joanna asked.

"There has to be something open, Jo," Jessica replied.

We all piled into Joanna's car and after driving around for a few minutes, we managed to found an all-night diner. For a while, we sat at the table in complete silence. No one wanted to be the first person to ask me what happened, and I wasn't going to say nothing til they did. One of these heffas won't be able to take it, and right on cue here comes Vickie asking, "Did you hurt him badly?" Everyone stopped eating and looked at her. I don't know what they were so scared of. Did they think I was going to flip out on them too?

"Oh my God, Vickie," Jessica said acting like she was scared of what might come out.

"Damn, Vickie. You had to be the one." I said.

"What Nic...I mean, I just want to know." Victoria replied.

"He's not hurt bad, just a little bruised that's all," I answered.

"Well, what happened?" Jessica asked. Now that Vickie broke the ice, Jessica felt better asking me her question.

"Nothing. We just had a little fight, that's all."

"Nic, little fights don't land you in jail," Joanna said.

"It really wasn't that big a deal, Jo."

"Uh huh... did he hit you again?" Jessica asked me with that I-told-you-so look in her eye. I hated when she acted like that.

"Again? What do you mean again? He's been beating you, Nic?" Victoria asked. I forgot that Victoria was the only one of us who didn't know how me and Steven get down.

"Stop being so dramatic Vickie. It ain't like he's wiping my ass all over the place. We just fight, that's all," I said to her.

I wasn't about to let these bitches turn me into a victim. I'm not one of those scared punk-ass women who curl up into a ball every time their husband walks into a room. I always held my ground with Steven; we would fight like most married people, but he never abused me. I wish they would stop trying to make shit bigger than what it was.

"Nic, at the hospital there's a support group for abused women. I could get you the schedule if you'd like," Jessica said to me.

"I don't need no damn support group, Jess. I'm not abused. Why can't you guys understand that?"

I was glad when Joanna changed the subject cause these bitches were starting to get me mad. I ain't helpless or weak. Shit, I think I proved that tonight. The conversation was going pretty good until Victoria's ignorant ass opened her mouth again,

"Well, that kind of behavior is expected anyway."

"What kind of behavior, Vickie?" I asked her. Sometimes she just said the dumbest shit, and I just had to check her.

"Well, you know, the uneducated kind - from people who just don't know how proper people handle disagreements," she said.

"You know what Vickie, I don't mean no harm, but you're full of shit," I said to her.

"What did I say?" Victoria asked.

"I'm glad I ain't all snobbish like you."

"But all I said was..." Victoria started to say.

"Shut the shit up, Vickie... me and my husband fight - it happens. Can't everyone have the perfect marriage like you. Oh I forgot. Your husband don't even tell you bye when he leaves the room. I guess that's how proper people handle it right?" I knew the time would soon come when I would throw that shit back in her face and it felt good too.

But the moment those words came out of my mouth I knew I had gone too far. The last thing I wanted to do was hurt Vickie, but she just knew how to push my buttons.

"No, my marriage isn't perfect, Nic. And, yes, half the time he barely looks at me, but at least he isn't slapping me around," Victoria responded.

"Alright guys, people are starting to look over here," Jessica said in a whisper.

"Oh shut up Jess. Ain't nobody even here," I replied to her. If I had known things were going to turn out like this, I would have asked them to just drop me home. I could use the sleep anyway. All of them were so damn judgmental. They didn't know how real life is. Screw them. I ain't gonna let them make me feel like shit.

"I'm moving to California!" I tried to look at Joanna to see if she was just saying something to get our attention and stop us from fussing, but the bitch looked serious.

"You're what?" Jessica asked the question for all three of us.

"I'm moving to California," Joanna repeated the words again, but I don't think any of us knew what the hell she was saying. Her mouth was moving, but none of us understood the words that were coming from it. "If it's because of me and Vickie arguing, girl you know we always do that." I said to Joanna.

"No, Nic. It's because I got that promotion and the company has decided that the position will be more effective in the LA office," Joanna responded.

"Well, I think that's great," Victoria said. What the hell is Victoria thinking? Did she just hear the girl say she moving across the country? I bet her ignorant ass thinks that LA somewhere in Maryland.

"You do, Vickie?" Joanna asked, sounding just as surprised that Vickie took the news so well.

"Yes, I do. There are some very influential people in LA," Victoria said.

"Vickie, I can't believe you."

"Well, it's true Nic," Victoria replied.

"Since we've met, we ain't never been more than a few minutes away from each other. Now she's saying she's moving across the country and you think that's great?" I responded.

"Nic, I'm not saying that I'm happy she's leaving. All I'm saying is that I'm happy for her opportunity," Victoria said.

"An opportunity that's gonna take her away from us? You're happy about that?" I asked Victoria.

"Yes, I am. She's worked hard for this. Why should she stay and settle just because we're unhappy? I say go, Jo. You've earned this." Victoria explained.

"Jess, are you alright?" Joanna was the only one who noticed that Jessica wasn't saying much of anything.

"No, I'm not Jo. You're leaving us."

"I'm not dropping off the face of the earth. We can still call each other every day. You guys can come up and visit, and I can come back every now and then," Joanna said.

"That's not the same, Jo, and you know it," Jessica told her.

"I know Jess but...listen, my company has a beach house in Ocean City and my boss said I could use it this weekend," Joanna said to the three of us.

"Oh so you're ass trying to leave us even sooner," I said to her.

"No, Nic, I want you guys to come with me. What do you say to a girls' weekend? I mean we all seem like we could use the break," Joanna replied.

Hell, that actually sounded pretty damn good to me. I could use the time away from all the nonsense right now.

"Shit, I'm down," I said. "Oh I may have to call Mitchell to see if I can go."

"Why wouldn't you be able to go?" Joanna asked. "It's only Ocean City. It's not as if we're leaving the country or even the state for that matter."

"I still want to check. I don't need no more problems," I replied.

"Actually I'm off this weekend, so why not?" Jessica said. I thought for sure Jessica would have taken longer to convince. She normally didn't like going away from Michael for a long time.

"Come on Vickie. You know you want to," Joanna said to Victoria and nudged at her from across the table where she sat next to Jessica.

"I just can't leave, Jo. I have obligations," Victoria said.

"Vickie, damn your obligations. When was the last time we got a chance to spend time together without our crazy lives getting involve?" Joanna asked her.

"I just don't know Jo." Victoria said.

"This weekend you won't be Victoria Combs. You'll just be Vickie. No obligations. No drama, just fun. You know the thing we used to have before our worlds got so damn crazy," Joanna explained.

"I know Jo, but, well, alright. I guess I could make it," Victoria said, finally giving in.

"Good. Why don't we all go home, get packed, get some rest, and then hit the road," Joanna suggested.

"What, Jo. You me today?" Victoria asked.

"Yes, Vickie. I mean today. It is Friday, and the weekend starts today. No hesitation Vickie," Joanna responded.

I was actually getting excited. The thought of leaving this place and getting far away from Steven's stupid ass got me all upbeat again. Shit, this was the first time all night that I smiled. Then I remembered why we were going. It ain't had nothing to do with me and my shit, but because Joanna was leaving. I don't know what I was gonna do without her crazy ass. Now I had to figure out some place else to go the next time me and Steven fought. Who else was going to leave me alone and just let me cool down without asking a whole bunch of questions? I was happy for her, but I just couldn't believe she was really going.

21

When I got home, I packed some of my things and lay back in the bed. I was really hoping I could get some sleep before we left, but I just kept thinking about how Mitchell had acted when he were leaving the jail. I thought about how my girls had seen that Mitchell and I were having problems, and I thought about what I was going to say to them. There was no easy way of saying that my marriage was over. How could I form the words to say that my husband didn't want me anymore?

A part of me did not want to go on this trip, but there was this other part of me that wanted to run far away from here. Maybe Mitchell would miss me enough to want me back; maybe he wouldn't even notice I was gone. I had to let him understand that I was not just sitting around this house waiting on him. I knew people thought that I was playing Susie Homemaker, but all I ever wanted was for our lives to be perfect. What's wrong with that? Other people had perfect lives why couldn't I? Who says that I didn't deserve this big beautiful house, with the wealthy husband, and fabulous connections?

I didn't know why Mitchell would consider throwing all that away. I had to believe that he would come to his senses soon and call off this silly divorce. In the meantime, I'd just act like it didn't bother me. I guess this weekend was a good idea after all. Let Mitchell wonder where I was for a change. No, I would tell him where I was going and then let him wonder if I was ever coming back. I got up off the bed and begin searching my room for a pen and paper. I was going to leave him a note and make the note as vague as possible. That way, all weekend long, he'd be wondering what I meant.

"Vickie, what are you doing?" I was shocked to see Jessica standing in the doorway of my bedroom.

"Um, I was just writing a note for Mitch to let him know where I was going," I replied.

"Oh you don't have to. He's the one who let me in. I already told him."

"Really, what did he say?"

"Nothing. He just said to have fun."

"You told him I was going as well?"

"Yeah. Why?"

"Oh nothing. I just wanted to make sure he knew."

That fact that Mitchell didn't care that I wouldn't be home for days really killed me. The least he could do was come upstairs and ask me what was going on or where I was going. I would have asked him. I would have wanted to know all the details about the trip. I would have at least told him to his face to have fun. I really wanted to cry but Jessica was staring right at me. My girls already suspected that something was going on between Mitchell and me. I was not going to do anything to let them know how serious it really was.

"Are you sure you're alright, Vickie?"

"Of course why wouldn't I be?"

"I don't know. You just looked like you might need to talk."

"Oh no I'm fine. Anyway what are you doing here?" I asked to Jessica trying to change the subject.

"I figured it would be easier just to come here."

"Oh... well I guess."

Jessica seemed like there was something going on with her as well, but I couldn't worry about anybody else's problems. My own problems were more than enough. I mean, I was in a mess. What were people going to think of me? I was going to be utterly humiliated. I could kill Mitchell for putting me through this.

"Why don't we call Jo and see if she's ready?"

"Why, are you ready to leave now Vickie?"

"Why wait? The earlier we get there, the more time we can have together."

"I guess so."

"I know so," I replied as I picked up the phone to call Joanna.

I couldn't wait to get out of here. Being someplace else would buy me the time I needed to figure out what I was going to say to people. It was obvious that Mitchell didn't care, so it would be up to me to try and make some sense of this whole thing. I mean, I could hear the gossip mill now: *We thought they were so happy. I wonder what went wrong? You know he found some young beauty and dumped Victoria.*

I was so pissed at Mitchell. I'd be the laughing stock of the entire city. All are friends were going to know. Nothing was going to be the same. I wouldn't be able to show my face around Baltimore.

"Hello." Joanna answered her phone.

"Oh...um...Jo...are you ready?"

"What? Ready for what?" Joanna asked sounding confused.

"To leave."

"Vickie, I thought we decided to get some sleep and then leave."

"I now, but I think we should get an early start. It'll give us more time."

"Vickie, I'm not in any shape to drive all the way to Ocean City right now."

"Well, I'll drive. Everyone can sleep in the car."

"What the hell is going on?"

"Nothing just get ready. I'll be there soon."

22

"What was that about?" Nicole asked me as I hung up the phone.

"Apparently your girl Victoria is all ready to leave now," I answered.

"Call that bitch back and tell her ain't nobody ready to go nowhere." "I can't do that. She's all excited."

"So what? Why we gotta jump 'cause Vickie's ass wants to do something?"

"Come on Nic. Just get up and let's get ready. You're just trying to start something with her."

I didn't like having to leave earlier than expected, but Nicole knew as much as I did that trying to fight Victoria was a losing battle. The girl could be totally oblivious to everybody else's feelings. No one wins with a person like that, and I, for one, was not in the mood to deal with the drama. My mind was still on overdrive with this whole David thing. I had just lost the only man I had ever loved, even if it was from afar. I didn't think Vickie or any of these girls could understand that. They've at least been held, kissed, and made loved to by the man they loved. But I haven't had any of that, and I never will.

When I thought about life without David, it was almost unbearable. I'd done everything I was supposed to do, so why did it seem that I had nothing to show for it? Sometimes I felt so alone and so lost. I'd always told myself that I would never be one of those silly women who looked to a man to solve all of their problems. But what if not having a man was the problem? What if not having the right man was the problem?

I was so confused and so torn. My heart told me that I owed it to myself just to lay it all out there with David and just see what happens. But my head told me to pack up all my shit and go to LA. This would have been so much easier if David would have just understood and said something that told me that if I stayed we would be together. I would be the biggest dummy if I followed my heart and stayed just to have David say, "Oh, sorry Jo. I never thought of you that way."

I laughed at stupid women like that who threw their lives away for a man that didn't even want them. Women could be running the world if we weren't so easily fooled by men. There are women who are highly educated and on their way to success when they get married, have kids, and decide that it would be best if they slowed down and raised a family. That's the biggest bullshit I'd ever heard. A woman who has drive always has drive and there is nothing that can stop that except a man who convinces her that it's "for the best."

I was not going to be one of those women. I couldn't be. The sad thing was, that was the kind of woman that David wanted and needed. He was the white picket fence, two kids, and a dog type of a guy. For most ordinary women, that would be the dream. He was what we women would call a good man. But I guess I was not the ordinary type of woman. I didn't know how I would survive in that type of a world. I hated predictability and normalcy. I didn't even know what normal was. Am I not normal because I wanted to wear business suits and carry a briefcase? Maybe I wasn't normal because I didn't know if I wanted kids or a husband for that matter. I hated the stereotype that women had to be one particular way. It just made women miserable.

Maybe living in misery was my fear. What if one day I woke up married to David with beautiful kids and a home but I looked at myself in the mirror and there it was; misery. I think I would just end up hating David, and he didn't deserve that. I didn't deserve that. God I loved that man. But what did I have to sacrifice just to be with him? How much of myself did I have to give up?

I always knew David and I were mismatched, but from the first moment I saw him, I loved him. I've tried to find a man who would fit me better, but I've always loved David; I always come back to him.

"Here I'm ready." Nic threw down her suitcase and stood in the middle of my living room looking like she was pissed at the whole world.

"Nic, why are you acting like that? How do you expect to have any fun?"

"I don't expect to have fun with that crazy chick."

"Nic, give it a rest and just relax. Vickie may just surprise you."

"I don't see how."

"Well I do. So smile and pretend like you're excited."

"I'ma smile but if that heffa says one wrong thing to me, that's her ass."

"At least you'll smile," I said to her with a chuckle.

If nothing else, at least Nic and Vickie would serve as my amusement for the weekend. There bickering would get my mind off my own issues. I sort of felt bad thinking of them like that, but I'll take all the distractions I can get.

David was just stuck on my mind. I felt like those crazy-ass love songs, where the person couldn't breathe or eat or sleep without the one they loved. I've always thought that they didn't know what love really was. I'd always thought that love didn't hurt, that everything fit perfectly like pieces of a puzzle. But maybe it was me who didn't know what love really was, because I was sitting there killing myself over a guy who probably only thinks of me as just a friend.

"Hey Nic." I called out.

"What?" Nicole answered.

"Do you love Steven?"

"Now why the hell you ask me that for?" She asked looking frustrated.

"I don't know. I was just wondering I guess."

"I ain't in love with him if that's what you're asking, but, I guess, some parts of me care for him."

"Is that enough for you to stay with him?"

"You know if this is a setup for some kind of lecture, save the shit, ok, 'cause I ain't in the mood."

"Relax, this isn't actually about you."

"Then what it's about?"

"I don't know. I guess I've just been thinking that I'm getting older, you know. Maybe I should start considering marriage and kids."

"Bitch please. You won't last one day being married with kids," she said with a slight laugh.

"That shit's not funny. What are you trying to say? I'm not wife or mother material?"

"No, I'm not trying to say that. I'm saying...Idon't know"

"What does that mean?"

"I don't know. You're just you. I guess I never pictured you married with kids."

"I never pictured myself married with kids." I liked my life, but how long could I live like this?

23

Joanna said she ain't trying to give me no lecture, but I knew she was. That bitch knew good and damn well I ain't love no damn Steven. How could I love a bastard like that? I just knew this whole trip them heffas gonna try and make me see the light. Shit. They needed to be worrying about their own messes. I was the only one who had my shit under control. I handled my business. They sitting around looking all depressed and trying to hide shit, like couldn't nobody see they were going through some serious shit. They ain't fooling nobody. But Nicole's the crazy one. Hell, I put my shit on full display. This the shit I'm in. My husband and I fought like crazy. Sometimes he got the best of me and sometimes I got the best of him. That was just how it went. But I bet anything that these bitches gonna use this weekend to try and make it seem like I'm the one with the issue.

They needed to know that I'm cool. In life we all got shit to deal with. My shit is just obvious, that's all. I didn't need the looks or the lectures or the judgments. I got mine under control. I knew how to handle Steven and ain't nobody scared, ain't nobody running and fuck anybody who thought I should.

I love my girls, but they looked at me like I'm the one with all the problems, and they have to fix me just so I could be right. Hell, I'm right. I knew who I was. I didn't need no one trying to fix me. Yeah, I screwed up and, yeah, I hated my husband, but, shit, in life you had those kinda problems. That didn't mean I ain't right or that I needed to be fixed. All I needed was to be left alone.

I didn't have what they had, but, hell, I had enough. I was happy with what I'd done with my life - well maybe not going to jail last night. But I was happy with everything else. Steven was a bastard, I couldn't stand him, and I hated the sound of his voice, but, hell, at least he was around. Some men knock-up women and then they're gone. Those women gotta struggle all by themselves. That was just something I couldn't do. How the hell was I supposed to make a life for myself with two kids hanging on my hip and no man to help. Me and my kids got to eat. So I'm gonna keep knocking Steven around, and he gonna keep knocking me around until our kids get old enough to take care of themselves. Then we could go our separate ways. That's it.

"I sure wish Vickie would hurry up," Joanna said as she walked back and forth between the sofa and the living room window.

"Jo, why you keep pacing around like a crazy person."

"I'm just ready to go."

Jo thinks didn't nobody know she lonely all the time, but I knew the bitch didn't sleep nights. Whenever I was over there, I heard her walking the halls or typing on her laptop. She needed to get herself together, and people thought I was the one who's all screwed up.

And if I got issues with knowing how to treat a man, then how come it's Vickie's husband who's on his way out the door. She's the one who didn't know how to treat a man. If I had a man like Mitchell I'd be so good to him that motherfucker wouldn't ever want to leave the house. I'd have his ass stuck on my tit. But Vickie got him feeling all bad and worthless. She should be the one in jail for mistreating a good man. All I did was beat the shit out of a bad man. Hell, I should be getting the damn key to the city for that shit. If every woman was whipping the ass of a bad man, I bet those motherfuckers would think twice before raping and mistreating any woman. That's what we need around here, a national whip a motherfucker's ass day. Every woman should be given a bat and allowed to whip the hell out of a motherfucker.

And everyone was talking about how my husband abused me. Jess was the first damn one talking about I should go to some meeting -her ass needed to be in a damn meeting if you ask me. She was the one being abused, and the bitch just sat there and took the shit. I dare a man cheat on me to my damn face. I would start two damn days, whip a motherfucker's ass day and whip a stink-ho day, where all the hoes of the world get their asses beat for fucking somebody else's man and acting like that shit ain't no big deal. Jess is the one who needed the support group. She needed to run her ass over to Cheating On Me Anonymous. For all the women whose men cheat on them and they just sat there watching like dumb ass bitches. For me, I knew Steven cheated. Hell I want him to 'cause he sure as hell ain't touching me. Let him go do whatever with whoever. I didn't even see it as cheating. He's living his life and I'm living mine.

"I think she's here," I announced as I looked out the window with Joanna and saw a fancy-ass car pull up; I just knew it couldn't be nobody but Vickie.

"Good let's go down and meet them," Joanna said.

That may not be a bad idea. I just knew that if Vickie brought her ass up here, all she gonna do is talk shit then I ain't gonna want to go. At least if she talking shit in the car, we'd already be on the way and I ain't had no other choice but to go. But if anyone of these heffas say the wrong damn thing to me, I'd start telling them about themselves.

24

Sitting in Vickie's car watching Nic and Jo as they pulled their luggage behind them made me wonder how easy it would be to pack my bags and move far away from Michael. It would certainly spare me so much pain and anger. But then what? I'd never known myself as a woman without Michael. He'd been in my heart for so long - hell he was my heart. No one could be expected to let that go.

I had cried so hard and so often for this man. But no one could tell me that Michael didn't or has never loved me. It was impossible to fake what we had. If only Michael could change. If only I was sure that he would be different. I think I could forgive Michael and try again, but I had to know that this would never happen again, that he would never cheat again.

Sometimes I thought that I must be the dumbest woman on earth. What other woman would put up with this crap. Nicole beat the hell out of her man, Victoria flat out ignored hers, and Joanna wasn't bothered at all. But dumb me, I was stuck on the same man who engaged me but didn't want to set a date. Then he sleeps with every woman he sees. What do I do? Absolutely nothing. I loved him too much to hurt him or risk losing him. That made me dumb. Most women would worry less about the man and more about themselves. But not me - not dumb old Jessica who was so in love with a cheat and a liar.

"Jess, you gonna stay in the front seat?" Joanna asked me.

"Yes. Why you want the front seat?" I replied.

"No I want you to sit in the back with me," she said.

"Oh hell no. I ain't sitting up front with Vickie," Nicole blurted out.

"And what is wrong with sitting up front with me, Nic?" Victoria asked her.

"Bitch, I know you ain't just asked me that question," Nicole replied.

"Alright, alright. I'm staying in the front and Nic you sit in the back with Jo. Ok, can we all just relax now?" I said with a bit of an attitude.

"Well, darn. What the hell got up your ass?" Nicole asked and the look on her face told me that I'd shocked her by the way I yelled at them. I didn't know why I snapped like that. I just felt so much anger that I could practically feel the steam coming out of my ears. The last thing I wanted to do was to take out my anger on my girls but I just couldn't stand the bickering, not while I felt broken. All I wanted was some peace and quiet. I just didn't want my girls to feel bad or attacked. I had to somehow control myself from lashing out, at least for this weekend. Besides, what would it profit anyone to take my anger over Michael out on my girls? Everyone would just end up tense and on edge.

"Ok, well I'm going to sleep. Wake me when we get there," Joanna announced.

"Jo, how the hell you gonna go to sleep when you're the one with the address to where we going," Nicole said to her.

"Nic, if Jess is going to sit in the front, then she's going to handle the directions, and I'm going to sleep," Joanna replied.

"Well, somebody needs to tell me where we're going," Victoria said. "Vickie, you mean this fancy ass car ain't got no GPS?" Nicole asked. "Must you cuss all the time Nic?" Victoria asked Nicole.

"Yes, bitch, I must," Nicole replied.

"Will you all just shut up! I'll do the damn directions. It's no big deal," I shouted.

"Alright, Jess, your ass got one more time," Nicole said to me.

By the look on Nic and the other girls' faces, I could tell they were starting to get tired of me snapping at them. But I couldn't help it. Every time I opened up my mouth, I screamed, and I had to go an entire weekend trying not to lose it. I couldn't even go two seconds. This whole thing with Michael was turning me into someone I didn't even know. I could feel myself becoming this angry irritable little bitch. That's just not me. I was always calm, but I didn't know how to be that any more.

There were all these feelings and emotions that I just didn't know what to do with. I didn't know how to let go of Michael; I didn't know if I should let go of Michael. I loved him. That's all that should matter. I could learn to trust him again. I knew I could, but didn't think I could learn to live without him. A life with Michael had been my dream. All I ever wanted was a home and kids and him as my husband. How could I claim to love a man if I'm not willing to hang in there with him through the tough times? No relationship is easy and I knew in my heart that Michael could be the man that I needed him to be. Why should I have to give up on him now? Yeah he had hurt me. But he had also been so good to me. He'd loved me and accepted me as I was without judgment. I didn't know who I was without him, without us.

I loved him, that was all that mattered. So I had to figure out a way to forgive him, to reach out to him, and to hang in there with him until he became a better man.

25

Lord I was glad we were finally there. Sitting in that damn car made my body even more sore. It felt worst then it did after me and that bastard fought last night. At least I slept the whole way there. I took some painkillers from Jo's medicine cabinet and the shit knocked me right out. But it done wore off 'cause I sure was starting to feel my back starting to hurt all over again. I was barely able to get out the car. That shit hurt.

The minute I got out the car, I could see Vickie's bougie ass looking at the beach house like the shit was a pot of gold. I couldn't blame her, though; the house was nice. I don't think I ever seen or lived in anything so beautiful. The ocean was just a foot away and the whole house was surrounded by sand. It looked just like one of those pictures you see in magazines.

Jo opened the front door with a key and, hell, the inside looked just as good as the outside. That damn house was like three levels. On the ground level there was a rec room with a big screen TV, a kitchen, and a bar, two regular size bedrooms, and off the kitchen there were French doors that led to the pool. On the midlevel, there were two extra large master bedrooms and two large bedrooms. Each bedroom had its own bath and deck. The top level had a great room with another kitchen and a third deck.

That damn beach house was like something out of the movies. With the exception of a little dusting and vacuuming, the house was well kept. The refrigerators and kitchen cabinets were filled with food, all the beds were neatly made, and the bathrooms were clean and fully stocked with bath soaps and towels. They fixed this place up just like one of them high-end hotels. I was ready to kick my shoes off and relax.

I got away from them other three heffas and found myself in the kitchen. I ain't never seen a kitchen so big. If I had a kitchen like this to work in, I could create magic. It had everything down to two ovens. Why anyone needed two ovens was beyond me, but it was sure nice to look at.

I didn't want to leave the kitchen but I figured I'd better go find me a bedroom and get settled. I had my eye on one of the big ones but by the time I got there, there was Vickie unpacking her shit.

"Vickie watcha doing?" I asked her.

"I'm unpacking," she answered.

"How you know this your room?" I asked again.

"Because it's the one I pick," she replied.

"What if someone else wanted it?" I continued.

"So?" she responded.

"So, you could've at least waited till we were all together before deciding what room to choose," I said to her.

The damn bitch acted like she didn't even hear me and kept right on unpacking. I was so tired of her acting like no one else mattered. She didn't even consider that maybe I might have wanted the room. I guess my poor ignorant ass don't deserve a room like this. Only perfect Victoria could have it.

"Nic, you need to relax," Victoria said in that smug tone of hers.

"Why? So you could just bulldoze your way through things? This ain't your house. You can't have the room you want. You gonna have to learn to share," I told her.

"Ok, Nic, if you want this room, have it. Besides, this could be the only experience you'll have in a place like this anyway," Victoria said.

"You're full of shit, Vickie!" I shouted.

"Why? Because I'm telling you the truth?" she asked so damn calmly.

"You know what Vickie. Keep the room."

"Well, thank you. Since it was yours to give."

"You little bitch, how…" I began to say.

I didn't even hear Jo and Jess come into the room cause I was so pissed at this bitch. It wasn't till Jo said, "Hey, what's the problem?" that I realize they were standing there and had heard me and Vickie arguing.

"Ms. High And Mighty decided that this room should be hers so she took it," I explained.

"Nic, did you expect her to take one of the smaller rooms?" Joanna asked me.

"No, Jo, but I at least thought she would ask."

"Alright, Nic. Why don't you take my room? It's about the same size as this one. Matter of fact, I think it might be bigger," Joanna said.

"I don't want no goddamn bigger room Jo!"

When I stormed out of the room, I could hear Vickie ask, "What did I do?" and Jess answered, "You were being you."

I really wanted to go back in the room and say, Yeah bitch you were being you. But if I had gone back, I would have slapped the shit out of Vickie. So I just had to get out of that house.

It wasn't but a minute of me sitting on the porch of the house until Jess came outside to check on me.

"Are you ok, Nic?" Jessica asked me.

"I don't know why I even came."

"You came to be with your best friends."

"Well, two of you are my best friends."

"Why don't you just talk to her, Nic?"

"I can't."

"Why?"

"Because she's right. I'm not like you guys and I don't belong in places like this."

"Hell, I don't belong in places like this my damn self and when was Vickie every right about anything?" Jessica asked.

"Jess you know I don't fit with you guys. I'm always the odd one out," I said to her.

"Listen, don't let Vickie ruin your weekend. With Jo leaving, it might be the last time we'll all be able to get together like this. Plus you fit, Nic. You always did."

Jess and the rest of them didn't get it. They don't have to go through what I have to go through. I ain't them and they ain't me. They ain't never gonna get it.

I must have flinched when Jess tried to pat me on my back 'cause I sure felt a sharp pain running down my back.

"What's wrong?" Jessica asked looking really concerned.

"Nothing I'm still a bit sore."

Jess lifted up my shirt and something must have really worried her, because she acted like I was at death's door or something.

"Shit, Nic. I thought somebody took a look at this?" Jessica asked in a panic.

"Girl, you know how them people do. Besides they said it ain't bad," I told her.

"Well it is. Come inside with me so I can take care of it," Jessica said.

I wish I could see what Jess saw. I knew my back hurt, but I didn't think it was all that bad. Sometimes Jess overreacts, but I sure was glad she was here.

26

I didn't know why Nic always acted as if I was the worst person on earth. I was so tired of having to defend myself against her. I wasn't going to censor myself around her. I will not shield Nicole from the truth. It was one thing to be sympathetic but it was something entirely different to encourage Nicole not to take control of her situation.

She was in a bad place. For some reason everyone else felt like it was ok to ignore it. Well not me. I would not stand for Nicole speaking to me however she wanted and acting as if I were to blame for all her problems.

"Vickie, maybe you should take it easy on her at least for the weekend. She's been through a lot," Joanna pleaded with me.

"I didn't do anything wrong. She's the one who came storming in here like she runs the place."

"I get it but that's Nic. She acts tough and carefree on the outside, but you and I both know that on the inside she's really hurting right now."

"That makes it alright? Perhaps if she wasn't being that way, she wouldn't have ended up in jail last night and I wouldn't be out $5,000."

"Vickie, I thought you said you weren't going to mention the bail money?" Joanna asked me, sounding as if she had gotten frustrated with me. I didn't know why she would; I was only speaking the truth. No one ever gives me credit for the things that I do. They always try to correct me when all I do is tell them the truth.

"No I said I wasn't going to mention it to her and I haven't."

"Vickie, let's just try and have a good time this weekend," Joanna said as she got up off the bed and headed for the door.

"That's what I'm here for Jo - to have fun, but I will not be censored." I told her as she walked out of the room.

I'm so sick and tired of people always putting me on notice. From my girls to Mitchell, everyone wanted me to be someone I'm not. I wish people could just accept me for who I am. It's like I was all wrong and everyone else is all right. I couldn't help who I am and you would think that if people loved you, they would love all of you.

Perhaps people just didn't get me. They didn't understand how hard it was to be me, having to cope with so much negativity and hatred. I was surrounded by so many fake people that I didn't know how to keep them straight. For once I just wanted people to be real with me. I was not a bad person - well not as bad as Nicole or Mitch would have people believe. So I'm not going to change who I am for anybody. I like having money and being able to buy nice things. I was not going to pretend like I didn't just because Nicole felt intimidated.

As for Mitchell, well, I loved him. I knew people might think that I didn't but I did. I just am not willing to overlook his behavior. So if he wanted a divorce, then that's fine. But if he thought I was going to go down without a fight then he had another thing coming. He promised me the world, and I intended to take it. I'm not giving up my house or my car or anything else that I have become accustomed to. I'm not going to be one of those ex-wives who ended up with nothing just because their husband has gotten bored with them.

A sweet smell coming from the kitchen prompted me to stop what I was doing and go find out what was going on. Jo and Jess were already there when I arrived. It appeared that Nicole had started cooking. She had always been a really good cook. I loved eating her creations, so I couldn't wait to see what she had whipped up for us.

"Oh my god Nic. I can feel the twenty pounds piling on right now," Joanna said as she sat at the kitchen table next to Jessica.

"Good, you've been looking kinda scrawny lately Jo." Nicole responded.

"Shut up, I'ma let that slide 'cause I'm hungry," Joanna said as she began to dish out food.

"Girl, you put your foot in this," Jessica said with a mouth full of food.

"You sure did," Joanna agreed.

Every bit I tasted seemed to be much better than the last. The food was amazing.

"Wow Nic. This food is slamming. You see, you can do something right," I said to Nicole. I was so impressed with her skills and so excited with what she had done. All I wanted was for her to know how proud I was of her.

"What the shit does that mean, Vickie?" Nicole asked with an angry tone.

"Nothing. I was just telling you how good your food is," I replied. I'm not sure what she had taken offense to.

"No, you wasn't. You were trying to say something slick. What, because I'm not a doctor or the rich, spoiled wife of an attorney or...or...whatever the hell Jo does, does that mean I can't do nothing?" Nicole said still seeming angry.

"That's not what I meant Nic...stop making a big deal out of nothing," I told her.

"Well, Vickie it is a big deal," Nicole said.

"All I meant was that we all have strengths," I said to her.

"Well Vickie, I'm sorry that my strengths took this long to hit you," Nicole said as she threw the dishes into the sink.

"Sorry you took this long to recognize your own strength," I said back to her. I was starting to get annoyed at Nicole's reaction.

"Guys why don't we all just relax and go take a walk on the beach or something," Joanna said, trying to interrupt our argument.

"You shut up Jo. This is all your fault. If you hadn't insisted we be friends with her because she had a car, we wouldn't be stuck with her ignorant ass now," Nicole yelled out.

That was the first I'd heard of that. I always thought that they really liked me. Boy, have I been a fool for all these years. I can't believe that I thought these girls were my friends.

"You guys just wanted to be my friend only because I had a car?" I asked.

"Well...just...you know...first impressions can be a bitch. Besides, Vickie, that was years ago. Things changed; we've changed," Joanna said.

"Hell no. Her ass ain't changed. She's still the same stuck-up bitch that we had to take pity on cause ain't nobody wanted to be her friend," Nicole said.

"Oh. So was that all that I was Nic? Is this friendship just based on pity?" I asked again.

"Yup that about sums up all these years of putting up with your ass," Nicole answered.

"Well fine. I have come to a place in my life, Nic, that if someone does not want to be around me, than I will not force them to. My car and I will be leaving first thing in the morning."

27

It was really early in the morning but I had to wake up this early. Between Nic and Vickie, yesterday was a complete failure. I had to figure out a way to make it right. For all Vickie's posturing, she was probably the most sensitive of us all. She always feels like she has to try hard to fit in. Sure Vickie could be annoying, but underneath, way underneath, she was a good person who did help her friends in her own way. It was just that sometimes she didn't understand that the things she said and the way she said them could be harsh.

I knew it appeared that I overlooked Nicole's problems, but I understood how serious they were. I get it. But I just didn't think the constant lecturing was necessary. When Nicole is ready, she'll fix her issues. My job was to be her friend, not the dictator of her life. If she was alright where she was, then I'd support that. Friendship is not build off of control; it's built from support, and I supported Nicole like I supported Jessica and Victoria. That's why I knew Victoria couldn't leave angry. We all needed each other, so I had to go to her room and tell her that.

But Victoria's room was empty. She wasn't there and neither were her things. I knew Vickie was pissed, but she wouldn't leave us here without a ride home. I ran down the stairs and out the front door and saw that her car wasn't there. I wasn't mad that she left us without a ride home, just the fact that she left us at all. This weekend was supposed to be about all of us just being together but everything seemed to be falling apart.

"Hey." Seeing Jessica standing behind me looking like I felt was more than I could handle. I had to sit just so my mind could grasp the fact that this may very well be the end of the four of us. Jessica must have felt the same cause she sat down beside me and held my hand.

"She's gone?" We turned to see Nicole standing in the doorway.

"Yeah. I don't know when she left," I answered.

"About an hour before you got up," Nicole said. I could tell Nicole felt bad about the argument, but she was too stubborn to admit it. After a while of just sitting on the porch and watching the road to see if we saw her car drive up, we went back into the house in complete silence. It was hard to think about Vickie out there somewhere all alone thinking that her friends weren't really her friends. It was hard to figure out what would be the right thing to say that would put my friends back together. I couldn't even tell Vickie how sorry we were because she wasn't picking up her phone. I must have called about a hundred times, but I guess she was just done with us.

Nicole tried to salvage what was left of the morning by making breakfast for everyone. Jessica and I sat in the kitchen as Nicole cooked. No one wanted to be the first person to say anything. I guess we just didn't know what to say. What could we say? We were all pretty much thinking that this weekend was over before it even started. There was a time when we could say the craziest things to each other and, yeah, we would get mad, even want to kick each other's ass, but five minutes later it was as if nothing even happened. I guess the older you get the less likely it is to bounce back from hurt feelings. I mean just looking at Nicole. I could tell that she'd never gone to sleep. I bet she must have paced in front of Vickie's door over and over again debating whether to go in and say something. But when pride and anger mix, the outcome could be the destruction of all that is good in your life.

"Is there enough for me?" I looked up to see Victoria standing in the doorway of the kitchen. I had never been so happy to see someone. I couldn't control myself. I ran right up to her and held her tight. I didn't know what made her come back, but I was glad she did.

"I just felt like, I don't know, maybe we needed to talk," Victoria said softly.

"Yeah, Vickie I think we do need to a talk," I replied.

"Alright, so go ahead then Jo," Victoria said to me.

"Me? Oh well...um..." I didn't really mean I needed to talk. I more meant that she and Nicole needed to talk.

"Vickie, when we first met, you were the most spoil brat any of us had ever seen..." Nicole blurted out.

"Nic! Come on," Jessica said looking like she was scared that everything might blow up again.

"No it's time for the truth. Vickie complained about every fucking thing and no one was good enough. It was damn annoying," Nicole explained.

Jessica and I both held our breath and waited for round two. This was getting us nowhere, but Nicole and Victoria were not going to let it go.

"You think I don't know how bad I am, of course I do. Why else would my three best friends hate to be around me and my husband cheats on me and now wants to divorce me!" Victoria yelled. For the first time I saw tears fill her eyes and I could see her try with all her might to not allow them to fall down her face.

"Oh my God Vickie," Jessica said and reached out to hold Victoria.

"No, don't feel sorry for me now, Jess, because I'll be fine. I'm always fine," Victoria said pushing Jessica away.

"Yeah bitch you are always fine, 'cause you play the victim so damn well that you got to be fine," Nicole said.

"Nic, can't you see she's hurting. Just give it a rest," I said to Nicole.

"No, I won't Jo. Her problem is she doesn't ever let anyone talk. She just assumes shit," Nicole said.

"What else do you want to say Nic?" Victoria asked.

"After we became friends, I understood you better. You still got on my damn nerves, but I could deal," Nicole said.

"You could deal? It doesn't seem like you're dealing. It seems like you hate me," Victoria responded.

"I don't hate you, Vickie. You have just been treating me like shit for all these years," Nicole said.

"How?" Victoria asked.

"Well, by acting like you're embarrassed of me or something," Nicole answered.

"I've never been embarrassed of you," Victoria said.

"Hell yeah you have. Every time you threw one of those uppity parties and not inviting me or if you do invite me you act like I ain't even there," Nicole said.

"First of all, I always thought you would be uncomfortable at my parties, and I do try to be around you, but I have other guests to attend to. What am I supposed to do? I'm being told by you that I need to hang around you and my mother's telling me to do something entirely different. I'm stuck," Victoria explained.

"You see what I mean, Vickie. You're playing the victim role again. Poor Victoria. Her mommy won't let her play with her friends. Bitch, please. You could stand up to your mommy if you wanted to. You're a grown-ass woman, Vickie," Nicole said.

"That's not fair. But you're right. I'm sorry I didn't realize how it made you feel," Victoria said.

"I'm sorry too girl. I know sometimes my mouth can get away from me. We do love you girl," Nicole replied.

Seeing Victoria and Nicole hug made me feel all tingly inside. It took a while, but I think they may finally be able to relate to one another, at least for right now. Let's see what happens in about an hour.

28

"What's your problem Jess?" Joanna asked me as we sat on beach chairs enjoying the scenes of the ocean.

"Nothing I'm just enjoying sitting out here on the beach. Why do you ask?"

"You just seem to be a million miles away."

"Jo, you're supposed to be relaxed when you're relaxing on the beach. That's the point."

"See that's what I mean all that unnecessary attitude. You've been having that since yesterday," Joanna said as she sat up in her beach chair.

"No I have not. I'm fine."

The truth was I really wanted to be away from all the drama. Being here with my girls almost felt like being around Michael. Every five seconds it was something different. It was like riding a rollercoaster and I was ready to get off. I so missed the hospital. Even on its busiest days, it would be better than sitting around waiting for the next fight or the next hurt feeling. I had issues of my own and dealing with everyone's problems was not what I had signed up for.

Look at how crazy this whole vacation had been so far. Nicole and Victoria had fought like cats and dogs and then Victoria made one of her dramatic exits and reentrances. Now both of them were sitting on the beach together talking and laughing like nothing even happened. Craziness.

If only they could just deal with their own selves for a while and leave me alone, I would be a happy person. But today just didn't seem like the day because even though I got my shades on and my eyes closed I could still feel Joanna's eyes staring me down. This crap is getting tiresome and I was ready to make my own dramatic exit.

"Jess, if he's cheating, then you need to kick his ass to the curb. You don't need no man holding you back," Joanna said.

"Says the woman without a man."

"Excuse me?" Joanna asked turning her entire body towards me.

"You heard what I said. I am so sick and tired of you always giving advice on someone's love life when you don't have one of your own," I said to her. All the while, I kept my shades on and didn't look in her direction at all.

"I don't need a love life to know when a man is no good, and your man is no good."

"Please, my man is just fine. We are in love and true love sticks it out. You would know that if you've ever been in love."

Joanna was getting me so frustrated. Every time something happened with Michael and me, the first thing out of her mouth was "leave him." What kind of a friend does that? She didn't ever tell Nicole to leave Steven and those two never should be on the same planet together let alone in a marriage. But Michael and I can work. All I needed was a little support from my girls, but I guess I'm not going to get that.

"What's going on?" Victoria asked as she and Nicole walked over to us.

"Nothing Vickie. Jess and I were just talking," Joanna replied.

"Oh hell, now these two bitches over here fighting," Nicole said. "No one's fighting, Nic. Like I said, we're just talking," Joanna replied putting on her shades and sitting back onto the beach chair.

"Well when talking gets loud that's fighting," Nicole said.

"Will everyone just give it a damn rest. We came here to relax and get away from it all and so far that hasn't happened yet." I told them.

"That's true, Jess. We did come here for that, but I'm your friend and I'm not going to see you looking all unhappy and not say anything," Joanna said as she sat back up and turned to me again.

"Jo, it's so funny how you're saying something when someone's unhappy, but you don't ever say something when someone's happy," I said to her, finally turning in her direction.

"What does that mean?" she asked.

"That means that I've been wearing this engagement ring for a while now and not one of you has said boo about it. Is that friendship?" I asked, looking at all three of them.

I wasn't going to stay there one more minute and have Joanna tell me how unhappy I seemed. My life may be a mess but I knew it could get better. I just needed to figure out how. All I needed was to talk with Michael, maybe there was a good explanation, or maybe he could make me understand what he was thinking, having some woman in my house and in my bed.

I had to leave. I couldn't stay and argue with Joanna any more. I just didn't have the strength to do it.

Victoria followed me back into the beach house asking, "Hey Jess are you ok?"

"I'm fine Vickie. You could have stayed on the beach. You didn't have to follow me."

"I know. But I just wanted to make sure you were cool. Do want to be alone?" she said.

"No...yeah...I don't know." I tried to explain to Victoria but I really didn't know what I wanted right now.

"You want to talk?" Victoria asked.

"Vickie what...did you...I mean how did you feel when you found out Mitch was cheating?"

"Well I didn't actually find out. It's more like a feeling."

"And you're divorcing your husband over a feeling?"

"The divorce was kind of his idea," Victoria said sounding as if she was not sure of anything.

"Are you willing to lose your marriage?"

"I don't know, Jess. I have my limits. Some people could be able to work through it. I just don't think I can."

"Some people like me."

"That's not what I mean. You've been with Michael a lot longer than I've been with Mitch, and you have a lot invested. I think when you reach your limit you'll know it."

"How do you know when you've reached you're limit?"

"You just know, Jess."

Victoria left me alone and I finally got the peace I wanted except I didn't know why I wanted it. Was I supposed to think about what to do with my relationship? Or was I supposed to just block it out completely as if it didn't exist?

I wish there was this magic potion that could make a woman stop loving a man anytime she wanted. But life didn't work that way. No matter how much a man hurts you, your heart can't stop aching for him. I wanted Michael. I wanted him sitting here with me, enjoying this beautiful scenery in this beautiful home. I loved being in love with him. I loved him being in love with me. How could I stop that? Maybe it was easy for Victoria because she didn't feel the same for Mitchell like I felt for Michael. If she did, she would be fighting just as hard as I was to keep her man. I couldn't lose him. It would be like losing a piece of myself and I would be incomplete.

29

I could see Joanna trying to act like she was all ok with Jessica calling her out for not knowing shit cause she ain't got a man. That bitch knew she was heated. It was all on her face. All someone got to do is look at her and you could tell she wanted somebody, playing like she was all cool with being alone. Yeah, it was cool to have that nice fancy job and all those material things but everyone needs someone in their lives to share the good and the bad. That was why I stayed with Steven stupid ass. At least he was there. Shit. I got the whole thing about being strong on your own and all; that's all fine and dandy, but my thing was once you'd done that then find you someone, even if it's just someone to argue with. Hell, at least there would be some sound in your home. Lord knows there's a whole lot of sound in mine.

I wished Jo would get that. She just needed to let go and find her somebody. But you tell her ass that, and she'd start preaching about how woman have been brainwashed into thinking that they need a man in their lives. That ain't what I say. I say it ain't brainwashing. It's the truth. Women do need a man in their lives. How the hell else we going to get the good dick? Even Oprah's ass got Stedman waiting for her to come home at night. Life gets lonely as hell. Who wants to live their life all alone?

"You feel like she does, Nic?" Joanna asked me.

"Like what?"

"Like I don't know what I'm talking about cause I ain't got a man."

"Well..."

"Cause I know that I may be making the biggest mistake of my life not taking a chance on love or that I may be running away but I'm good with my decision," Joanna said interrupting me.

"Darn, Jess said all that in the little bit of time or that's how you feel?"

"I don't know how I feel anymore, Nic. I used to know exactly what I wanted for my life. Now I'm just not sure," she said in a low voice.

"All I know is if I find a man who felt about me half the way David feel about you, I would hold on to his ass like my ass is drowning and he's the damn last life preserver," I told her.

"He kicked me out his house...what kind of feeling is that?"

"Girl, please. That man done kicked you out so many times that shit ain't even funny no more."

"Yeah, I know. But this feels different, Nic. This felt like goodbye for good."

"No it ain't. That's just David pissed cause you're leaving. He'll get over it. But you do need to decide what to do and soon cause as fine as he is some hoe waiting right there to scoop him up, and it might be my ass."

Joanna just sat back in her beach chair, put on her shades and began to stare into the ocean. She obviously didn't feel like laughing at my joke, and I didn't know what else to say to her. So I also just sat back and put on my shades.

30

It was later on in the afternoon when Victoria suggested that we all go shopping on the boardwalk. We walked for a while and then sat down on a bench that gave us a clear view of everything going on. After sitting for a few minutes, Nicole, Joanna, and Victoria got up and started walking.

I wanted to get up off the bench, but something caught my attention. There was this older couple maybe in their late fifties or early sixties, but they were still quite attractive. The two of them sat together on the beach effortlessly. There was comfort that surrounded them. I watched as that old dude took a peek at every young girl passing by in a bikini. It wasn't in a nasty old man kind of way just in an appreciative sort of way. But every time the woman would catch him watching, she would pinch him and then the both of them would laugh and kiss.

I wondered if they had some secret that no one else had. Why didn't she get mad that he was looking at other women? Why did he have to look at other women when he had someone next to him that is obviously devoted to him? Obviously it didn't bother her. Maybe they're still together because they keep working at it. Maybe they both know that neither one of them are going anywhere. I guess that's how Michael and I are. I don't have any intentions on leaving Michaels and I don't care how many women he's been with, he always stays with me.

"Jess you coming?" Joanna asked. The two of us could never stay mad at each other for very long. We don't really say sorry, we just move on to the next thing. I guess being friends for so long, we both understood that sometimes things get said out of anger, but true friendship can handle anything.

"Um, I'll catch up. I have to check in," I replied.

But it wasn't the hospital I had to check in with; it was Michael. My moment of truth was finally here and it was time for Michael and me to talk.

"Hey baby." Michael's voice was just as deep and smooth as it ever was and the sound of it lingered in my ears. "You having fun with your girls?"

"Yeah, we're having a great time."

"That's good baby. You know I miss you right?"

"Do you really

"Off course I do. You're my heart, girl."

"How can I be your heart and you do what you did."

"Baby, I'm sorry. I got drunk and got stupid."

"You couldn't think of a better lie other than you were drunk?" I asked him. I could feel myself getting angry all over again.

"Baby it's not a lie. I..." Michael's voice got lower.

"Save it, because I can't handle hearing another lie right now. I'm so tired of it all Michael."

"Wait, so you're saying you don't believe me? I bet your girls are up there in your ear talking all kinds of crap about me. But I'm not lying to you, Jess."

"My girls aren't saying anything cause they don't know. I've been a fool Michael, and I don't know what to do anymore."

"You don't know what to do? Well do you love me?"

"Yeah. That's the problem."

"No, it's not a problem. If you love me then trust what I say."

"What are you saying?"

"That I'm a changed man. For you I can change. I love you and want to spend the rest of my life with you. That bitch took advantage of the fact that I was drunk. That's all that happened. Do you believe that?"

"I don't know Michael."

"Baby listen I'll get in my car and be up there in a couple of hours."

"No don't. I just need some time to myself to think."

"Are we gonna be alright baby?"

"I don't know."

Michael tried to tell me he loved me again before I hung up the phone, but I couldn't handle hearing it. Part of me wanted to believe him. I knew how he gets when he goes out. He drinks a lot and girls or groupies throw themselves all over him. It's all part of his job; he's one of the highest rated DJs in Baltimore, so it makes sense. But God there was this other part of me that says he is taking me for another ride. When the hell was I going to get off?

———

I finally caught up to Joanna, Nicole, and Victoria standing outside of a tattoo parlor trying to get Victoria to get a tattoo with them. I stood back for a while and watched them interact. Nicole and Joanna knew good and well that Victoria was not going to get a tattoo even if it was temporary. But they pushed the subject anyway just to aggravate her. Victoria's personality was one in a million; the more aggravated she became, the funnier she got.

"Vickie, it's temporary," Joanna said to Victoria.

"Oh, no. That's nothing but the devil's mark, Jo, temporary or not," Victoria replied.

"Oh Lord, it's Holy Ghost Hour," Nicole said.

"It is not, Nic. It's the truth. Our bodies are our temples and I will not defame mine," Victoria said.

Nicole was the first to notice that I was standing there. I didn't even realize that I looked distressed. I was actually enjoying watching them.

"Jess, you ok?" Nicole asked.

"Yeah, Nic. I'm fine."

"Did something go wrong at the hospital?" Joanna asked me.

I shook my head but I didn't want to speak. Something told me that the second I opened my mouth everything I was feeling and thinking would come flowing through. I just wanted to enjoy the moment and let my girls enjoy the moment as well. But sometimes you just couldn't stop the tears, and they just came rushing out before I had time to stop them.

"Damn, Jess, Did the patient die or something?" Nicole asked coming over to me and wrapping her arms around me. I didn't realize how much I needed that. It allowed me to release some of the pain that had been burning a hole in my heart for so long.

"You didn't call the hospital did you?" Joanna asked. Sometimes it amazed me how much Joanna knew me. There's nothing I could hide from her.

"Who did you call?" Victoria asked.

"That dog," Nicole said.

"What dog?" Victoria continued to ask.

"Damn, Vickie. Michael!" Nicole yelled.

"Oh," Victoria said, finally getting what was going on. "I was so stupid." I said softly.

"No you're not," Joanna said.

"Yes I am, Jo. He lies over and over and I fall for it every time. That's stupid," I replied.

"Sure is," Nicole agreed.

"Shut up, Nic. Jess you're not stupid. It's ok to love someone that strongly," Joanna said.

"Yeah. Jess. I know where you're coming from. Look what I'm going through with Mitch. Sometimes it's hard to let go. That doesn't make you stupid," Victoria said.

"Ok, if I'm not stupid, then why would I be considering going back to a man who slept with another woman in my house in my bed?" I asked to them.

"Cause you stupid as hell," Nicole said.

"Nic, shut up. Jess, that's not stupid - stupid. That's love stupid," Joanna said.

"What the shit you talking about Jo?" Nicole asked turning to give Joanna crazy look as if she should have known that there was not a difference between the two. And maybe there wasn't. Stupid was just stupid. There's no different type that makes one lesser than the other; if you're being stupid for a man, then you're stupid in life period.

"What if I were you and the same thing happened? What would you do?" I asked Joanna.

"Um...before or after I kicked his ass?" Joanna replied.

"That's right. Hell, whip his ass to the damn white meat." Nicole's laugh made me forget for a moment, but only for a moment.

"Alright, Jess, so you tend to be a little gullible. That doesn't make you stupid and it certainly doesn't gave Michael the right to take advantage of you. It's the best part of you," Joanna said.

"Yeah, the fact that you'll fall for anything has kept us entertained many a days," Nicole said with a chuckle.

"Thanks, Nic. I'm glad that I provided your entertainment," I said to Nicole.

"You're welcome, girl. But you need to get your shit together. That's all I'm saying," Nicole replied.

"Listen, we all need to get our shit together and start fresh. I think we should get that tattoo to show that we're not taken anybody's crap anymore," Joanna said.

"Now Jo, I said that I'm not going to put none of that devil's mark on me and I meant it," Victoria said, trying to back away from us.

"Oh Vickie, you need a little devil in your life," Nicole said to her. "I don't care what you say Nic. It's heathenish," Victoria said.

"Vickie, it's only temporary and we can put it in a spot only we know about," Joanna told her.

"No, Jo, I'm not doing it," Victoria replied and folded her arms. "Oh you're such a punk," Nicole told her.

"Look, Nic, I don't care what you call me. I'm not putting any mark of the devil on my body," Victoria said.

"Vickie, you are getting this and I don't give a damn if we have to tie you down," Nicole said.

"You can't make me, Nic," Victoria said.

"Shit, yes I can. Watch," Nicole told her, then turned to me and Joanna. "Anyway what we going to get?"

"Two horns probably," Victoria said.

"That's not a bad idea Vickie," Joanna said laughing.

"It sure ain't, Jo. I think we should have them pointy with daggers," Nicole said to Joanna with a wink.

"I was joking!" Victoria yelled.

"Why don't we get this butterfly?" I saw this picture on the wall of a multi-colored butterfly that spread its wings across the page. It had a look of tranquility and contentment. It was free to live life on its own terms to fly as high and as far as it wanted without remorse, regret, or fear. It was the perfect beginning to a new life that was once lost.

31

"Would you quit playing with that thing, Vickie," Nicole said to me.

"No, Nic. I can't believe I let you guys talk me into getting this tattoo."

"Vickie it's fake. It ain't gonna last but for a few days."

"So, I still defiled my body."

"Oh please, Vickie. Besides I think I might make my permanent," Nicole said as she admired the tattoo on her arm.

I didn't care what Nic said, things like this didn't belong on the human body. What would my pastor think? What would my mother think? The kind of people who got things like this were jailbirds and drug users. Oh my God, I'd put myself in the company of those people. What had I let these girls do to me? I was so glad this thing was on my arm. Maybe I could cover it up so no one would see; it please Lord, don't let anyone see it.

"I bet Mitch will think it's sexy," Joanna said with a smile.

"I don't care what Mitch thinks, Jo. Beside he hasn't thought about me in months."

"What do you mean? Ya'll ain't doing it?" Nicole asked.

"Nic must you be so vile," I said to her.

"Shit it ain't like I said *fuck*," Nicole replied.

"Wait a minute. This is about to get good. Let's grab some wine and take this to the living room. I need to be relaxed to hear this," Joanna said.

Joanna ran ahead of us to find where they kept the liquor, and Nicole and Jessica jumped on the sofa with such eagerness in their eyes like they were children about to be told their favorite bedtime story. I had no clue why I'd even said anything at all. As much as I loved these girls, it was none of their business what I did or didn't do in my bedroom. Bedroom business was for the bedroom and no place else. That's what's wrong with the world now. We are so quick to tell each other every aspect of our lives; it is absolutely ridiculous.

"Alright I'm back, so let's hear it. You and Mitch are not getting it in," Joanna said as she ran into the living room where the rest of us were sitting.

"Jo, come one," I said to her.

"Yeah, Jo, you ain't got to be so vile," Nicole said with a loud laugh.

"Funny, Nic. Very funny," I told her.

"Come on, Vickie. I bet we can help. I mean I told you guys my business today," Jessica said, and was the only one who did not find this the least bit funny.

"Alright. No we aren't getting it on. We haven't for some time now," I confessed.

"Damn, that's why your ass act like that...You're horny," Nicole said.

"No, Nic. I am not horny. I just don't know why he doesn't find me attractive," I told them.

"I don't think that's true, Vickie," Joanna said, finally getting serious.

"It is true, Jo. Why else would he be with other women," I said to her.

"Vickie have you seen Mitchell with other women or has he told you he was with other women?" Joanna asked.

"Why would I need to wait for that to happen first, Jo? I know what I know," I said to her.

"It just doesn't seem like the Mitch I know. That's all I'm saying," Joanna said.

"Who is the Mitch you know? Is he the one that sleeps in another bedroom? Or maybe he's the one who stays out all night and then comes home without any explanation as to where he's been, 'cause that's the Mitch that I know," I explained.

"Vickie, maybe you should just talk to Mitchell. I think that he loves you so much. I just don't see him doing that to you," Jessica said.

"Didn't Michael do that to you?" I asked to Jessica.

"Hell, yeah. We all seen that," Nicole blurted out.

"I was talking to Jess," I told Nicole.

"Well I'm answering, and what she trying to say is Mitch was so sprung on your ass that he didn't even know there were other women out there. That motherfucker actually gave your spoiled ass everything you want. You just need to do a better job hanging on to him," Nicole said to me and took a swig of wine out of her glass.

"Excuse me?" I asked.

"You heard me, bitch. Get yourself some see-through lingerie and get to work," Nicole replied.

"And don't forget the pumps: red ones," Joanna said.

Nicole and Jo began cackling like two hyenas as if me in see through lingerie was some magical wand that would erase everything. They know good and well that I'm not that kind of person.

"I don't even know where to find something like that," I told them.

"I got some," Joanna said.

"I bet your ho ass do. Go on and Let Vickie borrow it," Nicole said laughing.

"She can borrow it anytime she wants," Joanna said.

"No I can't," I replied.

"Well you better do something, girl. You need that man," Joanna said as she filled her glass full of wine for what looked to be the tenth time.

"I do not need Mitch, Jo. He needs me," I told her.

"Bitch, please. You need someone to worship you and that motherfucker does, so you need his ass so get to learning the karma sutra," Nicole said.

"Oh my God. Nic. You are so disgusting," I said to her.

"Listen, Vickie. Forget what those two are saying. Talk to Mitchell. I bet that's all he wants is for you to hear him," Jessica said.

"Damn, Jess. I see why Michael cheats on your ass all the time. You need to get to learning the kama sutra too. What the hell is the talking shit; put it on him. He ain't gonna never leave," Nicole said.

"Oh really, Nic? You know the kama sutra so well, then why don't you and Steve get along better?" Jessica asked Nicole.

"Cause I can't stand his ass, Jess. But you best believe he ain't going nowhere. He knows where it's at. Shit you see he always come home don't you," Nicole told Jessica.

Nicole had such a disgusting way of putting things, but in a way, she and Joanna were right. I could be a bit uptight and perhaps I could try and be more sensual for Mitchell. After all, he is my husband. It wasn't as if I'm running the streets with a different man. There's nothing wrong with me being free with my husband. I think I could do this. No I don't think I could. It's just not proper. I shouldn't have to resort to such behavior just to keep him home.

"Alright, Vickie. Now I was not going to say nothing cause it's Mitch's secret to tell but..." Nicole started to say.

"But what?" I asked her.

"Now I don't know about him sleeping in another room, but I do know where he be at nights," Nicole said.

"You do? Where and with whom?" I continued to ask.

"He's teaching at the law school at nights, part-time...but I think he wants to make it permanent," Nicole explained.

"Permanent? As in quit his job at the firm permanently?" I asked in shocking.

"See that's why he didn't want to tell you cause your bougie ass only thinks about money and status and not what's good for your man," Nicole said.

"That's not true. I just didn't expect this. I mean I need a moment to take it in. Mitchell wants to be a teacher...ok...a teacher...I can handle this...a teacher?" I said trying to let the information sink in.

"Vickie, why don't you breathe. I don't think it's your typical teacher it's a law professor. That's pretty prestigious, I think," Joanna said.

"It don't matter the title, Jo. Looka here, Vickie. Now I don't know if he got some chick on the side but after I talked to him, I know he loves you and he would change his mind in a heartbeat if you asked him to. Just don't ask him to. That man needs some kind of happiness. Hell, it's bout time he do for himself for once," Nicole said.

I have entered the twilight zone because Nicole is actually right. How could I have missed this? How could I have ignored some part of Mitchell that was so important?

"So Vickie, you want to borrow my lingerie and pumps or what?" Joanna asked, filling her glass once again.

"Yes, I think I will," I said.

"Hell yeah, bitch. Give it to him girl," Nicole said laughing and clapping her hands together.

"Now Vickie I'm not offering up my pumps and lingerie cause I think he's cheating. I just think you lucked out in the husband department, and it's about time you show that man how proud you are of him. He's done right by you," Joanna said.

"Give it to him, girl. That's all my ass is saying," Nicole told me while raising her glass in my direction.

Joanna was right. It was time I show him how much I appreciated him. Mitchell had done everything I had ever asked of him. He'd given me everything I'd ever wanted. I had the life I'd dreamed of and it was all thanks to Mitchell and it was time to tell him that I was grateful.

32

"Jo you're drunk!" Jessica shouted at me.

"No I'm not Jess."

"Then why are you laying on the floor like that?" she asked.

"Because it's comfortable."

I was not drunk I was a little bit relaxed, but not drunk. Jess knew better than that; I never got drunk. Other people got drunk, but not me. Jess was crazy, always thinking somebody drunk.

I wondered what David was doing right now. He was probably with the bitch. I wondered who she was. Whoever she was, I knew she was not cuter than me. And he knew she wasn't cuter than me. I didn't know why he always acted like an ass sometimes. I was so sick and tired of it. I kept looking like a dummy. Well I wasn't dumb, and if he wanted somebody else and not me, well so be it. Shit, I was sexy and successful. Hell, many men would crawl on their knees if I asked them to just to be with me; the hell with David.

I had to pee, but I felt so good lying there that I hated to get up. Besides, I didn't feel like walking all the way to the bathroom. But if I didn't go I was liable to pee all on this floor and myself. Shit.

"Jo, where are you going?" Victoria asked me.

"Damn, Vickie. What, are you my keeper?" I asked to her.

"Sorry, but you look like you about to fall on your butt," she said. "No I'm not. I have to pee," I told her.

"Then why your ass looking around like you forgot where the bathroom was?" Nicole asked.

"No, Nic. I'm looking for my phone," I responded.

"What the shit your phone got to do with you peeing?" Nicole asked again.

"I just wanted my goddamn phone. Is that a fucking problem?"

"Here, hell," Nicole said shoving my phone into my hand.

"Thank you. Now where the hell is the bathroom?"

"Take your ass down the hall and don't pee on nothing that ain't the toilet," Nicole said.

"Fuck you, Nic," I told her as I headed down the hallway towards the bathroom.

I could hear those little bitches laughing. They still thought I was drunk but I was not. This was one big ass bathroom; the toilet had to be about ten feet from the door and it was cold as hell. As extra as this house was, couldn't they spring for a warm toilet seat?

Why the hell did I have my phone? Oh yeah I wanted to call his ass and give him a piece of my mind. I knew he didn't think I was going to let him get the last word. Shit he must'a forgotten who the hell I was. It was time I remind him.

"Hello," David answered, sounding like he was shock that I called.

"I got one thing to say to you David... well maybe more than one... but however many it is you gonna listen," I told him.

"Jo? Why do you sound like that?"

"Sound like what? I sound like nothing."

"Are you drunk?"

"Why the hell does everyone keep asking me that? No I'm not drunk, and stop trying to change the subject."

"What's the subject, Jo?

"You and your audacity to kick me out your house. What the hell was that? Are you crazy?" I asked him, not wanting an answer. I just wanted him to hear me.

"Jo, why don't we talk about this when we are both in our right minds."

"Hell no. We gonna talk about this now 'cause I'm tired of this shit."

"You're tired? That's funny."

"What's so funny about it? You think I can't be tired?"

"I'm sure you can be, Jo. But you haven't been the one at a standstill."

"I don't even know what the hell that means. But I haven't even told you that one thing yet."

"Well go ahead, Jo, cause I can't wait to hear this."

"You, David, you are the man that I think I love."

"What did you just say?"

"See all that game, all the games. You heard what I said. I said I love you and you play acting."

"Jo, we really need to talk about this later, when I'm sure you mean what you're saying." David said sounding like he had a smile on his face.

"Hell yeah, I mean what I said. What you think I'm a liar now?"

"No, but this is really not a good time, so I'm going to pretend that this conversation didn't happen, and when you get back, we can really deal with this."

"No, don't pretend shit. See that's the problem. You always want me to be something I'm not. Who's to say that I gave up everything I've worked for and run into your arms and then you just kick me out. Then I'm left with no job, no future, and worst of all, no you. Then what?"

"Jo...Jo..." David called to me.

"What! I think I just fell."

"Why don't you go to bed."

"Ok."

"And Jo, I know you probably won't remember this in the morning, but I love you too."

"Ok, Bye now."

33

Nicole and Victoria were in the living room listening to some old school music. I wasn't really in the mood for reminiscing on days pass. The present was already hard for me to handle. I went to check on Jo but she was passed out on her bed. The night was beautifully still so I went and sat on the front porch. There were people still on the beach even at this time of night and someone was shooting firecrackers and having a bonfire. It felt good just to sit there and watch people enjoying themselves.

Being by myself sometimes felt freeing. There was no one to worry about, no one to hurt your heart, no one to argue with, no one to make you cry. At this very moment, it was just me, and I loved it.

I would sometimes catch myself thinking about what my life would be like if I lived like Joanna. She did what she wanted, focused on only herself, and lived life on her terms. We joked around with her a lot about it, but at least she knew who she was. I didn't have a clue about Jessica. All I knew was Jessica and Michael. If someone were to ask me where I saw myself in five or ten years my answer would be married to Michael, but that wasn't the question. The question was where did I see myself, me just me. The answer to that was, I don't know. How pathetic was that? How could an educated woman like myself not know who she was without her man? I wondered if the problem wasn't Michael but me. I kept waiting on him to change and be the man I wanted him to be, but maybe I needed to change and be the woman I needed to be.

"Oh my God. Are you alright?" I saw this lady limping on the sand as she passed our house. She looked to be in such pain that I instinctively ran to her. I grabbed her by the hand and turned her to me. I wanted to get a better look at her.

It was her, the lady from earlier in the day who had sat on the beach with her wondering eye husband. Her face showed agony and she reached for her ankle.

"Oh, I slipped coming down one of those stairs off the boardwalk, and I think I really hurt my ankle," The woman explained.

"Do you mind if I take a look at it? I'm a doctor," I said to her.

"Of course, as long as you don't charge me," The woman said with a chuckle.

"No, I wouldn't. Come take a seat over here." I led her to the stairs of our house and knelt down before her. Her ankle was a little swollen but nothing appeared to be broken. "It seems to be a minor sprain. When you get home, make sure you keep it elevated and put a cold compress on it. It should be okay." I told the woman after examining her ankle.

"Well thank you. I sure would have hated to have broken my ankle. What is your name?" the woman asked me.

"I'm Jessica... Jessica Mathews."

"Well it's a pleasure to meet you Dr. Mathews. I'm Rebecca Lewis," The woman said.

"Please call me Jessica. I leave the Dr. Mathews at the hospital."

"Why? You've earned that title. Young black women need to be proud of all that they've accomplished. I hate it when I see a successful black woman beat the odds and pull back on their celebration of it because they fear being called a bitch or a diva. Own who you are Dr. Mathews."

"Thank you Mrs. Lewis."

"That's Judge Lewis to you."

Judge Lewis let out a chuckle and patted me on my back. She appeared to have such an ease and confidence about herself that it became a bit infectious. For a moment she had me feeling like "I'm woman hear me roar." I loved being around women like her. Now I understood why she wasn't bothered with her husband looking at other women; she knew who she was and what she had to offer.

"Would you like for me to help you home or do you want to call your husband to come get you? I saw the two of you earlier."

"Oh, if you could help me home that would be great. He's probably already in bed by now. I'm more of the night person then he is."

I helped Judge Lewis up and held her hand as we walked towards her beach house. She noticed my ring and smiled at me asking, "You're engaged? Is that why you and your friends are here? To celebrate? I noticed you all as well."

"No, actually we just wanted to have a girls' weekend."

"Well there's nothing wrong with that. Sometimes it's good just to ditch all the men and have some girl time, you know."

"Well, you and your husband seem to be really happy. I really admire the two of you."

"Honey, that is called thirty-one years of trial and error. But yes, we are happy; I guess that's what happens when you find the person you were meant to be with."

"I guess so. I noticed he has quite the wondering eye."

"Oh, honey, yes. He's always been that way, steering at one young thing after another; he's a man who appreciates the beauty of a woman."

"And that doesn't bother you?"

"No, why should it? A man doesn't stop being a man just because he's married, any more than a woman stops being a woman. We will always appreciate the opposite sex and there's nothing wrong with that."

"You don't consider that cheating? Don't you think if he loves you, he wouldn't even consider another woman?"

"Oh, Lord, no. That's not cheating, and cheating has nothing to do with love. See a man can look at another woman but still love you more than the air he breathes. Love is what brings two people together, but respect and trust is what keeps them together. I trust that my husband will never take it any further than looking, and he respects me enough to only look. That's what's kept us going all these years."

"Wow," I said amazed at her relaxed comfort in the relationship she and her husband had.

"Well, here we are Dr. Mathews," Judge Lewis said.

"Oh, ok. Remember to elevate your leg and keep something cold on it, and if you need anything, I'm just a few doors down."

"Thank you so much for your assistance, Dr. Mathews."

"No, thank you Judge Lewis."

"What did I do?"

"A lot."

I stood there watching as Judge Lewis went into the house. She had given me a sense of clarity that I had never had before. Yeah, Michael loved me. I think he always had and I knew I will always love him but I didn't trust him and I couldn't say for certain that he respected me. So then what did we have? I wanted to never have to question what my man was doing when I was not around. I wanted to never have to wonder what I'd be walking in on every time I opened my front door. I knew that Michael and I didn't have what it took to sustain our relationship. I just didn't know if I had what it took to leave.

34

Why my ass always the first person up all the time? These bitches needed to know how to handle their damn liquor. Hell, Vickie ain't even drink nothing and her ass still couldn't get up. I didn't expect Jo to wake up anytime soon, as much as her ass drank last night. That girl knew she was something funny when she got a couple of drinks in her. She was always saying or doing something that her ass knew she wouldn't have if she'd been sober. I was just glad she passed out before she ran outside butt-ass naked or something.

Man I loved this kitchen. I couldn't stop cooking. I ain't realized how much I loved to cook until I got here. I got all these ideas running through my head 'bout what I wanted to make and they real good stuff to. Why my mind ain't never work like this before, I'll never know, cause Lord knows my kids be asking me to make all kinds of stuff but all they get is the same old stuff. Shit, that's all I could afford. But this feels good. Ain't no telling what I could do with all this food.

Damn, I realized I ain't checked on my kids or really thought about Steven in a while. I mean his name be coming up but I don't be thinking about him. This was the longest I'd gone without cussing his ass out. I bet he was happy wherever he was. But I do wonder what my kids were doing and if they were alright. I knew my mama was taking good care of them. I'd hoped this didn't make me seem like a bad mother, but I didn't want to have to deal with the kids or with Steven for a while. We were leaving tomorrow, and I could deal with them then. But right now, I just wanted to cook.

I was busy in that kitchen for almost an hour before I even heard one person moving around. Damn them heffas didn't know how to handle their liquor.

"Hey what are you doing?" Victoria asked as she came into the kitchen.

"What it look like, Vickie? I'm cooking," I said to her.

"I know that. I mean what are you cooking?"

"Just sit down, Vickie. You'll see."

I put a plate of food in front of Vickie and waited to see what stupid shit she had to say. I just knew she was about to say something. That girl got something wrong with the filter between her brain and her mouth; if it was stupid or ignorant you'd better believe Vickie would say it.

"Mmmm this is good, Nic. What is it?"

"It's an omelet. I just put a twist to it. You really like it?"

"Yes I do. My cook has never made anything this good before."

"I'ma take that as compliment, Vickie."

"It was. I wasn't trying to start anything."

"I know, Vickie. You never are."

You could never stay mad at Vickie. She's laughable really. She didn't mean no harm but damn that girl sure knew how to work a nerve.

"Nic, you know all I meant before was that you could be really good at this."

"At what?"

"At cooking. Maybe you could be a chef or a caterer or own your own restaurant."

"Girl, please. You talking nonsense."

"That's your problem, Nic. You don't think bigger."

"No, I think real. How the hell I'ma do all that with two kids tied to my hip."

"Anything's possible. You should just consider it."

"Vickie anything's possible in your world. You always forget we live in two different worlds."

"It's not that different. You could have anything you want. You just have to not be afraid to reach out and grab it."

"That's easy for you to say."

"Why do you keep saying that?"

"Cause you don't know how hard it is reach out and grab what you want. Your husband always hands you whatever the hell you want."

"That's not true, Nic."

"The hell it is. You won't make it one day having to struggle for shit."

"So I don't get it?"

"No, you don't. That's why you need to hang onto that man."

"I am not going to hang onto some man who does not want me."

"Bitch, please."

"I know you and Jo think I'm crazy and that Mitch is so into me, but you guys don't live with us; he's not what you think."

"Vickie, that man gave up his dream just to give you what you wanted, and I mean all the shit you wanted."

"That's not true. His dream was to be a lawyer and he is. What did he give up?"

"Girl, sometimes I think you're too dense to be real."

"What does that mean?"

"Remember when Mitch interned for that nonprofit in law school?"

"Yeah, so?"

"So didn't he really like it?" I continued to ask, hoping that she would soon catch the hell on to what I was saying.

"I guess but what does that have to do with anything."

"Lord girl, that's what he wanted to do as a lawyer, not some stuff shirt corporate big firm motherfucker."

"That's ridiculous. Why would he have gone on to the firm if that's not what he wanted?"

"Because you wouldn't be Victoria the almighty if he hadn't. It's what you wanted."

"I did not."

"Really, Vickie?" I asked, amazed at how in denial Victoria really was.

Damn, she was too dense to be real. At least I got why my man acted the way he do; he's an ass, but that damn girl ain't got a clue. If I had a man like Mitchell who would bent over backwards to make me happy, hell, maybe I would own a restaurant by now. But my ass was stuck with this broke ass bum.

Some bitches didn't know how good they had it. I got so tired of bitches who got a good man but fight their damnedest to find something wrong with them. Them hoes needed to spend one day living with the bastard I got. Shit, they ain't got to look very hard that motherfucker will just show himself in the first two seconds. I bet they'd be glad to go running back to their men then.

Hell, I ain't saying I wanted Mitchell, but when you been with a bad man for so long, you sure knew how to appreciate a good one.

35

God, my head was throbbing. I didn't even know what got into me last night. I didn't ever drink that much. How the hell did I even get into bed? The last thing I remembered was lying on the living room floor talking to my girls. Maybe one of them brought me to bed. I am way too old to be getting so drunk that I black the hell out.

I couldn't even move. I smelled something cooking but the scent was making me feel sick. Oh yeah, I was way too old for this. I thought the best thing for me to do was to stay in bed for the rest of the day; hell, probably the rest of the week. I swear I will never drink again.

"Jo, you okay?" Jessica asked as she slowly came into the bedroom.

"No. I think I may be dead," I said to her with my face smash against the pillow.

"Oh girl, you're alright. you're just hung over," Jessica said sitting on the edge of the bed where I was lying.

"Jess, if you ever cared about me, you will take one of these pillows and suffocate me," I said to her.

"You'll be alright," she said again.

"No, I won't. You're a doctor. Don't you have something to make me feel better?" I asked her.

"Yeah, advice. Don't drink till you pass out," she said with a chuckle.

"Thanks," I said to her.

"No problem. That one's on the house," she said still chuckling. Jess wasn't doing much to make me feel better; actually all the talking was making my head hurt more. I just needed to lie there in the dark with some peace and quiet, but it appeared that Jess had no intention of leaving. I've seen that look on her face before; it's that I got something on my mind and I need to talk look. Of all the times that she needed to talk, why does it have to be now?

"Jo are you happy?" Jessica asked me.

"Well not at the very moment."

"You know. What I mean is, are you happy with your life?"

"I guess."

"Come on, Jo. Seriously," Jessica said as she laid down next to me.

"What do you want me to say Jess?"

"I just want you to answer honestly."

"Honestly I don't know what happiness means," I told her finally peeling my face off my pillow and turning on my back.

"You don't know what it means?"

"I mean I can define it, but I don't know what it means to me. Why are you asking?"

"Well, it just doesn't seem like you hesitated to take the job in L.A. So I thought that you were happy with the direction your life is going."

"Jess, the truth is I haven't accepted the job in L.A."

"Wait, but you said you were going."

"I know but I'm not sure if I want to go."

"Why?"

"I guess I'll miss you guys. Won't you miss me?"

"No. Joking. Yeah, I'll miss you, but Jo, I do want you to be happy," Jessica said with a laugh.

"I know, Jess and I want you to be happy too. That's why I get on you about Michael, I just worry about you."

"I know I worry about me too."

"I guess we both have to figure out what happiness means to us."

"I guess we do. Anyway I'll leave and let you sleep. Oh Jo, one more thing," Jessica said as she got up and walked towards the window.

"What?" I asked lifting my head to see what she wanted.

That crazy heffa opened the blinds to my room and the sun sunk into my eyes like a sharp needle. If I could've gotten out of this bed, I would have so kicked her ass. I flung the covers over my head and tried like hell to go back to sleep but my cell phone started ringing like crazy. I wouldn't have answered it, but the sound was like daggers piercing my head.

"Hello."

"Hey Jo." The voice on the other end said.

I recognized David's voice right away. I knew he would be the one to make the first move. But now it was my turn to play hardball. I was going to treat him as cold as he treated me. He needed to know what it felt like to have somebody make you feel like shit.

"What do you want David?"

"I was just making sure you were alright."

"Why wouldn't I be?"

"You don't remember anything do you?"

"Anything like what?"

"It doesn't matter. When will you be back tomorrow?"

"Why?" I asked since David was sounding and acting strange.

"Because I think you and I need to meet face to face and talk."

"Well, I don't think that would be possible David cause I have a lot to do when I get back."

"Jo, I think it's important that we do this before...before you leave."

"Well, if you remember David, I came to you to talk and you didn't have time, so I'm not going to drop everything now that you're ready."

"Jo..." David started to say something but I didn't feel like hearing it.

"Look David, I got to go, okay."

I didn't even give him a chance to say goodbye. I didn't know what he thought we had to talk about. I was tired of this thing with David. I didn't even know what it was but I didn't like it. Yeah, it was probably my fault for not being honest with him about my feelings, but realistically us being in a relationship would never work. I adored him as my friend, but him as my man - I didn't know about that. I was just glad I never told him how I felt.

36

"Oh I am not going in there." I don't know why I always let these girls talk me into doing things I knew I shouldn't be doing. They were determined to corrupt me; first the tattoo, and now this cesspool of sin they called a nightclub. When Joanna finally decided to wake up, she thought it was a great idea that we go to the club and, of course, Nicole and Jessica agreed. So there I was out voted and in the mist of hell.

I mean, just look at these people, the women were barely wearing clothing and the men had on extra big jeans and oversized shirts. There were huge men who stood outside the door and made sure no one had any weapons on them. I mean really . . . . weapons? What kind of place is this? The music thumped so loudly from the inside that it seemed to shake the sidewalk where we stood. I knew for sure that I could not be seen in a place like this; what would people think? Not even Nicole or Joanna could talk me into doing something so ridiculous.

"Come on Vickie it's time for you to practice how to be spontaneous," Joanna said pulling at my arm.

"Jo this is not spontaneous; this is just moronic," I respond trying to pull myself back.

"Vickie don't think, just do," Joanna told me.

"Damn, Vickie, you always scared of something," Nicole said.

"I'm not scared Nic but this is not my type of place."

"Listen Vickie, we'll just go in for a few minutes and then we'll leave. Plus I don't think anybody you know will be in here anyway," Joanna said.

"Jo's right Vickie. If we don't like the place, we'll just leave. It'll be alright," Jessica said to me.

I'm not going to win against all three of them, but I swear I am out of here the minute I hear gun fire.

When we got to the door, we were facing a four-hundred-pound linebacker who looked at us as if we were criminals; perhaps that was because only criminals come to a place like this. I tried again to run, but Joanna and Nicole caught hold of me and held out my hand as the linebacker stamped it and then waved us in. Inside the club was even louder than the outside. It was horrible in there. There were people on the dance floor doing things that I knew had to be illegal. Drunken men were coming at us from all angles. These people were way beneath my standards. I looked at my friends, and they seemed to actually be enjoying themselves. It made absolutely no sense how they could enjoy a place where the music was so loud that it was impossible for anyone to even hear themselves think.

"Hey guys, guys!" I yelled at the top of my lungs, but Nicole, Joanna, and Jessica didn't hear me even though they were standing right beside me. Then Joanna pulled me towards the bar and yelled to the bartender, "Three gin and tonics!" I shook my head no at Joanna but when the bartender brought our drinks, Joanna pushed one in my face and shouted, "Just try it. Be spontaneous!"

The taste almost made me gag. It was so strong that I was barely able to get down the first sip. The three of them watched me with smiles on their faces. It seemed as though they were on the brink of full-on-gut-busting laughter. I took another sip and then another. Pretty soon the sips became easier to digest and were going down smoother and smoother. I didn't know what made me do that but before long I started to relax.

I had this urge to try drinks that I'd seen people drink or heard them talk about like a martini. But before I could, Jessica stopped me, "Oh no. The last thing you should do is mix drinks." Then they pulled me to the dance floor and we began to dance. But the dance floor was so crowded that I soon lost track of my friends. When I looked around, I realized that I was dancing in between two guys I didn't even know, but for some reason I wasn't bothered. I just went with it. I was feeling so good that I forgot myself for a while and started doing the type of dances that had disgusted me when I first walked in.

I was having such a good time that before I knew it, I was on the stage with the half-dress dancers and began to move as they were. I could see the shocked look on my friends' faces, but they wanted me to be spontaneous. Well here it is and it didn't feel half bad.

When I turned my head I saw the very cute DJ motioning me to him. What the heck, you only live once right. I jumped in the DJ booth and started dancing with him. Then he gave me the mic and I heard this loud voice that sounded like mine yell, "Get your hands up, everybody get your hands up!"

I didn't even notice when Joanna, Nicole, and Jessica got to the DJ booth. I just felt them pull me away.

"Hey, I'm not ready to go yet," I told them.

"Oh yeah you are," Joanna said.

"No I'm not Jo. I'm having a good time, plus I could spin on the wheels of lead," I replied.

"Do you mean wheels of steel?" Jessica asked.

"Oh yeah, that's it. Wheels of steel." I leaned up against the DJ and grabbed hold of him. His arms were so strong and firm that I didn't want to let him go.

"Well maybe next time Vickie," Joanna said pulling me off the DJ and continued pushing me until we were outside the club.

"I'm glad the both of you found this funny," Jessica said to Nicole and Joanna who were laughing hysterically by the time we left the club.

"Hell yeah. This is funny Jess. Look at her," Nicole said to Jessica.

"I'm sorry Jess, but this is a side of her that we never thought we'd see," Joanna added.

"Sure is. You think she's gonna be mad at us...I mean when she sobers her ass up?" Nicole asked.

"I don't know. If she is, it don't matter cause she really needed this," Joanna said.

"Who needed what?"

"No one, Vickie. Nic and Jo just talking...come on let's get you home," Jessica said to me as she grabbed hold of my hand and started leading me down the road.

I wasn't ready to go home. The night was still young and people were out having a good time. I saw some kids on the beach having a bonfire.

"Where the hell you going?" I could hear Nicole shouting at me, but I was going to those kids, and I was going to have fun. Those kids looked so free and energetic, I had to join them. I heard Jessica say to Nicole and Joanna, "Oh my God. I think we created a monster." I don't know what their problem was. I was merely doing what they wanted me to do and having a pretty good time doing it. I have never had this much fun in my life.

Those kids had the music going and they were dancing around the fire, and I couldn't help but join them. But here comes Nicole, Joanna, and Jessica again to pull me away. I don't know what their problem was. I was having a ball. This must have been what it felt like for them. For the first time I understood why they went out every night in college; it was fun.

Before reaching the foot of the stairs, my stomach began to twist and turn. It felt as if I had just gotten off a roller coaster after eating a full-course meal. "Oh no," I moan.

"What's wrong?" Nicole asked. I think Nicole could see that I was in pain. "Girl you better run your ass to the bathroom." Nicole opened the door and I darted for the bathroom. All I saw was the bottom of the toilet and it smelled like rotten eggs.

"You alright Vickie?" Joanna asked me as she came into the bathroom and knelt down next to me.

"No, Jo. I feel like I'm about to die," I replied.

"That sounds about right," Nicole said coming into the bathroom as well and pulling my hair away from my face until I was done. Then she led me to the bed. Jessica came over and put something cold on my forehead. "Just relax, Vickie. You'll feel like crap, but you'll be alright."

As I lay there with the room spinning around me, I realized why I never went out with them; it's fun for a moment, but you sure pay for it in the end.

37

Damn, I didn't want this day to come; I ain't ready to go home. That probably made me sound like a bad mother, but, hell, mothers need to take a break from their kids every now and then. I was actually enjoying myself. I ain't had this much fun in a while.

Again I was the first to get up but I hoped that everybody would stay sleep for a while; I wanted to be by myself. It just seemed like a long time since I'd been by myself. I love my kids but being here made me realize how much I still wanted to do something more. I still think it's hard for a mother to do a lot, but, hell, maybe it ain't impossible. I still had some thinking to do. One day I'm sure I'd figure everything out, but today ain't that damn day.

It's kind of crazy how people take themselves for granted. I guess it's cause nobody seems to know what they're worth. I sure ain't got a clue. How can someone like me be like, yeah, I sure could be somebody? What the hell was I supposed to be but what I am: a mother and a wife trying to make it in this hard-ass world. But, shit ain't nothing wrong with trying. Maybe I could see what I could do with this cooking thing. I knew Steven gonna try and make it hard, but fuck him. I was so damn tired of Steven. I really should get rid of his ass, but I knew he aint going nowhere. I was just gonna do me.

"You up early girl." Joanna said as she came on to the back porch where I was standing.

"I'm always up you're the one who stays asleep all day," I replied.

"That was yesterday, Nic," Joanna said, giving me a nudge.

"Whatever bitch. Come on, let's get ready to leave," I said to her and turned to go inside the house.

"Vickie and Jess are still asleep. Let's wait for them to get up. We got time. You in a hurry?" Joanna said following behind me.

"Hell no. Shit, I can stay longer," I replied, walking into the living room and sitting down.

"Me too, girl," Joanna said and sat across from me.

"Jo, what you doing with your place when you leave?"

"I don't know I really haven't thought about any of that."

"Why not?"

"Between all of ya'll dramas, I haven't gotten the chance. Why you asking anyway?"

"I don't know. I was just thinking."

"About taking over my lease?" Joanna said with a slight grin.

"Girl, I can't afford what you pay."

"About me keeping my lease and letting you live there?" she asked again with a side eye.

"Maybe."

"You ready to try this as a single mother, Nic?"

"Shit, women do it all the time Jo, I ain't gonna be trying something new."

"I know and I have no doubt you can do it. I just want to make sure you're ready. It's not going to be easy."

"What the fuck, Jo. You think I'm a weak bitch? Hell, ya'll keep telling me to leave Steve. Now I'm saying I want to."

"I keep telling you to be happy. I don't want you with Steven, but I also don't want you to rush into something that's going to leave you in an even worse situation."

"Alright Jo, So what you want me to do?"

"It's not about what I want you to do. That's how you started out with Steven. Your parents wanted you to marry so you did. Nic, what do you want?"

"Jo stop trying to get so damn deep."

"I'm not. I just want you to do some real thinking."

Me and Jo were about finished packing before Jessica and Victoria decided to get up. I could understand Victoria's ass not getting up early, but Jessica's ass was dragging around like she ain't got nowhere to go. They needed to get themselves together I ain't gonna be waiting all day.

I may not be ready to go but hell I got kids waiting on me. These heffas ain't got to worry bout all that.

"Ya'll bitches need to hurry the hell up. Me and Jo are ready to go," I said to Jessica and Victoria.

"Nic, why are you shouting?" Victoria asked.

"Cause it's time to go Vickie and you walking round her with your hair looking like who done it and why. Please go get your shit together," I replied.

"I don't feel like doing anything right now. Can't we leave tonight?" Victoria said as she slumped down on the sofa.

"Hell no. I got kids to get home to. Now go slap a ponytail in your head and start packing. Matter of fact, I'll pack for you cause you liable to go in the room start sleeping again."

I had to make that damn Vickie get up and go to her room; she needed not drink no more cause the bitch couldn't handle it. She also didn't know how to keep her stuff together. All Vickie's clothes were all over the place; it took me forever just to find her shit. Then it took me even longer to pack her shit the way she liked it, while she laid her ass on the bed giving instructions.

"Vickie, I thought I told you to put your hair in a ponytail?"

"I don't have the strength. Nic."

"Girl, get your ass up and come here."

I slapped a tight-ass ponytail on Vickie and she was ready to go. All I knew was by time I get downstairs everybody better be there with their shit or else somebody getting left. Sure enough by the time me and Vickie got down the stairs, Jessica hadn't even changed her clothes.

"Alright I'm bout to slap the shit out of somebody." I said the minute I saw Jessica sitting there.

"Nic, I know I was just bringing my luggage downstairs. Give me five minutes and I'll be ready to go," Jessica said passing by me to go up the stairs.

"Five minutes, Jess. Don't make me come up there and drag you out this house," I said to her.

It seemed like damn near twenty minutes had gone by with me, Joanna, and Victoria waiting on Jessica to bring her ass down the stairs so we could go. I was just about to go up there and drag her down when she came running. "I know I know, I'm over five minutes, but I'm ready now. So let's go."

38

Oh God, I'm home. I hadn't really been back here since I saw Michael and that girl in my bed. Everything pretty much looks the same; I didn't think Michael had been here either. At this point, I didn't care where he was as long as he stayed there. I was in such a state of peace that I didn't want anything or anyone to ruin it.

I went to my bedroom and saw the same sheets on my bed that Michael used with that other woman. I snatched them off and started to put them in the laundry basket, but for what? Every time I saw them, all I would do is think about what he did; so I threw them away. I didn't need any reminders of Michael or his cheating ways. I was done with all that. As a matter of fact, I didn't even want to feel like I was lying on their body fluids. I put on some gloves, took a bottle of Clorox and washed the bare mattress. I scrubbed it down as hard as I could. I would have thrown the whole mattress away, but I paid way too much money for it. When I was done I let the mattress dry, then I sprayed it with perfume to get rid of the smell. Maybe now I could move on with my life-one that didn't include Michael.

But my life did include me being the best doctor I could be, and I hadn't checked on any of my patients the entire time I was away. I needed to go to the hospital for a while, even if it was just to say hi and leave. I needed my patients to know that they could count on me. I guess that's what I took away from the trip. At some point in everyone's life, we need to know that someone is there who we can count on. Life sucked when all you have is yourself, when no one is ever there to prop you up when you fall or wipe your tears when you cry. I guess I'd been thinking that Michael was my someone, but I needed to let that go. The worst thing than not having someone is having the wrong one-the person who makes your problems worse than they already are or who actually is your problem.

I'd cried till I was tired of crying. I didn't think any more tears could come out of my eyes anymore. I'd experienced the crazy blind love, but what I needed now was trust and respect. I wanted to walk alone on the beach late at night knowing that my husband of thirty-plus years was waiting for me without another woman to keep him company. I wanted that everlasting, unwavering, unchanging love, and Michael wasn't it.

The hospital was pretty quiet, and I had checked on a few patients who seemed to be doing well. I was on my way to check on some more when I bumped into Dr. Reynolds who actually looked happy to see me. I hoped he didn't want me to assist him with anything cause I was ready to leave at any moment. I was off the clock and had no intention of working.

"Hey how was your weekend?" Dr. Reynolds asked me.

"It was pretty good. How were things here?"

"Um...quiet. So what did you and your friends get into?"

"A bit of everything. I think we kinda reverted back to our college years and forgot that we were a little too old for certain things."

"There's nothing wrong forgetting your age every now and then. I know when I get with my boys, we tend to do the same thing; it's a good stress reducer."

Dr. Reynolds had a way of putting me at ease and putting a smile on my face. He was such an easy-going guy. It's no wonder he was so popular around the hospital. I noticed that he began to stare at my fingers. I had forgotten that while I was scrubbing down my mattress I had taken off my engagement ring. The crazy thing was I didn't even miss it. Maybe that's because I really didn't miss Michael.

"Um, are you still engaged? I mean I don't want to be nosy or anything. If it's none of my business, feel free to tell me that."

"No, it's ok. Actually I'm not sure what I am. I guess I'm just weighing my options right now."

"Oh. Well, could one of those options possibly be dinner with me?"

I was a little surprised. I guess this is what Nicole and Joanna meant by me being dingy, because I didn't think that Dr. Reynolds liked me in that way. I just thought he was really friendly. Well, what do I do now? He was a great guy who was really sexy, but I thought the same thing about

Michael and before I realized who he was, I was already so in love with him that I couldn't let him go. I still didn't know if I had let him go. Would it be weird for me to go out with someone before actually breaking up with someone else? I knew Michael did it all the time but should I stoop to his level?

"The truth is Dr. Reynolds..."

"Todd" He corrected me.

"Todd, the truth is I'm still involved and until I get that situation figured out, I don't think I can date anyone-not right now at least."

"I can understand that as long as you can understand that I'll probably keep asking until you finally say yes."

God, that man was smooth but getting involved with another smooth brother was the last thing I needed. I had to get away from this man quick before all that sexiness seduces me.

All the way home I kept thinking about Dr. Reynolds. I mean, it would be good to go on a date with a guy that wasn't Michael and just compare the two. Sometimes I wondered if other relationships were like mine and Michael's. Maybe that's the bad you have to go through to get to the good. How would I know the grass is greener on the other side? Dr. Reynolds or any other man could be worse than Michael-a whole lot worse.

I opened my front door to find my house filled with flowers and candles and soft music. Then Michael appeared from around the corner dressed in his best suit like he was on his way to a funeral or something.

"What are you doing here?" I asked Michael.

"I wanted to surprise you," He replied.

"Well I'm surprised alright. But why?" I said to him trying to keep my distance.

"I thought that after our last conversation, we needed to reconnect again. I love you, Jess, and I can't live without you."

"Michael, I thought I told you that I needed time to think?"

"Yeah, you did but..." Michael started to say.

"But what you couldn't respect that." I said, interrupting him.

Respect, wasn't that what Judge Lewis was talking about. Does Michael even know what that word means? I felt like breaking into Aretha Franklin's song "R-E-S-P-E-C-T," find out what it means me. It was so obvious that he didn't have a clue.

"Michael, you need to leave now."

"But baby..."

"No you need to leave right now. I'm done," I said not letting him finish his sentence.

"What do you mean you're done?" Michael asked me.

"I mean I'm done with us. Enough is enough Michael. You don't need me. You need to be free and I love you enough to let you be free. I also love myself enough not to hold onto someone who doesn't want to be held," I explained.

"Jess, your friends have gotten into your head, and you're saying things you don't mean. So, I'm going to let you think about what you're saying. Just remember that once we're done, we're done. There's no coming back," Michael said as he walked out the door. The thought of Michael not coming back scared me; the thought of being without him forever scared me.

39

Okay, so I was supposed to be sexy and appealing; well how should I do that? Mitchell was going to be home any minute and I didn't even know how to put this thing on. Why didn't I have Joanna show me before I left her house? Matter of fact, why didn't I just say no to Joanna and Nicole? At some point in my life I'm going to have to stop letting them talk me into things. I didn't even think Mitchell liked lingerie. I'd never worn it for him before, and it was never a problem. Well, at least he never said it was.

I didn't know what I was doing. If he walked into the bedroom, all he'd see was me standing there naked holding a black lacy slip-looking thing trying to figure out if the underwear was supposed to show. He was going to know right away that I didn't know what I was doing, and there goes the sexy element. I must be out of my mind with insanity; my husband was going to laugh at me. But, oh well, things couldn't be any worse than they already were.

Oh good Lord. I don't think my body was made for something like this. It was cute though, and I did feel kind of womanly with it on. I tried the heels to see what it all looked like all together. Oh...yes... that...wow. I saw what Joanna and Nicole were talking about. I sort of felt sexy. But this God-forsaken thing was still on my arm. I thought it was suppose to wash off after a while. Well, I've taken a few showers since getting it, and it was still on. Mitchell is going to think I've lost my mind. I was standing in the middle of our bedroom with this slip on and a tattoo. I thought I'd lost my mind. Never again would I listen to those girls. I needed to change before Mitchell got home. What was I thinking? Oh my God, I was officially insane.

"Vickie?" I could hear Mitchell calling my name from behind me.

"Mitch...um hi...you're early," I said turning around to face him.

"I didn't know you were back." Mitchell said as he let his eyes graze up and down my body.

"Yes, I got back awhile ago," I replied starting to feel a bit uncomfortable with his staring.

"Were you expecting someone?" Mitchell asked me with a confused look on his face.

"No, why would you ask that?" I replied.

"Why are you wearing that?" he asked me.

"Um well...um for you, I think. If you don't like it I'll take it off it was crazy anyway. I know I look stupid," I responded.

"No Vickie, you look good. I'm just not sure what I'm supposed to do with this. Why?" he said all the while standing in the doorway as if he was stuck in place.

"I thought that maybe we could spice up our relationship," I said to him.

"Spice up...that doesn't sound like you talking," Mitchell said, finally walking into the room.

"Off course, it's me talking. I'm the one standing here half nude, I may add," I replied.

"No Vickie, it sounds like someone talked you into this and you're just using their words," Mitchell said.

"What? Who?" I asked.

"I don't know the same someone or some ones who talked you into getting that tattoo...and it's nice by the way," Mitchell said pointing to my arm.

"Thank you. It's temporary-at least it's supposed to be. Joanna and Nicole did think that I needed to loosen up a bit," I explained.

"And let me guess, that's Joanna's," he said this time pointing to what I was wearing.

"Yes," I answered.

Mitchell walked over to the bed and sat down. He looked disappointed. I was sorry if I didn't look the way I should in this thing, but the least he could do was not make me feel like the ugly duckling. I didn't get it; I took a stand and he threw divorce papers at me. I tried to be sexy for him, and he was disappointed. What did he want from me?

"Vickie, I wish that no one had to tell you to try with me - with us," he said with his head bent.

"What do you mean?" I asked him.

"Vickie, you know the first time I saw you, I was like, Wow there's the woman that God made for me. I wanted to give you the world. I was sure, and I still am, that you were the answer to my prayers. I just wish that I was the answer to your prayers," he said.

For the first time since I met Mitchell, I saw his eyes fill with tears. He was such a strong and proud man that I had forgotten that he was just a man. I didn't know how, but I think I may have broken his heart. My Mitchell, the man who had given me the world, I had broken his heart. He got up to leave and I had to say something. I had to let him know something; something from my heart, from my soul.

"Mitch I..." I tried to say something, but nothing could come out.

"It's alright Vickie. I get it. You know, you do look really good, but the funny thing is you didn't have to wear that to spice things up. All you have to do is lie next to me fully clothed and give me your heart, your whole heart," Mitchell said. This time he lifted his head and looked into my eyes. "I had the divorce papers drawn up and I left them in the desk draw...I'm sorry that it has come to this Vickie."

I watched helplessly as Mitchell left the room. Mitchell does have my heart, and I don't know why he couldn't see that. I don't know why I didn't show him that? I thought the problem was with him, but it's me. I was the one destroying this marriage. I couldn't go on hurting him. I figured the best thing to do was to let Mitchell go. He needed a woman who would give him everything, and I couldn't do that for him. He deserved someone better than me.

I went over to my desk and took the divorce papers out. It was time to sign them, it was time to let go of everything: this house, the car, and the money. It all belonged to Mitchell, and I had no rights to any of it, not after all the hurt I'd caused him. I didn't want any of it. I owed him that much. I went through the pages where it discussed dividing up the assets, and I scratched out everything that was left to me, then I signed. I hoped that by letting him go, he'd find someone who could make him happy.

40

"Hello Mr. Stephen, This is Joanna. If the offer is still on the table, I would like to accept. Please give me a call back and let me know when you would like for me to be in L.A." I couldn't believe I just did that. I guess this means I was actually going to it, I was actually moving away. I just hoped I was making the right decision. It was hard sometimes to decide what was best for you when there were so many things to consider. How do you know you're doing something that's going to make you happy? How could you know if your life was supposed to go in that direction? All I knew was that I want that job. I'd given so much of myself to my work, and I deserved this job. The only problem was why did I have to give up everything that I loved just to have something that I wanted?

Why does life always work that way? You always have to give something up just to get something. Vickie may say that it's just God's will, but sometimes I wondered if God could possibly be that cruel. I loved God, but if I had to suffer heartache and loss just to get something that I'd earned through hard work and perseverance, then how much could God love me?

I wanted it all. I know I said that a woman couldn't have it all, but, God I wanted it all. I wanted a husband and beautiful kids and a great career. But most of all I didn't ever want to wake up one day and wonder what the hell happened to my life. Why didn't I give something a chance? I'd never been a fairy tale type of girl, but I did want the fairy tale. I just didn't know if the fairy tale existed; hell, I wouldn't know what to do with it if it did.

I needed to face it; I was the stereotypical career girl, the one who had the nice house, car, clothes, but no man and no life. Yes, I was that girl. Hooray for me, I've finally made it to the top, and I was standing there all alone. I used to say that being alone didn't mean being lonely. And I still think that's true, but if you're not careful being alone can cross the line into Lonely Girlville within a blink of an eye.

I caught myself starting to cry. I had to hold it together. There was nothing to cry about; this was what I wanted, what I deserved. There was no time to feel sorry for myself now; I'd worked for this and now I had it.

My thoughts became disturbed by a knock at my door. "Who is it?" I wished that when people knocked at your door they would at least have the decency to answer you when you asked, who's there. No one even knew I was back yet. For Christ sake, they could at least give me a day to get myself together.

"David what are you doing here?" I asked the moment I opened the door and saw him standing there.

"Well, I said we needed to talk when you get back. Can I come in?" David said.

"Yeah, I guess, but I thought I said we didn't have anything to talk about."

David walked passed me and into my apartment like he didn't even hear what I was saying. God he smelled good. I needed to control myself. I always lose my mind over this man. That's why he gets the best of me every time. This time I'm going to be strong.

"I see you've started packing," David said when he saw the boxes I had all over my living room.

"Yeah, so?"

"So you're still going?"

"Yeah. Why wouldn't I?" I said, confused as to why he thought I would stay.

"Well I guess after our conversation before, I thought you might have changed your mind."

"Why would I have changed your mind?"

"You don't remember the conversation I'm talking about," David said as he sat down on my sofa.

"David you've been hinting about some conversation. What the hell are you trying to say?"

"Alright, two nights ago you got drunk...really drunk from what I could tell."

"Yeah so...wait how do you know that?"

"Because you called me and said some interesting things."

"I did? Like what?"

"Well, you got on me about kicking you out of my house and pretty much said I wasn't shit."

"Yeah, well that sounds like me."

"You also said something else."

"What?" I asked, all the while standing over him with my arms folded.

"You said you loved me," he said looking up at me.

"What? No...are you sure it wasn't Jess or Nic or sometimes Vickie plays on the phone." I replied, trying my best to make some sense of what he was saying.

"No, it was definitely you."

"You're a doctor. You know that alcohol can speak through people and make them say things that they don't mean."

"Really, is that how alcohol works?" he asked with a smile.

"Yes, it is, and I'm ashamed of you for not knowing that. You should know better."

"That's interesting cause I wasn't drunk at all and I said it," he said as he got up to stand in front of me.

"Said what?"

"I said I love you."

"To who?" I asked trying to wrap my head around what David said.

"To you, and in fact, I'm completely sober right now, and I'll say it again, Joanna Stewart, I love you," he said as he gently grabbed a hold of my hands and stared into my eyes.

What the hell just happened? Did I hear what I thought I heard? Okay I couldn't breathe. Why didn't he come five minutes earlier with all this love talk before I accepted the job? Oh my god. David just said he loved me. Was I hearing things? I needed a moment to process this. Joanna, girl, relax and breathe. DAVID JUST SAID HE LOVES ME!

"Oh my god, David. What the hell? What am I supposed to say?" I asked taking my hand away.

"I would hope you would say it back," David said with a smile.

I looked at David and, yeah, I did love him. I've always loved him. But I was not what he needed. He deserved so much more than I could give him.

"Okay, truth. Yeah, I do love you. I think I've loved you since the first time I saw you. Oh my god, I can't believe I'm actually saying this out loud to your face right now."

"I think it's about time don't you."

"No there is no right time."

"Why not?"

"Because then what? I'm going to be that girl chasing a dream and you're always going to be that guy who's ready to settle down."

"Is that what you think?"

"Eventually my ambitions will destroy any relationship we may have and then I'll lose you. David, I rather have you as a friend than not have you at all. I just want you in my life."

"Jo, I think you're selling me short, but most importantly I think you're selling yourself short."

"No, I'm not."

"Yeah, you are cause you're living with the delusion that I don't know who you are and what makes you happy. I do and I'm still here. Yeah I want to settle down, but I don't want to do that with just anybody. I want to settle down with you. I want you to have everything, but you have to want it too."

"David, there's no such thing as having everything."

"Yes, there is. You just have to go for it," he said, holding onto me. He continued, "I will never ever regret being with you, but I don't want you to ever feel as though you gave something up to be with me. I think you need to decide what's going to make you happy, not just right now, but for a lifetime. No matter what you decide, I'll always be in your life." David kissed me on my lips for the first time since we met. It was short and without tongue, but I've never been kissed like that before. I felt a surge of energy racing through my body. When he left I was alone again.

41

Boy, I was glad I got to spend the whole day after getting back without Steven. I'd hoped his ass never come home. I bet he was too scared to come back after that ass whipping I gave him. From what I heard, he ain't been seen by no one since then. My mama said he was too shamed to show his no-good ass around here. I hoped he kept on running. I've finally made up my mind that I was gonna try to make something out of myself and I didn't need his ass telling me no kinda bullshit.

I spent the day looking on the web at nearby cooking schools and I think I might have found one. Damn, I was sure starting to get excited. Even my mama thought it was a good idea. She agreed to keep my kids when I went to class; I just might be able to pull this off. That damn Vickie might have been onto something. Maybe all it takes is to just go for it.

"Mamie, why you keep smiling to yourself?" my daughter asked me.

"Cause I'm happy Keshia...Mamie's happy," I told her.

"Why?"

"Cause Mamie's going back to school."

"Why?"

"Cause Mamie's going to learn to cook."

"That's silly Mamie. You already know how to cook."

"I know how to cook for you and your brother but I'm gonna learn how to cook fancy type food."

"Wow," she said with those big brown eyes of hers stretched out.

"Yeah, and maybe I might open my own restaurant or something like that. How that sound?"

"I like that," she said with a smile and came over to me wrapping her arms around me.

"Me too baby...me too." I replied, squeezing her tightly.

I must have been lost in my own dreamland and not paying much attention 'cause the next thing I knew, Steven's bum ass was standing in my living room looking all kinds of messy. He looked like he'd been sleeping outside the whole time I was away. It don't matter where he'd been long as he knows he gotta go back there, cause he sure as hell can't stay here.

"Keshia, take your brother in the room," I told my daughter.

"Okay Mamie...hi daddy," she tried to get her dad's attention, but he was focused only on me.

"Hey," he said to her like she were some stranger on the street.

This stupid motherfucker. That's all he got to say to his kids. He ain't seen them in days and all he got to say was hey. Man, fuck him. I shoulda kicked his ass out a long time ago.

"Steven, you can't stay here."

"This my house aint it?" he asked angrily.

"Shit, barely. Anyway I don't know what's going on with that shit that happened before, so until it's settle you can't be here."

"The shit settled, I said I wasn't pressing charges," he said taking a couple of steps towards me.

"I bet you did. My lawyer said you should have some charges yourself," I told him.

"Where the fuck you get a lawyer from?" he asked looking angry and calm at the same time.

"That ain't got nothing to do with you. I still don't want your ass here," I said to him.

"Well, too damn bad cause I ain't leaving," he said.

"Why the fuck you want to stay some place that don't nobody want you?" I asked him.

"Cause this my place. You always acting like you running shit." he said putting his hands in my face.

"Steven get your fingers out my face," I told him.

He was ready to start again. Now if I were to do something, I be the one back in jail. He ain't gonna have me catching another case. I'm walking away and ignoring his ass. All Steven wanted was for me to do something. I ain't playing his game.

"Where the fuck you going?" he asked as I started to walk away from him.

"To mind my business."

"Stupid bitch!" Steven yelled and jumped in my way.

"Whatever, just start packing your shit and make an exit." I told him, still trying to get away from him.

"I told you, I ain't going no fucking place!" he yelled again and grabbed at my arm hard.

"You know what, Steven, you ain't got to go. I'll go and take the kids with me. First thing tomorrow, I'll call the welfare place and tell them they need to find me someplace else to stay," I tell him, yanking my arm away.

"And where I'm supposed to go?"

"I don't give a fuck."

"You fucking bitch!" Steven yelled and grabbed at my arm again even harder.

"Steven get your fucking hands off me!"

Steven's face made an expression I ain't never seen before. Since I met Steven I ain't never been scared of him, but for a moment I got really scared. His eyes looked like he had something planned, and it wasn't anything good. The hair on the back of my neck stood up straight and chills ran down my body. Something didn't seem right. I pulled away from Steven and tried to run to find something to scare him with, but he grabbed me again and slapped me across my face so hard that my whole head spun clear around. When I turned back towards Steven, there was something shiny in his hand. I couldn't tell what it was, and then he made a motion. I felt something sharp go through my stomach. I grabbed hold of my stomach to see what it was, but my hand was covered in blood. Then something else sharp ran through my stomach again and then again and then I seemed to feel it all over my body.

The room was fading. I put my hands to my face, and it was completely filled with blood. Oh my God, this motherfucker is stabbing me. I wanted to swing on him, to take that knife back and stab him with it, but I couldn't move. My legs seemed not to be there and I could feel myself dropping and there was the floor pressing against my face.

I heard the door slam and then I felt these small hands on my back. God please don't let him hurt my babies. Somebody help my babies.

"Aunty Jo, Mamie's not moving. She can't get up. Mamie wake up, wake up Mamie. Please Mamie wake up."

Baby I'm here. You're going to be alright. I'm here, baby. It's okay, I'm okay.

42

My hands were shaking holding the steering wheel. I knew I was going fast trying to keep up with the ambulance. I had to slow down. I got Keshia and Donte in my back seat, and I kept trying to reassure them that everything would be alright, but I didn't even know that myself. I couldn't think straight. Why didn't I insist that Nic stay with me for a while? How could I not think that things could go this far? What the hell was wrong with me? My best friend could be dying right now and it was all my fault. What was going to happen to her kids? How were they ever going to understand this? I didn't even understand it.

It took us forever to get to the hospital. I got the kids out the car and held them on either side of me. I tried to cover their eyes as the paramedics got Nic out the ambulance, but I could hear them calling for their mom. I held their hands tight and followed the gurney through the hospital doors. The moment I walked in, I saw Jess and David standing there. Jess was frozen in disbelief and the both of them looked at me, waiting for me to say something. I couldn't. I stood there holding tight to the kids' hands with my face wet from tears and my clothing soaked with Nicole's blood.

This male doctor and some nurses took Nicole somewhere, and I couldn't see her any more. I didn't know what was happening to her. I looked at Jess for some comfort, but she was shaking and crying. I didn't know what I was supposed to do. Where am I supposed to go? What was I supposed to do with the kids? I needed to know where they took Nicole. I needed to know if she was okay.

"Jo, can you hear me?" David was standing in front of me trying to get my attention, but I just wanted to see where they took her. David continued to ask, "Jo are you hurt? What happened?"

"He stabbed her. He stabbed her," I said softly.

"Who?" David asked me with concern on his face.

"Where did they take her?" I asked in a whisper.

"They're taking care of her. Come on, let's get you and the kids to the lounge."

Waiting for us in the lounge were two police officers. I didn't want them to question the kids because I could feel how scared they were. They held onto me so tight, and I was not going to let anything or anybody hurt them. I had to take care of them for Nicole; she would want me to make sure her kids were alright. But these police officers kept asking them questions and the more they asked, the more the kids cried. Finally I had to say, "could you please just give them time? Please."

"Ms. Stuart we need to figure out what happened and only the kids know," The police office said.

"What do you need to know? Their mother is lying there fighting for her life. Just leave them alone and go catch the son-of-a-bitch who did this," I said to them almost shouting.

"Alright Ms. Stuart. I think we got all we need for right now anyway," the police officer said as they got up to leave.

No one was getting near these kids not as long as I was around - not the cops and definitely not Steven. I only wished I had gotten there sooner. I would have killed him with my bare hands.

"Aunty Jo, is my Mamie dead?" Nicole's daughter asked me.

"Oh no, baby. Your Mamie's the toughest woman I know, and the doctors are doing everything to bring her back to you," I said to her, wrapping one arm around her and the other around her brother.

I think I just lied. Nicole could be dead, and they just don't know how to tell us. She may have been dead by the time she got to the hospital. How do you tell a child that her mother is dead and her father is the one who did it?

I've never had motherly instincts, but I hugged these kids like they were my own. I didn't want to let them go. They needed me; they needed reassurance and right now I was the only person who could provide that. Suddenly nothing mattered but them. Everything in life seemed so petty in comparison.

Jessica came into the lounge and I thought she was going to tell us something, but she just sat there wiping her tears. Neither one of us said anything to the other. We both didn't seem to know what to say.

"They wouldn't tell me anything I don't know why." Jessica seemed not to be talking to anybody in particular. She just seemed to be talking just to say something, not really to start a conversation.

David had left us a while ago, and I was hoping that when he returned he might have news, but he came out and there was nothing new.

"They're still working on her. Do you guys need anything?" He asked as he sat down next to me and the kids.

"No we're ok." I said to him.

"Listen Nicole's mother just arrived. Jo do you want to go see her?" David asked me.

"Yeah that'll be good," I answered.

I tried to get up and leave, but the kids refused to let me go. So I took them with me. David brought us in this room that was filled with Nicole's family. The kids ran over to their grandmother and gave her a big hug. She held them so tight almost as if she was checking, in her own way, to see if they were alright and safe. I didn't know what to tell them. I didn't feel like I belonged. Nicole's sister came over to me and gave me a hug. She offered to take the kids home so that they could get some rest. It seemed reasonable to me, but I just didn't want them to leave my sight. What if Steven came back and got them? Who would be there to protect them? He knew where Nic's sister lived and how to get to her. I gave Nicole's sister the keys to my apartment and told her to stay there. At least that way, I knew that Steven couldn't get to them.

After the kids left, David walked with me back to the lounge where Jess was still sitting. It seemed as if she hadn't moved the entire time. I know Jess, and sometimes she can't handle stuff. She's not as strong as the rest of us. I was afraid that she might fall apart or begin to lose it. I could see it in her eyes; she was so confused. I didn't know what to say to her. How could I make this better for everyone?

"Did you call Vickie?" I asked Jessica

"Yeah, I called her right after they brought Nic in."

"Oh, okay," I replied not really knowing what I should say next.

"She should have listened to me and left a long time ago."

"That's not what she wanted."

"No, that's not what you wanted."

"What does that mean?"

"Jo, if you had once told her to leave, maybe she wouldn't be in an operating room with holes in her body," Jessica said with such anger that it caught me off guard.

"What? This is my fault?"

"You knew long before any of us did and you did nothing," she said with a slightly raised voice.

"What the hell do you mean I did nothing? I was the one who let her stay with me all the time. I did what I could."

"Oh Jo, shut up! Face it your selfish. All you ever care about is what's good for Joanna and the hell with anybody else. That's who you are. All you had to do was tell her to get some help but that was way too much for you. That was too much drama for Joanna to get involved in. Well Jo, look around. This is what happens when you refuse to deal with shit. But all you and Nic did was laugh about it, like it was nothing, like it didn't matter. So yes, Jo, this is your fault and yes I do blame you," Jessica said, and by this point she was completely yelling.

I just stood there while Jessica yelled at me. What could I say? That she was wrong? I don't think she was. I failed my best friend. I messed up. I took off running and didn't even know where I was going. I heard David calling my name, but I just kept running. I passed Victoria and she tried to stop me, but I just kept running. I found this empty room that looked like it was for a patient. I curled up on a chair by the window and just cried. David somehow found me in the room and held me.

"Jo, you know that Jess didn't mean what she said. She's just scared," he said kneeling in front of me.

"No, she's right David. I knew years ago what was happening between Nicole and Steven, and I did nothing. You know, Nic and I had never had an argument or a fight."

"Really?"

"Nope and that first night when she came into my room with her eye all swollen, something in me wanted to say something, but I didn't want to fight with her...I didn't want to lose my friend."

"Jo, that doesn't mean that this was your fault."

"Maybe not, but it does mean that Jess was right. I am selfish. I run from things rather than run to them. I made myself believe Nic when she said she could handle it," I replied.

"Alright, do you have your moments of selfishness? Yes, you do. No one knows that better than me. But Jo, there's no wrong or right way to deal with this type of situation. The truth is this isn't the typical abusive relationship. It was kind of a give and take so you did what you knew to do and that was to be her friend and there was nothing wrong with that."

I don't know why David put up with me or why he was always there when I needed him, but I was so glad that he was here.

43

"Jess what's going on? Why did Jo run out of here like that? Did Nic get worse?" I walked into the waiting room and could feel the tension and didn't know where it was coming from.

"I don't know what's going on with Nic. They won't tell me anything, and as for Jo, well she just can't deal with the truth."

"What does that mean?"

"Don't worry about it Vickie."

"Well, I don't know why the hospital won't tell you anything about Nic. You're a doctor here for Christ sake. Mitchell sits on the board. I bet they'll tell me something. Let me go try," I responded and tried to walk towards the door.

"Vickie, sit down! The last thing the hospital staff needs is you throwing your weight around. Just wait, like we're all doing."

Jessica's tone was completely uncalled for. All I wanted to do was find out about Nicole. She could at least let me try. I guess she was scared like we all seemed to be. I just wished I knew more. All I know is that Nicole was brought to the hospital after Steven stabbed her; but how bad was she stabbed? Was it just a flesh wound? Was she awake or unconscious when she came in? Somebody needed to tell me something and by the way Jessica was acting, I didn't think she wanted to be that person.

I just had to keep reminding myself not to panic. I mean this could be nothing. For all I knew Nicole could come walking out that door at any moment. She could be just fine. I had to stay positive. It was obvious that Jessica and Joanna had given up, but I was not. The God that I served is a great God, and he wouldn't let Nicole leave us like this. We just had to pray and keep the faith. I knew she could make it; she had to make it.

"Is her mother here?"

"Yes she's in a private room for families."

"What about her kids?" I continued to ask, trying to get a better sense of the situation.

"I don't know."

"What about..."

"Damn Vickie, stop with the twenty questions. Okay!"

"Jess, I'm just trying to find out what's going on." I told her, but she hardly looked at me.

"Well then, you should have been here earlier."

"I came as soon as I heard. Why are you acting like this?"

"Vickie, you want to know what's going on? I'll tell you, Steven stabbed her four or five times while there kids were in the other room. Then he left her there to die and she still might," Jessica said with so much aggression that she didn't even sound like herself.

"Jess, we can't think like that. We should just keep praying for a miracle."

"Vickie, why don't you just sit there and pray. I'll be over here drinking my coffee and waiting to hear what her doctors have to say."

Jessica has completely shocked me. This wasn't her normal demeanor. She wasn't this abrasive and rude. She must be really scared. That must mean that Nicole could really be dying. Oh Lord God, please don't let this be happening. Please don't take my friend.

"Vickie, are you alright?" I looked up to see Mitchell running into the waiting room.

"Mitchell, how did you know I was here?" I asked, standing up to greet him.

"I went home and the housekeeper told me what happened. How's Nicole?"

"We don't know anything yet."

"Hello, Jess," Mitchell greeted Jessica by putting his hand on her shoulder.

"Hi, Mitchell," Jessica responded and managed to give a half smile.

"Do you both need anything?" Mitchell asked.

"No we're fine Mitchell," I answered.

"Well do you need me to find out what's taken so long?" he asked again.

"Oh no, Jessica doesn't want us to throw our weight around," I replied, giving Jessica a side eye.

"I only meant you, Vickie," Jessica replied, meeting my side eye with one of her own.

"Whatever, Jess. We'll just sit here and wait," I said and sat back down.

"That's fine with me," Jessica replied.

Mitchell sat down next to me without saying another word. But he must have seen how Jessica's attitude and Nicole's condition was affecting me, because he reached over and grabbed hold of my hand. For a moment, I wanted to ask him why; after all, it was only a few hours ago that he was all too ready to leave me. But I really needed him here with me now. I really needed my husband and the feel of his hands against mine gave me the comfort I needed. I wasn't about to do or say anything that was going to ruin it.

A few moments later Joanna came in with David. She looked a mess. I'd never seen Joanna look so disheveled. Her eyes were bloodshot and her clothes where soaked in blood. It was obvious she hadn't been home since she came in with Nicole. I felt so bad for her. I could see her pain; I felt it since it was the same pain I was having. But the pain she was feeling must have been even worst since it was her who saw Nicole lying there. What she must be going through. I ran over and gave Joanna a hug. I hardly wanted to let her go. She was always so strong and fearless. But as I held her, I could feel her weaken. The Joanna I knew wasn't there. What had replaced her was pure fear. I almost broke down myself, but then where would that leave us. Joanna was in no shape to take charge, and Jessica was acting like one of us had been the one who had stabbed Nicole. So that just left me.

"Jo, how about I get my housekeeper to bring over some clothes for you. At least then you could get out of these."

"That would be good, Vickie. Thank you."

"You know, I also could see if she could bring some food for us and for Nic's family. I'm sure they're starving," I said out loud not really talking to anyone.

"Yeah, thanks Vickie. That does sound good," Joanna said in a quiet tone.

Joanna sat down next to David and curled up against him and almost disappeared. I called my housekeeper and gave her specific instructions on what to do. I urged her to come quickly; I didn't know about anybody else but I was positive that at any moment the doctor was going to walk through those doors and tell us that Nicole was just fine.

When I was done talking to my housekeeper, I needed a moment by myself. I was good at giving orders but taking care of other people was a bit overwhelming for me. It was hard to push your own feelings to the side and worry about how someone else was feeling. This is something new for me. I guess I never had to deal with other people's feelings; maybe nobody made me, or maybe I didn't care enough to make myself. It was obvious that my friends were falling apart and they needed me to do something; I couldn't let them down.

"You know Vickie, every now and again you surprise me," Mitchell said to me.

"What do you mean by that, Mitchell?"

"Just by the way you're acting now and by signing the divorce papers without asking for anything."

"You've already read it?"

"Yeah you left it sitting out on the desk. I guess you were in a rush to get over here," he said.

"Oh...well Mitchell. I can see that I've caused you a lot of hurt, and I don't want to continue doing that. I know you don't think I do, but I do love you, Mitchell, and I just want you to be happy."

"You think me being happy is having all the money to myself?"

"It's not about that. I don't want to fight with you anymore. You should have your peace and someone who can provide that for you."

"Vickie, the money was never mine. It was yours. I did all this...I got all this for you because I wanted you to be happy."

"I guess I didn't know that before."

"Do you now?"

"I don't know sometimes I think so many other things cloud my head and it's hard to appreciate all that. But I want to be better Mitchell, it's just not going to happen overnight. Let's face it, I've been this way my whole life."

"Yeah, but I see some glimmer of hope. That's why I tore up the divorce papers," Mitchell said to me.

"You tore them up? Why?" I asked him shocked that he would make such a move.

"Because I don't want to divorce you, Vickie. I can't be without you. I thought you wanted to divorce me," Mitchell said as he held my hands.

"No, Mitchell when I married you, I meant for it to be forever. Just please be patient with me, okay."

"For the rest of my life." He said kissing me on the lips.

Mitchell's kiss felt like a lost love had finally returned home. His arms around me reminded me of why I married him. Most women pray for this, but my prayers were actually answered. God sent me the perfect man.

44

I couldn't believe that this was happening. Why wouldn't they let me in the operating room? Todd knew that I could be useful. What if something went wrong? What if Nicole woke up and panics? I should be in there. She should hear my voice to know that everything was going to be alright. I'm a good damn doctor I should be in there. I needed to be in there. God please let her be alright.

I knew I was too hard on Jo, but I was just so mad. I knew something like this could happen. I saw it all the time. But they didn't want to listen to me. That was the problem. No matter what I said, no one listened. I would always be little dingy Jessica. I could scream at the top of my lungs and my voice will still be hard to hear. I just needed Jo to hear me for once. I needed her to know that I have a say too; that she should have let me lead instead of ignoring me and letting Nicole handle this all alone. Oh my god, how scared she must have been. I bet that was the most helpless she had ever felt. And no one was there to help her. We should have stayed one more day at the beach. Something was telling me that we should have stayed. Why didn't I insist that we stay? Why didn't I refuse to leave?

This was taken too long. It's not supposed to take this long. There must be some complications - maybe a blood clot or maybe she's bleeding internally and they can't find the source. Maybe they got her on the operating table too late. Todd's a good doctor. I'm sure he's doing everything he can, but he should have let me in there.

Maybe I should apologize to Jo. She's not acting like herself. I guess we're all not acting like ourselves. How could we? We've never gone through anything like this before. The last time we were in the hospital with Nicole, she was having Donte. How will we ever be able to come back from this? It's funny. I deal with life and death on a daily basis, but I don't think I ever really appreciated how life altering it is until I saw them wheel Nicole in on that gurney. Is it even right to pray for a miracle, knowing what I know about medicine? I just want my friend to be okay. I want everything to go back the way it was. How crazy is life? One moment we're all together making memories that will last a lifetime and the next we're sitting in a hospital in complete silence waiting to hear whether our best friend is dead.

"Hey guys listen, I got some food here and coffee. I took some over to Nic's family and...well, here's the rest. Oh, and Jo here's some clothes. Why don't you go and get cleaned up. You don't want Nic to see you like that when she wakes up do you?" Victoria said as she came back into the waiting room with her hands full and Mitchell following close behind.

"Thanks, Vickie," Joanna replied.

I watched Vickie lead Joanna to the restroom, and it dawned on me that she hadn't shed one tear yet. How could she not have cried? Joanna and I are beside ourselves, but Victoria is like ice. She just goes around taking care of everything and not crying. I wonder if she thinks that this isn't all that serious? Or maybe she's being typical Victoria and trying to get the attention for herself. I mean how could she not cry?

"Jess, why don't you eat something?" Victoria asked when she came back.

"I'm not hungry Vickie?" I replied.

"Come on Jess, you've been working all day. You need something to keep your strength up," Victoria said.

"Vickie, what the hell is wrong with you?" I said to her. This calm Victoria was new to me, and I couldn't figure out if she was being helpful or if she really didn't care about Nicole.

"What do you mean?" Victoria asked looking confused.

"Why don't you care about what's going on?"

"I care Jess. I'm just trying to keep it together."

"Why?" I asked again, not knowing what to make of this Victoria.

"Who else is going to? You? We're all falling apart. I'm just trying my best to keep this all together," Victoria said.

"I'm sorry, Vickie. You're actually doing really great."

"You think so?" She asked with a smirk.

"Yeah, you got Jo to wear that ugly sweat suit, and you know when all this is over, she may just choke you out for it, right?" I said to her with a giggle.

"Hey, I think that suit is kind of fly," she replied.

That was the first time we laughed. Vickie being in charge was a thought that used to scare me; hell, it use to scare us all, but she's actually good at it. Joanna came back wearing a very pink oversized sweat suit and sneakers. She must have been out of it, because it didn't seem to bother her. But the sight of her wearing it made me chuckle a bit. "What are you laughing at?" Joanna asked

"Nothing. You just look really nice Jo," I said to her, trying to hold back my laughter.

"Whatever," Joanna said as she passed by me.

"Look, I'm sorry for what I said," I told Joanna.

"No you're not," She said.

"Okay, maybe I'm not sorry for what I said, but I am sorry for the way I said it," I replied.

"Jo, do you accept Jess's apology?" Victoria asked.

"No," Joanna answered without focusing her eyes on either one of us.

"Jo, come on," Victoria said.

"Vickie ,I don't want to deal with you guys right now. Okay, just leave it alone," Joanna said.

"Okay listen, our best friend is in there fighting for her life and we need to pull it together. Jess, you can't blow a fuse at everyone and Jo you can't shut down now...I'm trying but I don't think I know how to fix this," Victoria said as she stood to address us.

"I don't either, Vickie. So like I said. leave it alone," Joanna replied.

I wanted to tell Vickie that she was doing good, but I could see for the first time since she got to the hospital how scared she was. I think Vickie thought that we would lose it for a minute and then we all would be back to normal. I never really realized how much Vickie looked to Joanna and Nicole for answers and direction; I never really realized how much I did as well. It was also becoming clear that so much of who Joanna was fed off of who Nicole was. The four of us were so connected that when one chain broke, we all fell.

"Listen, why don't I go back there and see what's taking so long. I promise to come back with some news," David said, getting up from where he was sitting next to Joanna.

I could see in Joanna's face that she didn't want David to leave. Although I was hard on her, I still felt horrible for what she must be going through. She was the one who saw Nicole lying there in her own blood. What an image to have to carry around in your head.

"When is everything ever going to be ok?" I asked myself not realizing that I said it out loud.

"That's never going to happen," Joanna said.

"What does that mean?" I asked her.

"We went away thinking all we needed was to get away from life for a while but it was a temporary fix. We hadn't found happiness. It was all a mirage - something to keep us from dealing with the world... our world," Joanna explained.

"I think you girls found what you were looking for a long time ago," Mitchell charmed in.

"What do you mean by that Mitch?" Victoria asked him.

"Because Vickie, you girls found each other and you were able to give one another a part of yourself that very few people get to see," he explained.

"Yeah, well that didn't save Nic, now did it?" Joanna said sounding a bit angry.

"But you're here for her now, Jo. The three of you...the four of you are going to be alright," Mitchell said.

Vickie sure lucked out with Mitchell. He just had a way of making you feel better and taking away some guilt that I think we were all feeling. I just don't think we could totally be alright until we knew for sure that Nicole was going to be alright.

⚬⚬⚬⚬⚬⚬

We sat there for almost another hour before I saw David coming and behind him was Todd still dressed in his scrubs. My heart started beating extra fast. I couldn't read their expressions. I didn't know if it was good or bad news. They were walking towards us in such slow motion. I was finally on the other side and I hated being here. I almost saw the expression on my face because it was the same expression I saw time and time again whenever it was me in scrubs walking in slow motion expressionless.

I could see Joanna and Victoria mentally preparing themselves for the worst. I just didn't want to do that; I couldn't. I needed to hear them say whatever they had to say before I could accept anything. Vickie was the first to stand and then I followed. Joanna stayed seated with a look of panic on her face. I had to hear. I needed to hear him say it.

"Well how is she?" Victoria asked impatiently when David and Todd got close to us.

"Mrs. Combs, I'm Dr. Reynolds," Todd introduced himself.

"Todd is she...is she dead?" I asked slowly.

"No Jess," Todd replied with a smile. "We did encounter some complications, but we were able to stabilize her. Luckily the knife didn't hit any vital organs, so I expect that she should make a full recovery."

"Oh thank God!" Victoria shouted out.

I couldn't control my excitement I went over and gave Todd a big hug. He'd saved my friend; he promised me he would and he did. Nicole was going to be alright.

"Has someone told her family?" Victoria asked Todd.

"Yes, I just did, Mrs. Combs," Todd replied.

"Thank you Doctor Reynolds," Victoria said.

Vickie and I both looked over at Joanna who had this big smile on her face. I was starting to see the glimmer of the Joanna I knew coming through.

"When can we see her?" I asked Todd.

"Not for a while. She's in ICU and needs to rest for the rest of the night," he said with a smile.

"Well, I'm not leaving," Victoria said.

"I am, Vickie," Joanna said, getting up and looking like she just broke free from some sort of confinement.

"You are Jo?" Victoria asked.

"Yeah, I need to go home and tell Nic's kids that their Mom is going to be alright. Plus I need to get out of this god awful outfit you got me in," Joanna said. "What were you thinking? Have you ever seen me wear something like this before?"

Joanna gave Victoria and me a hug before leaving with David. It seemed like the instant Todd told us that Nicole was going to be alright this cloud of incompleteness went away.

45

When David and I got to my apartment it was dark and it seemed clear that the kids had been asleep for some time. Nicole's sister was lying on my sofa and awoke the moment she heard us come in. Her face looked lighter, and I knew before I even said anything that she had heard that Nicole was going to be alright. She left after I suggested that she go to the hospital to be with her family. I figured that Nicole would want all of her family around her. She never would have to worry about whether her kids were alright because I was going to make sure they were; but what she needed most was to feel supported and loved.

I went upstairs to check on the kids and they were lying on my bed sound asleep as if nothing had ever happened. They looked so innocent and so at peace that I wondered how Steven could have caused them so much pain. Did he not know the damage that he'd done, not just to Nicole but to these children who had to watch helplessly? How would they ever be able to erase the image of their own father stabbing their mother? How will Nicole ever be able to explain to them how things got this bad? I pray that they would be alright, that they will not forever be emotionally scarred by this. But then again, why wouldn't they? This isn't your normal everyday thing. How many kids have to go through this? It's going to take a lot for Nicole to help her kids move past this. Hell, it's going to take a lot for her to move pass this. She's going to need everyone's support. How can I support her from way across the country?

I guess it was in that moment that I realized that there were some things more important than ambition. I'd been working and striving for so long that I think I had forgotten that there were people who needed me, people that I needed. Accomplishments aren't worth much when there isn't anyone there to cheer for you; then again, at some point in your life you have to realize that those same people who are cheering you on also needed you to cheer for them. This is where I needed to be.

When I came back downstairs, David had poured me a glass of wine and was waiting for me on the sofa. I sat next to him sipping my wine, thinking that all these years I had pushed him away but he never went anywhere. Every time I needed him, he was there. I always thought that I was way too strong and independent to be tied down to some man, but tonight taught me that I was not as strong as I thought. In my weakest moment, there was David. He seemed to know just what to do, just what I needed. I suppose that's what people mean when they say everyone needs someone. I thought those people were just being naive; times have change after all. But maybe I was the naive one. I never knew how much I needed someone to count on until the moment came when I couldn't count on myself; I actually never thought that moment would come.

For years I had been working and building myself so that I could reach a level where nothing could harm me, where I had more than enough strength to carry myself through anything and still had some left over to carry everyone else. But the time came and, well, let's face it, Victoria showed more strength then I ever could. So what was it all for?

"David, I'm sorry if I ever made you feel as if you were not enough for me," I said to him not being able to look him in the face.

"You didn't."

"I didn't?" I asked looking at him.

"No," he answered with a smile.

"Oh...well...good," I responded, not knowing what to say next.

"I mean you tried to but I knew it wasn't about me."

"What do you mean by that?"

"Jo, you've always had so much going on that you never tried to make room for me or anyone else. You have always been on this quest to be more and do more. But you see when a man truly loves a woman, he loves every part of her, including her dreams and ambitions. So, Jo, it wasn't about me not being enough for you, it was about you realizing that you were enough for me."

"When did you get deep?" I asked him with a chuckle.

"Girl, I've always been deep. I'm like an undercover poet...a word master if you will," David said. "See that's the smile I wake up thinking about every day."

"If you keep throwing all this sweetness my way, I may end up with a toothache."

"Well you better call the dentist, girl, cause I got a whole lot more where that came from," David said wrapping his arms around me. There was that kiss again, the one that made my whole body shiver and my knees buckle. And there were those eyes, the ones that stared at me as if they could see right through me to the part of my soul that was hidden from the world.

I can't believe I wasted this much time denying myself this great man. I have been so silly. My career is still so important to me but for the first time I'm wondering about that other side of life - the side that has someone who has a glass of wine waiting for you after you've had a hard day or holds you up when your legs are too week for you to stand. I wonder how it would be on that side. Is it as magical as all the fairytales make it sound? Right now at this moment with David's arms around me and his lips softly kissing my neck, I think I believe in fairytales.

"David there's something I have to tell you," I said pulling away from his lips.

"Right now?" he asked smiling.

"Yeah right now."

"What?"

"I love you."

46

What the hell was this bright ass light in my face? And why couldn't my eyes focus right? My whole damn body hurt. What was going on? Where the fuck was I? What happened? Oh yeah, that bastard stabbed me. Wait then did I die? Oh hell, I died and there was that damn white light. Well then why the hell couldn't I see nothing? Ain't I supposed to see angels and shit? Or hear harps playing or something? Ain't none of that happening. Shit maybe I ain't made it up to heaven. Any minute now the devil may be coming at me laughing bout getting my soul.

But why the hell couldn't I move? This was supposed to be how they took you to hell? By tying you down so you couldn't fight to get back to heaven. Shit, I was glad to be in hell and I intended on waiting right here till Steven's ass got here cause we got some unfinished business. So don't tie me up devil I ain't fighting to leave. I couldn't believe that bastard. Wait what the hell happened to my kids? Oh, if he hurt my kids...okay come on Nicole girl, what do you remember? All I remembered was blood everywhere. What if some of the blood belonged to my kids? I shouldn't have let him in the front door. God please let my kids be alright.

"Mrs. Bennett...Mrs. Bennett can you hear me?" a voice called out but I couldn't tell if it was a male or female.

Oh Lord, the devil done started calling my name. I ain't even gonna answer him till he unties me. I needed to be free for when Steven arrived; I got to be able to swing on his ass.

"Mrs. Bennett...can you speak? How are you feeling? Would you like for me to get the doctor?" The voice kept asking these questions.

Doctor? What the shit is a doctor doing in hell? Why people in hell wearing white? Why am I lying down? And what the hell is all this beeping sound?"

"Where am I?" I forced myself to say.

"You're in the hospital, Mrs. Bennett," the voice said.

"What happened?" I asked as my vision began to clear and I could see long hair hanging over me.

"You suffered some stab wounds," the voice, a woman, said.

"Where..." I started to ask.

"Wait a minute, here's the doctor," the woman said.

"Hi, Mrs. Bennett. I'm Dr. Reynolds. Are you in any pain?" This really fine doctor asked.

Hell yeah, I'm in pain. How the hell someone gonna get stabbed and not be in any pain? Lord, if this simple ass is my doctor, then I know I was gonna die for real now.

"Where are my kids?" I asked him.

"They're fine. They're with your friend Joanna."

Oh thank God. Jo got my kids, and I know if she got a hold of Steven, she'd take care of him; that's my girl.

"Steven?"

"From what I hear he's in police custody. But right now Mrs. Bennett, I need to know if you're experiencing any discomfort," The fine doctor asked.

"Yeah, a little."

"Alright I'm going to examine you quickly," Doctor Fine said to me.

This doctor may be fine, but I hoped he knew what he was doing. These damn doctors always examining something and still don't find nothing.

"Hey, how is she?" Jessica asked as she poked her head in the door of my hospital room.

"Ask her yourself," Doctor Fine told her.

"Hey Nic," Jessica said creeping in the room like she was scared to come in.

"Jess," I said happy to see someone I know.

"Girl, don't you ever scare us like that again," she told, me holding onto my hand.

"Where's..." I tried to ask her.

"Everyone is fine. You just need to concentrate on yourself," she said, interrupting me.

"My kids?" I asked.

"They're good, Nic. I'll tell Jo to bring them by when you're stronger; I know you don't want them to see you like this," she said to me.

Jess was right. As much as I wanted to see my kids and make sure for myself that they were alright, I didn't want them to see me like this. They might get scared and think that I'm dying or something. No, my kids couldn't see me - not just yet. I needed to be up and out of here before they could see me.

"Hey, guess what? They caught that coward Steven hiding at one of his boy's house in the closet," Jessica said with a big smile.

"Did they shoot him?" I asked smiling back.

"No they didn't. Mitchell is making sure he gets what he deserves. So you need to get better cause you are missing a lot of juicy stuff."

"Like what?"

"I promise to tell you when you get better."

"When are Jo and Vickie coming?"

"They'll be here later but first your mom wants to see you. Your whole family been here waiting for you to wake up."

I could feel tears dripping down my face. How scared everyone must have been. Jessica wiped my face and gave me a kiss on my forehead.

"You're fine now girl and you're going to stay that way." I saw her give a look to that fine Dr. Reynolds guy as if the two of them were communicating in some sort of silent code. I may not know that doctor but I knew Jess, and if she says I'm gonna be alright, well then I believed her.

Shit, right now I felt really good; I ain't feeling no pain at all. My eyelids were getting heavy though. I think I need to sleep for a while. Damn, I felt good. I didn't know why, but I wish I could always feel this way. This shit was good.

47

"Thank you for taking care of Nicole, Todd," I told Todd as we stood outside Nicole's hospital room.

"No thanks needed, Jess. It's my job," he said with a grin.

"I know, but you're quite good at your job."

"Well thank you. That means a lot coming from you," he said. "But how are you doing? I mean I know it must have been a rough night. Have you been home at all?"

"No, not yet, but I'm doing better now. I guess I keep thinking that if I go home something would happen and I won't be here to help."

"Well look, she's fast asleep and will probably be that way for awhile. So you should go home and get some rest. Doctor's orders."

"Oh you're ordering me now?" I asked him with a chuckle.

"Yes, I am. I want you rested when you decide to go out with me."

"Still pushing."

"I told you I would," he said. "Listen go home if anything happens, I promise you'll be the first person I call."

"You promise?"

"Cross my heart."

Going home wasn't on my to-do list, but Todd was right; I was exhausted. I could barely keep my eyes open. Sticking around here wasn't doing anyone any good. Talking to Nicole and knowing how good of a doctor Todd was eased my anxiety and made me feel a bit comfortable about leaving the hospital. Besides, I hadn't been home in almost two days and my bed was calling my name. I took a final peek at Nicole, just to make sure she was still breathing, before leaving.

My house was still filled with the candle and flower scent from when Michael was here. I couldn't believe he thought all it took to win me over were a few lousy flowers and some cheap candles. He needed to be a way better man for me to ever give in to him again. All these stupid pictures of us on the wall have got to go. I had no clue why I was smiling in them; I had a cheater wrapped around me who wouldn't know the truth if it fell from the sky and knocked him on the head.

I needed to do some serious cleaning. I needed to get rid of basically everything that reminded me of Michael. I refused to be that woman again, to be with that man again. I didn't even know why I thought it was okay to love him so hard that I somehow stopped loving myself. I was basically torturing myself every single day of our relationship. I don't think I was ever really happy with Michael. I didn't know why my heart got stuck. The truth was my heart was still pretty much stuck. How fast will I be able to get over that kind of stupid blind love that was still so strong and so real? The one thing that happened to me while I waited to hear if Nicole was going to be alright was that I realized how life can change in an instant. I was not going to waste another moment on a man that didn't make me happy.

I still wanted the romantic proposal and the beautiful wedding, and knowing myself, I'm probably going to love hard again. But I'm just going to make sure that it's with the right man. Mr. Wrong can certainly destroy your life, sometimes without you realizing it and sometimes he can even end your life. It's not worth wasting a moment on Mr. Wrong.

"Hey, Jess." Michael said as I walked through the front door.

I couldn't believe that Michael was here again. What was it about him that made him believe that it's ok to just show up whenever?

"So what are you doing in my house?"

"Jess, this is my house, too, if you remember."

"Michael, I know you're not about to do this right now are you?" I asked him in disbelief of his nerve.

"No, baby, I'm not. I've actually been waiting for you to come home. I heard about Nic and I wanted to call you, but, well, you know how we ended things."

"Yeah, I know."

"Jess, I don't know why you're being like this. I just wanted to make sure you were alright. I mean, I can do that can't I?" he asked as if I should be grateful that he was there.

"Michael, it's not that I don't appreciate the fact that you're checking on me, it's just that I can't be around you, not now."

"What's so wrong with being around me?"

"Because I still love you."

"Good, because I still love you too. So let's work this out, okay."

"No Michael. There's nothing to work out," I replied. "I need you to hear me. I'm letting you go not because you cheated on me or you lied, because I think I will always forgive you for that, for some stupid reason, but because I need to find my happiness and it's not with you."

"But, baby, you're my happiness," he said as he walked towards me.

"No, I'm not and that's the difference between us. I love and respect you enough to let you go and find the kind of life that makes you happy, but for as much as I have giving you, you don't seem to love and respect me enough to do the same," I explained to him.

"I don't understand, baby," Michael said as he wrapped his arms around me.

"Michael, I don't hate you. I'm not even mad any more. I'm just done. I've reached a place where I know that I got to take care of me for once," I said, stepping out of his grip.

"Okay, Jess, I can give you that. I don't want you to ever doubt that I never loved you cause I did—I do. You were the first girl in my life who ever loved me like that, and the last thing I ever wanted to do was to cause you pain, but it seemed like that's what I did. For that I'm sorry."

"I know you are Michael, and I don't doubt that you did love me. I just wanted you to be more than what you were, and for that I'm sorry."

"So what now?"

"Now we part and wish each other the best of luck."

"I do hope you find your happiness, Jess. You deserve it."

"Thank you, Michael."

As Michael walked out the door, he took with him the old Jessica and left behind a brand new woman who wasn't afraid to express herself anymore. I refused to worry about hurting someone's feelings only for my own feelings to be hurt. From this moment on, I decided that I was going to put myself first. I needed to figure out who I was as a single entity and how I could stand on my own two feet. I would no longer be so desperate for love that I accepted it in whatever package it was wrapped in. I deserved better than that. It was time to clean up my life and the first order of business was changing my locks.

48

Finally, Mitchell moved back into our room. I hadn't realized how empty his side of the closet was without him there. I was so glad we had gotten through all this mess, and I think Mitchell and I were starting to understand one another now. At least we're trying. This marriage was so important to me. Mitchell's such a special man, and I don't know how many of them are still left so I needed to make sure I held on to this one. I wasn't sure how all this domestic thing works, but I'm sure that I was willing to find out. There's nothing more important to me at that moment than taking care of my home and my man.

I lucked out with Mitchell and I knew that now. It seemed absolutely ridiculous for me to have acted the way I did and treated him the way I did. In all honesty, I did see Mitchell as a way to become somebody in Baltimore, aside from my parents. I wanted people to see me as influential in my own right. All that was for nothing, because none of those people who I was trying so hard to impress were there for me last night. It was Mitchell, the one person who I didn't pay much attention to, who held my hand. I didn't want to be Baltimore's most elite anymore; I wanted to be Mitchell's wife.

"Victoria, sweetie, what on earth are you doing?" my mother asked me when she found me in my closet.

"Hi, Mother. I'm putting away Mitchell's clothes."

"Why don't you have the help do that? Isn't that what they're there for?"

"Yes, I suppose, but I wanted to do it for my husband."

"Oh, sweetie, you sound preposterous. Why get your hands dirty for that man?"

"Because I want to, mother, and that man is my husband."

"A husband that you're divorcing, and I hope that you have made sure that you do not leave this marriage with nothing. Don't let him pull some of his lawyer tricks on you."

"Mother, Mitch and I are not divorcing."

"What? Why not?" she asked sounding shocked.

"Because we discussed it, and we both feel as if we should give our marriage another chance."

"Really? So is he's prepared to let the other woman go?"

"Mother, the other woman was me."

"Victoria, you are making absolutely no sense. How could you have been the other woman?"

"Because I wasn't allowing myself to fully love Mitch as I should. At some point I left the marriage and I shouldn't have. If last night taught me anything it's that it's important to hold on to people who truly love you and Mitch does."

"Last night? Oh yes I heard about your little friend's problem."

"Her problem, mother! Nic was stabbed by her husband with her kids in the other room that's more than a problem."

"Victoria, I've told you about that girl. Things like that will always happen to people like that. It's just the way they live," my mother said sounding cold and uncaring. I wondered if that's how I sounded to Nicole all these years. I heard my voice coming out of my mother's mouth, and I didn't like it.

"Mother, you've said some crazy things before, but I think that takes the cake."

"Sweetie, I'm being honest, and for you to use that to have some kind of an awakening that Mitchell is this incredible man that now you have to do manual labor to prove yourself worthy of him is insane. You don't see me doing that for your father, do you?"

"No, mother, I don't and that's why I'm doing this."

"What does that mean Victoria?" she asked me angrily.

"Mother, I did have some kind of an awakening. My eyes opened to who Mitch really is and I liked what I saw. And mother don't take this the wrong way, but I decided to love him better than you love daddy and to treat him better than you treat daddy."

"So, I'm some sort of monster that doesn't love her husband? Is that what you're saying?"

"No, mother, that's not what I'm saying."

"Good, because all I have ever wanted for you was someone who would give you all that you deserved and treated you like the princess that you are."

"I know, mother, and I've found that someone, his name is Mitchell, and he treats me better than a princess. He treats me like a queen."

"Well then, I guess when you got all that, you don't have much use for me."

"No, mother, that's not what I'm saying. I love that you care so much, but I need you to respect my husband and my marriage, and I also need you to respect my friends, especially Nicole. She's a great person, mother. She's always had my back and last night I almost lost her. You should really get to know her. Life is too short to worry about class and status," I told her as I held her hand.

"Well, perhaps," she said tapping me on my hand and walking out the closet.

I hoped I hadn't hurt my mother's feelings, but it was time I said some of these things; my mother needed to hear them. It wasn't about me being the good, obedient wife. It was about me being his partner, someone he could count on. If he was broken, I need to fix him. Mitchell had been doing that for me and my friends for the longest time, and it was about time I started doing the same for him. I think somewhere deep down, my mother understood that; at least I hoped she did.

"You're not mad at me, are you mother?" I asked, following behind her.

"Of course not Victoria. Well, I'd better leave you to your work," she said heading to the bedroom door.

When my mother opened the bedroom door to leave, there was Mitchell standing on the other side looking ever so happy. He spoke to my mother, but I think she was still too upset to speak back. For some reason, I don't think that bothered Mitchell much; it didn't bother me much either. I was finally in a good place in my life, and I knew that eventually my mother would come to accept that. But until then, I had everything I wanted in Mitchell.

The way he smiled at me and hugged me gave me assurance that we were headed in the right direction. Mitch was right in a way when he said that he wasn't the man I had prayed for; he actually exceeded my prayers.

I got more than I ever thought I wanted in Mitchell. I kind of felt bad because I knew that I could be a handful, but he seemed to be willing to hang in there with me. How fortunate I was.

"Are you alright?" Mitchell asked.

"Yes I think I am."

"Well I never really heard you stand up to your mother like that before. You just insist on surprising me."

"You were eavesdropping."

"I didn't intend to, but yes I heard what you said."

"Well, I thought it was time."

"Vickie, I don't want you to think that you have to be a completely different person, I rather like your snotty attitude," Mitchell chuckled.

"Oh, I'm changing everything about me. I just think it's time I try being a better me. Besides, I saw a different side to myself last night and I felt good about that person."

"I'm proud of you Vickie, and I just have one request."

"What's that?"

"Could you put that lingerie back on? It was really sexy." he grinned.

"Wait a minute you acted like I was standing here in a trash bag."

"I know and then I had to run and take a cold shower. It's been a long time baby," he said as he walked up close to me and grabbed hold of my hand.

"I know, so wait right here."

I went digging way back in the closet where I had thrown the lingerie, thinking that I was so not the right type of person to wear it. Hearing Mitchell say that I looked sexy made me actually feel sexy for the first time in my life.

I didn't want him to wait long so I quickly got ready and came out heels and all. He seemed impressed. This was the beginning of our life together as it should have been. Mitchell picked me up and carried me over to the bed and before long he was making my entire body ache with pleasure. God I missed this man.

49

"Hey big head you up?" Joanna asked walking into my hospital room.

"No, I'm asleep with my eyes open. Jo, get your stupid ass in here. I done died and come back and your ass still asking dumb questions." I said to her.

"I'm going to let that slide cause you're lying here with tubes all stuck in your body, but I'm about tired of people talking crazy to me."

"Who else talking crazy to you?"

"Jess, the little heffa yelled at me and hurt my feelings."

"Oh, bitch. You ain't got no feelings, and it's bout time Jess starts speaking up around here."

"Whatever, I do got feelings and I don't appreciate people not respecting them," Joanna said trying to act like she was mad.

"Okay, then I'm gonna pay you a compliment. You did real good with my kids. Thanks, Jo, for taking care of them."

"No thanks needed, Nic. When I got to the house and saw you lying there with them looking so scared, I ... no thanks needed," Joanna replied looking like she wanted to cry.

"It's crazy, huh? Who would have thought that his dumb ass would go this far. I was scared, Jo. I really was. I thought my life was bout to end right then and there, and besides my kids, I ain't done nothing to be proud of."

"You're insane. You've done a lot to be proud of, Nic. You somehow managed to raise two strong and smart kids, hold down your home, and still keep me in check. Now that's a tough job."

"That ain't no lie. But I still want to do more."

"You will. You've got time now."

"Hey, everybody alright?" Victoria said walking into the room like it was her stage.

"Why ya'll keep coming in here asking dumb ass questions?" I asked. They know I'm not alright. I've been stabbed.

"Well I didn't know what else to say," Victoria replied.

"Don't worry about it, Vickie. She's just back to her old mean self," Joanna told her.

"Vickie, why the hell you look like that?" I asked her when I saw how much she was smiling.

"Like what?" she asked.

"All glowing and shit," I replied.

"Ooh Vickie had sex and it was good too," Joanna said and burst into a loud laugh.

"Jo, must you sound like a twelve-year-old," Victoria responded.

"Hell yeah, especially since you finally had sex this decade."

"That's just overly dramatic; I am married."

"And I hope it was with your husband. Hell, I don't care who it was with. Your shit was dry. I'm just glad you got some," I told her.

"Oh my God, you guys are so vulgar. But if you must know, yes my husband and I have decided to work on our marriage, and, yes, we did what married people do in a marriage," Victoria said, trying to sound eloquent about it.

"Oh, Vickie, stop the shit you had some wild butt-naked sloppy sex," I said to her.

"It was not sloppy, Nic."

"But it was good," Joanna said still laughing hysterically.

"Are you two done?" Victoria asked us.

"Wait did he like the lingerie?" Joanna inquired.

"Yes, Jo, he thought it was sexy."

"Good girl, I got more that you can have."

"No, Jo, that one is about all I can handle."

"Good morning." Jessica came into the room dressed in her white coat like she was about to examine someone.

"Well, what the hell. All ya'll coming in here today?" I replied.

"I just came to check on you I didn't know Jo and Vickie were here."

"Well, they are. Now what the hell story you got, Jess?"

"I don't have a story, Nic."

"Hell yeah you do. I'm awake now. Ya'll know Dr. Fine who operated on me? Well, those two were standing over me yesterday looking like they were about ready to throw me out of the bed and use it themselves."

"Nic, that is not true. We haven't even been out on a date yet."

"Yet. You do know that *yet* implies that you're going to be going on a date with him," Joanna said.

"Well I just don't know yet," Jessica said.

"Wait what about Michael?" Victoria asked.

"That ship has sailed, Vickie," Jessica answered.

"Bout time," Joanna replied.

"Thank you, Jo, for your support. Anyway when are you moving?" Jessica asked, sounding like she wanted to get off the subject.

"Trying to deflect the topic are we? Well I'm not moving; I told my boss that I needed to be here in Baltimore, and if the job needed someone to be in L.A., then I wasn't the right someone," Joanna explained.

"Jo, you quit your job?" Victoria asked in shock.

"Hell no, Vickie. That would be crazy. My boss realized that I'm good at my job, and if he let me leave, I'll just end up at a competing firm. So he's allowing me to do the job from right here in Baltimore. I mean, I'll have to sometimes fly to L.A., but I'm staying where I'm needed."

"Bitch, please. You staying for David," I told her.

"Hell, yeah. But I also got to thinking about what if I wasn't here and this had happened. I wouldn't have been able to forgive myself knowing that I wasn't nearby when Keshia called. I need to be here with my three best friends," Joanna said.

"Oh, I'm glad you're staying cause I kinda owe you for going off on you the other night. I was stressed girl. You forgive me?" Jessica said to Joanna.

"I guess, but you're going to have to go out with Dr. Fine and give me very explicit details," Joanna replied.

"Alright, Jo. I promise that if and when I decide to go out with Todd, I'll call you and tell you everything; even though I do that anyway," Jessica said.

"How come you only gonna tell Jo? Hell, I want to know too! Shit it's bout time you got rid of that motherfucker and moved on to something that fine," I told her.

"Alright, I'll have a big conference call with the three off you and tell you everything," Jessica said.

"Well, I don't need to know; that's your business," Victoria said.

"Vickie, you're just saying that cause you finally got business of your own," I told Victoria.

"That's right, Nic. And speaking of my business, we would both like for you and the kids to come stay with us after you get out of here," Victoria said.

"I can't do that, Vickie," I replied.

"Why not? We've got the room; I mean you can basically have a whole wing to yourself," Victoria said.

"Now you know we would get on each other nerves by the second day," I responded.

"I know, but I still want you there. Please," Victoria begged.

"Only for a little bit. Just till I get on my feet and start my classes," I said to her.

"Classes? What classes?" Joanna asked looking like she was shocked that I would even consider going to someone's class.

"Why do you look like that, Jo? I can't go to class? I have you know I intend on going to cooking school," I told her.

"I think that's great, Nic," Jessica said to me.

"Yeah, me too," Victoria said rubbing my arm.

"I wasn't looking any kind of way. I just hadn't heard you talk about going to cooking school before. I like the idea. Hell, you can cook for me anytime," Joanna said.

"Thanks Jo," I replied.

"I have an idea," Joanna said.

"Oh Lord," I replied.

"No, Nic, it's good. The trip we did, let's do that every year. I mean, to different places," Joanna said.

"Jo, are you serious?" Victoria asked.

"Yeah, Vickie, I'm serious. I think it's time that we celebrate each other and our lives, the good and the bad. We made it through ladies. After all these years and no matter who comes in and out of our lives or how much pain we've endured, we've still got each other; we're still standing strong together," Joanna said.

We all grabbed onto each others' hands. Life ain't great and shit happens that will damn near kill your ass. But with a few good friends who got your back, nothing is impossible.